THE BLIND RUN

THE
BLIND RUN
Brian Freemantle

BANTAM BOOKS
TORONTO · NEW YORK · LONDON · SYDNEY · AUCKLAND

THE BLIND RUN

A Bantam Book / August 1986

First published in Great Britain in 1985

Library of Congress Cataloging-in-Publication Data

Freemantle, Brian.
  The blind run.

  I. Title.
PR6056.R43B5   1986   823'.914   86-3621
ISBN 0-553-05161-X

PRINTED IN THE UNITED STATES OF AMERICA

MV   0 9 8 7 6 5 4 3 2 1

For Terry and Penny, with love

What's in a name? that which we call a rose
By any other name would smell as sweet.

—Shakespeare, *Romeo and Juliet*

THE BLIND RUN

Prologue

"The prisoner will stand."

Charlie Muffin did, but awkwardly. They'd allowed the familiar and mourned-for Hush Puppies during the trial, molded and scuffed into comfort, but his feet still hurt like a bugger from the remand-prison boots.

The court was sparsely filled, because the entire hearing had naturally been in camera, no public and no press, and officials reduced to the minimum, just the red-robed judge and the bewigged, raven-cloaked counsel, with their instructing solicitors behind. And the short, limited procession of witnesses, the barest of formalities, because Charlie hadn't denied anything. There wasn't anything to deny, after all.

And a deal was a deal.

He hoped.

The first to give evidence had been Cuthbertson, the Director he'd made to look a right prick, still pompous, still purple-faced, still blustering. Still a prick. Then Wilberforce, the deputy who'd deservedly gone down with the Director to whom he toadied, pastel-shaded as Charlie remembered, bony and sharp-elbowed and with an Adam's apple that went up and down like an uncertain weather cone. Another prick.

It might have been a misleading impression, heightened by the emptiness of the court, but Charlie imagined the present

Director had distanced himself from his predecessors. Charlie looked toward Sir Alistair Wilson. The Director looked back expressionlessly. Wilson seemed to find it easy to distance himself.

". . . Charles Edward Muffin . . ."

Charlie went to the judge, the reflection interrupted. Hallet, recalled Charlie. Or was it Habbet? Something like that. Port-mottled face and cheeks that wobbled when he talked; if he were allowed the red coat and the white wig after work he would have made a good Father Christmas. Yo Ho Ho and twenty years.

". . . upon your own admission, you are guilty of a serious offense under the Official Secrets Act, a traitor to your country . . ." began the man.

Not true, thought Charlie. But they'd never understand; nor had they tried to. Their way it fitted into the box files they tied with pink ribbon and then sealed, with wax. It was easier, in a world of boxes and patterns.

". . . you conspired with the Soviet Union and exposed to Russian detention not only colleagues in the field but your superiors . . . the Director himself . . ."

There was a movement in the well of the still court as Cuthbertson shifted in his seat, embarrassed at the reminder. Best service I ever performed for the country, thought Charlie. Difficult to convince anyone of that, though.

The judge coughed, thickly. ". . . upon your behalf learned counsel has entered arguments of mitigation. Much has been made of a very recent incident, when, still undiscovered by British authorities and therefore beyond capture, you nevertheless served as a decoy and led to the destruction of a major spy ring, acting not only against this country, but the West as a whole. Much has also been made of your original action being not that of a traitor but of a rebellious, vindictive man intent only on retribution upon those in authority whom it appeared ready to betray you in their own right . . ."

At least the old bugger was mentioning it: he had to, Charlie supposed, to appear fair. Not that there was any likelihood of his entering an appeal. Not part of the promised deal.

". . . they are arguments and pleas that I dismiss entirely. The matter of your being a decoy has been put to every witness who has appeared before me and every witness has denied the suggestion . . ."

Because they're lying sods, even under oath, thought Charlie. None of them would have lasted a day in the streets, the streets—and the gutters—where he'd existed for twenty years.

". . . there can be no mitigation, no excuse, for what you did. You are a traitor, to be treated as such. Upon you, Charles Edward Muffin, I am imposing the maximum sentence permitted me under the law, that of fourteen years' imprisonment . . ."

Charlie looked to Sir Alistair, alert for the smallest indication. The Director's face remained unmoving. Charlie felt a sink of uncertainty, the sort of sensation he'd known far too often.

1

At first, in the early days and weeks and months, Charlie's immediate awakening impression had been one of the smell, the overnight urine and the odor of too many bodies too close together for too long. It didn't come any more. He'd become accustomed to it, he supposed. Like he'd become accustomed to everything else. Recognizing the good screws from the bad screws. And the important prisoners, the hard bastards who ruled the jail, from those who accepted that rule. And the all-male marriages, some happier and more contented than those he'd known outside, where the wife had been a woman. And the weapon making in the engineering shop: knives honed like razors and spikes sharpened to impale an arm or a leg, even a bone if it got in the way. And the use of tobacco for money. And the black markets that existed: marijuana was available, because he'd watched and smelled prisoners smoking it. He'd not seen the cocaine, but he didn't doubt that it was around because he'd seen the snorting and been offered it in the first month. And booze. Charlie knew he'd have to make a contact soon, to get a drink. It had been a long time. Too long.

The prison was never completely quiet: always something metallic seemed to be hitting against something else metallic. This morning it was a long way off, on a faraway landing and Charlie gave up trying to guess what it was. He lay with his

4

hands behind his head, staring up at the barred window; in the growing light, it looked like a noughts-and-crosses board, set out in readiness. Early on he'd actually used the reflected pattern that way, a mental checkerboard, playing games against himself. Not anymore.

He wished he could remember, precisely, when the smell had stopped being noticeable. It was important—basic training—to count days and weeks and to record events within them that mattered. That was the way to survive. To stop being aware of time was the first step toward becoming institutionalized. And that wasn't going to happen to him. He knew the days and the weeks, even if he couldn't remember the smell: fourteen months, three weeks, and five days. When he got up, it would be six days. Establishing a regime was part of the training, too; he always made the count as soon as he got out of bed. Fourteen months and three weeks and six fucking days! And not a word. No approach, no "don't worry" messages in the cells below the dock. No nothing. So they'd done it to him again. He'd trusted Sir Alistair Wilson; thought him a good bloke, like the Director who had preceded Cuthbertson.

Charlie stirred, aware of the metallic sound getting nearer. At least he'd lived: perhaps Wilson considered the bargain ended there. He'd only pleaded for that, after all, Charlie conceded; just his life.

Charlie looked away from the window and its neatly divided squares, to the table bare of any personal mementos and the stiff-backed chair and the pisspot he couldn't smell anymore. This wasn't life. Or rather it was, the sort of life he'd read about as a sentence and not thought anything about, because when he was free to get up when he liked and go where he liked and do what he liked it wasn't possible to imagine what imprisonment for life meant. He knew now: Christ, didn't he know now!

Charlie swung up off the bed, feet against the cold floor, head forward in his hands. Stop it! He had to stop the despair because that was another collapse, like forgetting to count the days or remember what was important in them. Despairing was giving up. And he wouldn't give up: couldn't give up. He never had. He was a survivor. Always had been. Always would be. Couldn't break him. No way.

Never been this helpless before, though.

He stood abruptly, angry at the self-pity. Needing actual movement against it, he went to the table and took from the drawer the calendar he was allowed. He was careful to sit, before making the inscription, and then circled the day which would give him his current total of imprisonment. Twelve years and nine months and one day to go unless he got parole. If he got parole. Three of the screws—three of the absolute bastards and one of them in charge of the landing—had told him the word was in and that he wasn't likely to get a hearing for years, even less a remission of sentence. He'd fucked the establishment. Now they were fucking him. Bastards, thought Charlie; real bastards. Always had been.

The sound on the landings had changed now, no longer a meaningless jangle but the slapping against the cell doors after the slop-out bell. Charlie swiveled from the desk and groped for his boots, wincing as he maneuvered his feet into them. He didn't try to lace them but left them undone. He buttoned his trousers and secured the belt and finally put on his tunic jacket. He was ready before the key chain rattled against the door.

As it began to open, Charlie reached down for the pot. When he could smell it, the ritual had offended him; now it was automatic, just as it was automatic to shuffle forward and be by the door as it opened out onto the landing.

Charlie decided he would probably have been more disgusted if he'd had to share a cell. Not solitary, the governor had explained: apart from the cell, he was just an ordinary prisoner. It was just that there was no one else inside serving a sentence for a similar offense and it was sometimes difficult to gauge the reaction of the other inmates. Better to be safe in the cell, where he could sleep unprotected and safe from attack. But apart from that he would be treated no differently from anyone else. Charlie had thought it was bullshit at the time, like so much else; he didn't think it now.

He blinked against the brighter lighting on the landing and

went flat-footed out to join the line toward the sluices. To Charlie's left, hung like spiders' webs between the landings, were the protection meshes to prevent from self-destruction a prisoner who could no longer fight the despair, or the death of those who had infringed an unwritten law and might be heaved over, to avoid the irritating forensic inquiry which might have disclosed the clandestine activity in the engineering shops. To his right the cell doors gaped, like the beaks of hungry, unfed birds. He couldn't miss the smell now: no one could, not even if they'd served twenty years and become accustomed to everything. Debris in a slowly moving stream of piss, thought Charlie. It was a fitting analogy.

Charlie had developed the prison walk, shoulders hunched and insular, his eyes away from any direct gaze and therefore possible challenge. He missed nothing, though. Never had. It was the beginning of the week and the shifts of the landing warders had changed; as soon as he rounded the bend, on the last run toward the sluices, Charlie saw Hickley and Butterworth.

They were two of the worst: bloody sadists. But clever sadists more obviously aware than the others that the prison was run by consent of the inmates and anxious to be friends with those who mattered, to the discomfort of those who didn't. Hickley, the one who'd told him there was no possibility of parole, was at the sluice entrance, so that he could control the approach, and Butterworth was inside the lavatory, supervising the actual cleaning. Charlie's eyes avoided theirs; it was a precaution he had learned.

The challenge came, from Hickley, an arm thrust out across his chest, halting him and the line beyond.

"Got another one of you bastards," said the prison officer.

Charlie knew he'd have to say something. "Yes," he said.

"Know what we did with spies in the war?" Hickley was ex-Guards.

"No."

"No what?"

"No, Mr. Hickley."

"We used to shoot them."

Bollocks, thought Charlie. Hickley had never seen a spy in his life; probably hadn't even seen combat. Hickley was a base camp type, a coal whitewasher and latrine scrubber.

"I think we still should," said Hickley.

Provided his didn't have to be the guilty finger on the trigger. Christ, how he'd like to have kicked the bullying bugger right in the crotch, thought Charlie.

"What's wrong with your boots?" demanded the officer.

"Nothing."

"Nothing what?"

"Nothing, Mr. Hickley."

"They're unlaced."

"There isn't a regulation," said Charlie, who'd checked.

"I like a tidy landing." Hickley was shaven-headed and hard-bodied from exercise and had a sergeant's voice that echoed, so that everyone along the corridor could hear. "Undone boots aren't tidy."

Charlie said nothing.

"So lace them up."

Charlie allowed the look, too brief for him to be accused of insolence but sufficient for the man who'd faced hostility on a hundred parade grounds to know he meant it. Then he knelt, cautious against upsetting either his pot or that of the man directly behind him, and secured his boots. He did it carefully, tugging each loop through its socket and taking his time over the knots; the murmuring and shuffling grew behind him and at last he was aware of Hickley's shift of impatience. Charlie went slowly on, adjusting and tightening the laces.

"Get up!"

"I haven't tied them yet."

"I said get up."

Charlie stood, as slowly as he had descended, to confront the officer. Hickley's face burned red, except for the white patches of anger on his cheeks.

"Be careful," said the man.

Charlie didn't respond.

"Very, very careful," insisted Hickley. He stood back, to let Charlie pass.

There had been an audience inside the sluices, as well as out, grouped around the center runway to see what was happening. Two, both long-timers, smiled just briefly in appreciation. Butterworth, controlling the main gangway, recognized his colleague's defeat.

"Move on!" he said. "Everyone move on!"

There was jostling and further delay, while the slowly moving line became organized again. Instinctively Charlie stopped by the main sluice, where it was widest and where there were most people, rather than go into one of the side drains where he would have been in a cul-de-sac.

"Move on," insisted Butterworth.

Doggedly Charlie remained where he was, letting other prisoners swirl and spill about him. He'd been backed into more blank alleys than this poxy lot put together and he didn't intend the last day of the third month of his second year to start with some officially inspired thumping because he'd made some prison officer look a bloody fool. He was aware of Butterworth's apologetic look to his friend beyond the doorway.

He realized that Prudell, who occupied the adjoining cell, had kept dutifully close to him. A Hickley man, Charlie knew; had to be because Hickley sanctioned the cell changes when Prudell got fed up with whatever prisoner he was screwing and felt like a change. And Prudell had sufficient muscle to keep the landing running smoothly.

"Shaken but not stirred, is it?" said Prudell, indicating the pot. He was a squat compact man serving eight years for grievous bodily harm: he'd nailed to his own desk the hand of a man who refused to pay protection money for a bingo hall in Haringay. The victim was sixty-eight years old.

"Something like that," said Charlie. He was ready for the push when it came, not just from Prudell but from someone passing behind, so he was able to avoid most of the urine from his pot and that of Prudell's. Some still splashed on his trousers.

"Told you to move along, stop causing a jam," said Butterworth.

Charlie put his pot under the rinse, scouring it out.

"Sorry about that," said Prudell.

"Why not lend me some perfume?" said Charlie.

"Anytime, if you're interested."

Charlie picked up the line, going out past Hickley and back along the corridor. Inside his cell he looked down, disgustedly, at his stained trousers. Maybe it wouldn't last long, he thought hopefully. Then again, it might. Hickley had lost face and in a place as minuscule and insular as a prison that was something that grew out of all proportion.

Knowing he would have to avoid any infraction of the regulations, Charlie was ready at the first sound of the washroom bell but inside the ablutions he hung back, waiting for the shaving area he wanted, abutting the wall so that he only had to worry about one side and that in constant reflection. He maintained the caution in the food line, because there were urns with scalding water. The porridge was slopped half in and half out of his bowl. Charlie didn't protest.

He was as lucky with the seat in the mess hall as he had been in the washing area, with his back against the wall. He saw Prudell smirking two tables away: the companion was new, someone Charlie hadn't seen before. Dark and very pretty: Greek or Italian, maybe.

Charlie had started eating by the time Eddie Hargrave eased in beside him.

"Saw what happened at slop-out," said Hargrave, his voice hardly above a whisper, talking prison fashion, lips practically unmoving. He was a graying, wisp-haired man who had been a schoolteacher outside. Charlie still found it difficult to believe that after murdering his wife Hargrave had tried to dissolve her body in a mixture of lime and acid, even though Hargrave had talked at length about it and why he'd done it, because he found her in bed with his brother. The brother had been the headmaster, responsible for the school curriculum roster: he'd given the man two free periods by mistake, instead of a history lesson which would have kept him at school. Hargrave had killed him, too. Hargrave was in charge of the prison library in which Charlie worked, as his assistant.

"The bastard picked on me."

"You asked for it, Charlie, scuffing about like that."

"Got bad feet."

"You cheeked him: shouldn't cheek someone like Hickley. He's authority and you can't beat authority."

That was something he'd never been able to learn, thought Charlie. "Careful it doesn't involve you," he said sincerely.

Hargrave shook his head. "No one bothers about me, Charlie. I'm not one of the hard ones but there's a kind of respect for a lifer."

"It'll pass," said Charlie.

"Be careful, till it does. You've got a long time to go."

"Yes," agreed Charlie, distantly. "Bloody long time."

"Papers have already been delivered to the library," said Hargrave.

Charlie mopped the last of his porridge from the bowl with a piece of bread. He supposed it was natural that Hargrave would want to talk about it.

"Did you know him?" asked the convicted murderer.

The name given throughout the trial, which he'd followed from the library papers, was Edwin Sampson, although if the man was the KGB agent the prosecution made him out to be then it would obviously have been part of the legend, the cover story to cover his time in England as an illegal.

"No," said Charlie.

"Papers say he worked in security. Thought you did that, too."

"It was a long time ago for me," said Charlie. "And there's a lot of different departments."

"They say he did a lot of damage."

"They always do."

"Word is that he'll come here, after sentencing."

For the first time Charlie started to concentrate. "Here?"

"That's the word from those who work in the governor's office; guilty as buggery, so they say."

"Hickley said something, at the sluices," remembered Charlie.

"That he was coming here?"

Charlie shook his head. "Just something about having got another of us bastards. Makes sense of the remark though, if he were coming here."

The bell sounded, ending breakfast. The departure from the canteen was slow, as usual.

"I want a drink," said Charlie. Like Hargrave, Charlie kept his head bowed, so no one would see even the words his lips formed.

"What?"

"A drink."

"That means Prudell: he's the supplier."

"I know."

"He'd shop you, Charlie."

"I know that, too."

Hargrave remained silent.

"I'd understand if you said you wouldn't get it for me," assured Charlie.

Hargrave sighed. "Money or tobacco?"

"Tobacco."

"How much do you want?"

"As much as I can get; I've saved up half a pound."

"It won't be easy," said Hargrave.

"I appreciate it, Eddie."

"Sure."

"I mean it. We could share it; the booze, I mean."

"Don't drink, not anymore," said Hargrave. "Pissed when I killed the missus, so I don't drink anymore. If I'd been sober I wouldn't have hit her so hard. Wouldn't be here."

"It'll be there, if you want it."

"What do you want?"

"Whatever there is."

"I've heard there's whiskey. And gin," said the older man.

"Whiskey, if there's a choice."

The mess hall was almost empty now. Charlie and Hargrave stood at last and joined the line to file out.

"Thanks, Eddie," said Charlie.

Hargrave didn't reply.

The morning was spent reindexing and replacing on the shelves the books that had been returned overnight, but Charlie was ready long before the first borrowing period, the half an hour before the midday break. The dark-haired boy he'd seen at breakfast that morning with Prudell was the first one to enter the library.

"I want a good spy book," said the boy. He lisped.

"There isn't one," said Charlie.

Sir Alistair Wilson had been disappointed with the Chelsea Flower Show. Or, to be more strictly accurate, with the roses. Because growing them was his hobby, they were all he'd bothered to see. He thought the attempt to hybridize the Provence Duc de Fitzjames was a disaster, like sticking the stem into coloring instead of preserving water, which made a mockery of the bloom. And the hybrids themselves were pleasing but not outstanding: only the Mullard Jubilee was worth anything more than a second glance. He left early and considered going to his club but then decided against it. If he entered the Travelers without an obvious luncheon companion he risked being ambushed by bores and he didn't want to relive an expedition up the Nile when the fellaheen knew their place and were damned glad of it or debate the superiority of mule over husky for an Arctic crossing. Instead he went immediately to the office. Although it was lunchtime and Sir Alistair wasn't scheduled back until midafternoon, his deputy, Richard Harkness, was in the office. Sometimes the Director wondered if Harkness slept on the premises.

"Disappointing show," said Wilson.

"I've never been," said Harkness.

"Wouldn't bother this year, if I were you."

"I won't."

"How's it look?" demanded Wilson. Instead of going to his desk he went to the window with its view of the Thames and the Houses of Parliament beyond. His right leg was permanently stiff from being crushed under a falling polo pony and it was sometimes more comfortable to stand than to sit. Today was one of those days.

"Good, I think," said Harkness. "Five obvious messages, four doubtful."

"Imagine the Russians will have intercepted?"

"Maybe not all," said Harkness, who was given to caution. "But some; I'm sure they will have monitored some. Be astonishing if they hadn't."

"Dangerous then?"

Harkness frowned at the question. He was a neat, proper man, pink-faced and tightly barbered: the suits were always dark and waistcoated and unobtrusive, the shirts hard-collared, the ties bland. People never remembered Richard Harkness: he didn't want them to. "It was dangerous, from the beginning," he said.

Still looking out over London, Wilson said, "Sometimes I think how safe and protected we are here. Not like the poor buggers out there in the streets."

Harkness, who was accustomed to his superior's occasional philosophizing, said nothing.

Wilson bent, massaging his rigidly stiff knee. "We're going to need a lot of luck," he said. "A hell of a lot of luck."

"Somebody is," said Harkness.

2

It took three days for the purchase to be made and Charlie was cheated. It wasn't Hargrave, he knew: the poor old sod was as much a victim as he was, bullied by Prudell into taking or leaving what he was offered. For half a pound of tobacco Charlie got a flat medicine bottle of whiskey, less than half what it should have been. As soon as he tasted it, Charlie knew it had been watered, too; he hoped it really had been water. Weakened or not, it was still marvelous. Bloody marvelous, in fact, the warmth of the booze feeling out through his chest and then deep into his gut, the welcome return of an old friend. Charlie knew it would be weeks before he could save up another sufficient quantity of tobacco and so he rationed himself, one sip in the morning, another in the afternoon, holding it in his mouth until it began to burn and then slowly releasing it, savoring its journey. Marvelous.

The library racks were metal, predrilled along the edge for any sort of adjustment or construction, to fit the room in which they were erected. They had a lip, about half an inch deep, and by selecting small-sized books he was able to create a secure hiding place for his bottle beneath them while at the same time maintaining the height to match that of the volumes on either side.

The rumor that the Russian spy currently on trial would be

committed to Wormwood Scrubs spread throughout the prison, increasing the pressure on Charlie. On the way back from the sluices one morning he was nudged—he never discovered by whom—at the landing stairway and if he hadn't been tensed against something happening and grabbed a guardrail he would have plunged down at least one set of metal stairs, toward the level below. There was never a seat for him in the recreation room, where there were fixed times to watch television, and if he stood other prisoners grouped in a mob in such a way that he couldn't see the set. Once, sufficiently alert again, he just managed to get his hand out of the way of the release of scalding steam from the tea urn and on two occasions he found a fly and a spider in his food.

Hargrave didn't sit with him anymore. Charlie didn't blame the man. Their only contact was in the library and even then surreptitious because there was a screw on duty.

"Seen it happen before," said Hargrave. They were shelf-stocking and Hargrave was in the line beyond, blocked from view by the intervening books so Charlie could only hear his whispered voice.

"How long does it last?"

"No telling."

"I'm pissed off with it."

"You're supposed to be."

"What can I do?"

"Nothing."

"I'm going to get hurt."

There was a pause from the unseen man. "It might stop, if you were."

"You mean I've got to let it happen! Don't be bloody stupid!"

When the silence stretched out, Charlie said, "I'm sorry."

At last Hargrave said, "It's your attitude, Charlie—fuck everyone. You treat the officers like idiots and you haven't aligned yourself with any group here in prison. No one likes that: you're supposed to conform."

"I don't conform."

"You're going to get hurt," confirmed Hargrave. "You've been inside long enough to know that. So far you've been lucky. Or clever. Or whatever. But it can't last. You can be smart-assed outside, because at the end of the day you can always go home, safe by yourself. But there's nowhere to go in jail. You're here. Always."

Completely concealed against any observation, Charlie grimaced. Why hadn't the bastards kept their promise! Where was the sodding deal! He looked along the rack, to the carefully regimented set of books hiding his precious booze. There wasn't much left: less than a third. He needed more.

"Take a beating, Charlie."

"Bollocks."

"Until you've been taught a lesson that all the landings in this block recognize, then Hickley's a cunt. You can't make prison officers look cunts, Charlie: not even if they are."

That night Charlie took the bottle back to his cell. He was careful, confident that he was unobserved, removing it from its concealment under the pretext of replacing some returned books and easing it down the waistline of his trousers, against the skin at the back, so the elastic of his underpants kept it in place; the trousers were sufficiently ill-fitting to prevent any bulge and his tunic jacket was low, as well.

There was sticky tape in the library, for basic repairs to torn books, and Charlie took some of that with him to the cell. The bottom of the lavatory pot was recessed, creating a small cavity, and into it he wedged the bottle, securing it with the tape.

Charlie sat alone, ostracized, during the evening meal and at recreation didn't bother to go to the television room, where he would have been an object of more amusement than whatever was showing on the screen. Instead he stayed in the cell, waiting for lock-up. He squatted on his bunk, back against the wall, feet on the bed edge, so that his knees were tight against his chest. The pot was the object of his concentration. He was trapped, just like Hargrave had said he was: there wasn't any comparison to anything he'd known outside, no matter how expert he had been. Tough spots, certainly: apparently disastrous on several occasions. But there'd always been room to move, to maneuver: somewhere, if winning was impossible, where he could run. He'd never cared that the odds were against him, because always he'd been able to think himself out. Which was an apt word. He wasn't out, not anymore. And wouldn't be, not for another twelve years and eight months and one week and one day. He was in, caged and trapped like an animal in a circus, and like an animal in a circus, confronted by men in uniforms, goading him with prods and sticks to snarl and fight. Except that in circuses the goads weren't supposed to hurt.

How much longer, for Christ's sake, before the doors were closed and he could get to the bottle! The landings and balconies outside murmured with activity, an anthill of humans. Or should it be subhumans?

Charlie was conscious of people passing outside his cell and of their gazing in. He didn't respond. It came at first, like it always did, by sound and not the sound of the final bell; a metal-against-metal noise, impossible initially to identify as doors being closed and secured, and then more recognizable, the solid clang and then the scrape of ratchets engaging cogs as the keys were turned. Charlie stayed gazing at the concealment pot. He swallowed, dry-throated, and ran his tongue tentatively over his lips. Not long now. Not sufficient to get pissed on: to forget even. Just the only direction in which to run. The sound was very near now, solid and positive, like corks being driven tightly into bottles. Charlie moved at last, putting his feet against the floor and sitting upright, looking expectantly toward the door.

Hickley filled the entrance, with Butterworth behind. And then Charlie saw two more warders as well and knew it wasn't lock-up time.

"Cell search," announced Hickley.

Set up, thought Charlie. Fuck!

He got to his feet. "Nowhere else?" he said.

"Not interested in anywhere else, just here," said Butterworth. As if fearing Charlie hadn't heard, he said again, "Cell search." He jerked his head. "Outside."

Obediently Charlie moved out onto the landing, putting himself between the two waiting warders. He stood with his back against the rail, gazing back in. Hickley and Butterworth were very good, working as a team, jabbing at brickwork for loose or disguised mortar, expertly stripping the bed and pressuring the mattress and pillow for anything concealed, then upending the actual wooden furniture, probing the undersides of drawers and frames, knowing every hiding place. They left the pot until last purposely, Charlie was sure. Hickley turned it over, the confident conjurer knowing the rabbit would be in place.

"What's this then?"

"I don't know."

"Never seen it before?"

"No."

"Perhaps it's a sample," said Butterworth.

"He's not on the hospital list," said Hickley, moving ponderously through their prepared joke.

Hickley withdrew the stopper and made the pretense of smelling the contents. "Whiskey!" he said, the voice that of someone making an important discovery. He came to the door, looking out at Charlie. "What you doing with alcohol in your cell?"

"Not mine," said Charlie stubbornly.

"Bullshit."

"Don't know anything about it."

"You're up before the governor," announced Hickley. "You're in trouble. Big trouble."

Asshole, thought Charlie.

The governor's name was Armitrage. He had a pink face, a lot of white hair, disordered clothes, and the distracted, absentminded demeanor of an academic. It was an impression heightened by his attitude toward the prisoners. He regarded them as a hopeful schoolmaster regarded unruly pupils, slightly bewildered and vaguely disappointed at their rejection of the trust he placed in them but always refusing to abandon the expectation that they would one day reform and make the world a perfect place.

"You've heard what Chief Officer Hickley and Mr. Butterworth have said?"

"Yes, sir."

"And you insist you know nothing whatsoever about it?"

"Yes, sir."

The governor looked expectantly toward the two warders.

"Nothing there during the cell search a week ago, sir," insisted Hickley, stiffly to attention. "He's sole-occupation, on your instructions."

Armitrage came back to Charlie. "It's a serious matter."

Charlie said nothing.

"I ask you again, what was a partially filled bottle of whiskey doing in your cell?"

"Don't know, sir. I'd never seen it before." Charlie was conscious of the tightness with which Hickley and Butterworth were holding themselves. Armitrage was a man who would never thoroughly convict without proof and by maintaining his ignorance, Charlie was denying that absolute proof. He was making it worse for himself on the landing, but he didn't give a fuck: things couldn't be much worse than they already were. Twelve years, eight months, one week, and one day. Dear God!

"I'm not convinced," announced Armitrage.

One way or the other, guessed Charlie. "Don't know anything about it, sir," he repeated.

Armitrage sighed, looking aimlessly around his desk. The office was in the highest block of the prison and the windows weren't barred. Charlie could see the barbed-wire-topped walls and then the White City beyond. There were some high buildings which he guessed were the television center, and beyond that, tufts of trees. Shepherds Bush straight in front, Charlie calculated; Notting Hill to the left. There were people out there, ordinary people, worried about mortgages and debts and girlfriends being pregnant and bosses not liking them and imagining that nothing could be worse, whatever happened to them. Lucky sods.

"What about fingerprints, Mr. Hickley?"

The chief officer went even more rigid. "There were none, sir," he said.

Because you were too bloody anxious, thought Charlie. If they'd waited, just five minutes after lock-up, they'd have caught him bang to rights. It had been instinctive to wipe the bottle, after securing it in its hiding place. Some things still were.

"Then there's no definite proof, is there?" said the governor mildly.

"Concealing it, sir," said Hickley desperately. "It's an offense to conceal liquor."

"True," agreed Armitrage. He turned back to Charlie. "You lose all privileges for a fortnight," he declared. "No recreation period, no tobacco, fined your work allowance, and confined to cell immediately after evening meal." The governor paused. Then he said, "Your employment in the prison library is a favored one. I won't take it away from you on this occasion. If there are any further infringements of the regulations, I will." The man appeared embarrassed at his own forcefulness.

He'd won, Charlie decided. Apart from the tobacco and the wages, he wasn't losing anything he hadn't lost already. He was still in the library, which was the important thing. Charlie knew they were trying to get him into one of the prison workshops, among too much noise and too many people. They'd try again.

"Remember what I said," warned the governor.

"Yes, sir."

Charlie marched militarily between Hickley and Butterworth from the governor's office, through the outer area and then back into the corridors leading into the jail. He didn't think they'd attempt anything openly against him but he still walked tensed against the smallest movement from either side. No one spoke. He reached his cell without incident, thrusting suddenly into it before they could trap him in the doorway. Hickley smirked at the fear.

"You should be frightened," said Hickley. "I'm going to get you. Really get you. Don't like smart buggers on my landing. Don't like them at all."

Charlie knew he meant it.

The restrictions were supposed to be a penalty, but Charlie actually found them a relief. He didn't smoke, so the tobacco represented only a currency, and the deprivation of that and of his official wages was bearable. He'd already abandoned the recreation period, and his feet, which ached constantly within the incarceration of the prison-issue boots, had always made exercise more of an ordeal than a benefit to his health: he far preferred walking back and forth along the length of his cell in his stocking feet. In his cell he was safe: protected. He recognized it as an institutionalized attitude; of fear, of Hickley and Butterworth and Prudell and God knows who else. So what? He was institutionalized. And he was scared. Shit scared. Worse than ever before. What made it worse was knowing he only had two weeks of safety.

The governor's decision meant he was escorted every day from his cell to the library and back again and that the warder in charge had to have him constantly in sight; obediently Charlie obeyed every rule, so there was no opportunity for any conversation between him and Hargrave. Despite the difficulties, the old man thanked him on the first day for not grassing and identifying him as the purchaser of the booze. It was during shelf-stocking, the best time.

"You're a good guy, Charlie."

"It's a minority opinion."

"There's a joke going around."

"About what?"

"The booze. Prudell diluted it, you know."

"I know."

"Do you want to know how?"

"No," insisted Charlie, swallowing with difficulty.

"He's a bastard."

"Right bastard," agreed Charlie. He felt sick.

"I wanted to be your friend, Charlie."

"I understand."

"I'm sorry."

"It's all right," said Charlie. "Stay safe."

"And you."

"I'll try."

"Try hard," murmured Hargrave. "I've seen this happen to people before in the nick. They end up mad."

It was on the fifth day of restrictions when he heard them coming along the landing, an hour after he'd been confined to the cell: it wasn't quite dark, the gray time of night. The cell light was on but it didn't seem to help much. Charlie pulled away from the door, hunched on the bunk, knowing intuitively where the footsteps would stop. They did.

It was neither Hickley nor Butterworth: Charlie thought he recognized one of the screws from reception but he wasn't sure. Between them was a comparatively young man, younger than Charlie anyway, still upright and looking about him demandingly. He had an outside haircut and the discomfited look of a new prison entrant, suddenly deprived of clothes that fitted him and put instead into the bluish-gray uniform that came only in stock sizes.

His nose wrinkled at the very entrance to the cell. "Dear God!" he said. "What on earth is this!" It was an exaggerated voice, stretching vowels and consonants, a voice that had responded to tutors and prep-school teachers and university dons and got respect from headwaiters and hotel doormen.

"Home," said Charlie. "There's no place like it."

The British embassy to the Union of Soviet Socialist Republics borders the Moskva River, almost opposite the Kremlin: the view from one to the other is uninterrupted and the story is that during his manic, despotic reign Stalin used to become apoplectic looking from his window to see the Union Jack rippling so close and so defiantly in the wind.

The communications center for the British embassy is a

peculiar room, deep in the basement and far below ground level; before workmen were flown in from London to tank the chamber, dampness from the adjoining river seeped through the walls and stained them. Appropriately, the discoloration was an iron red, not the green of mold.

The brickwork they created remains. Within it has literally been built another room, suspended from the roof and from the base and the sides by single steel struts, so that it looks like a module created for physics instruction. There is a medieval-type drawbridge, linking this suspended chamber to the one outside. It is withdrawn—like the castles of the Middle Ages—from inside, so that the suspended structure is completely isolated apart from its support bars and those are swept weekly by electronics experts, to ensure no listening attachment has been installed upon the diplomatic and secret radio traffic that emanates from it.

Progress is usually synonymous with improvement. For signals transmissions—clandestine transmissions, that is—it isn't so. Microwave relay is the easiest thing to eavesdrop on, particularly when an embassy is so close to a suspicious seat of a suspicious government.

By the sixth week of the coded messages being relayed to London, they were being intercepted with complete clarity if without any understanding at Dzerzhinsky Square, Moscow.

That's the headquarters of the KGB.

3

The man shuddered as the cell door closed solidly behind him, turning to stare at it. Charlie remembered doing the same; everyone did, the first time. After several moments the man moved further into the cell, his belongings collected in a rolled-up towel. In his swamping tunic, Charlie thought he looked like a shipwreck victim rescued on an island of big men. The newcomer seemed aware of it as the impression came to Charlie, looking down at himself as if for the first time, plucking disdainfully at the rough cloth with his fingers. He put the towel roll on the empty bunk and gazed around, at the table and the chair and the wall rack, briefly at Charlie and then, for the longest time, up at the narrow triangle of light from the only window. Charlie waited and saw the abrupt sag of his shoulders.

"Christ," he said, hollow-voiced.

"You get used to it."

The man started, as if he'd forgotten Charlie's presence. He turned to face Charlie and said, "Sampson. Edwin Sampson."

He offered his hand. The instinctive politeness of public school, thought Charlie. He allowed the briefest contact between them, not bothering to stand. Sampson frowned at the rudeness.

"I know who you are," said Sampson. "They told me."

"I read about you," said Charlie. "The beginning of the trial, at least."

"Thirty years!" said Sampson. "That's what I got. Thirty years." He looked again toward the window.

"You must have done a lot of damage."

"That sounded critical."

"It wasn't meant to sound anything."

"You can hardly bloody talk: there isn't a section in the department that doesn't know what you did," said Sampson viciously. "If you hadn't managed to run until the Treason Law limitation ran out, you'd be doing thirty years too, most probably."

"I wasn't criticizing," repeated Charlie wearily.

"Everyone said you were bloody rude: people who could remember you, that is."

Sampson swore with a small-boy defiance, as if he were trying to shock. Charlie swung back onto his bunk, lying with his hands cupped behind his head. He had bigger problems than worrying about offending a snotty-voiced little bugger who'd sold his country down the river. Charlie hadn't done that; no one but he could ever accept the qualification, not even the damned judge to whom it had been so patiently explained, but it was the truth. Charlie knew he wasn't a traitor.

"What am I supposed to do?" asked Sampson. There was a plaintiveness about the question.

"Why not make your bed?" suggested Charlie, nodding toward the folded blankets. "This is recreation period but you don't get it first night in."

"Recreation?"

"There's a television room, place to play chess and draughts and things like that."

"Why are you locked up then?" demanded the younger man.

Clever, thought Charlie. "I'm on restrictions . . . punishment," said Charlie.

"What for?"

Charlie sighed. "In prison you don't ask anyone what they're doing time for and you don't ask about their punishments. You don't ask about their background or their families. In fact you don't ask about anything. This is the nick, son: not a public school."

"That was another thing they said about you: that you're an inverted snob," said Sampson.

"I don't give a shit what they say about me," said Charlie. It was all past: too long past.

"Is it bad? In here, I mean?" The nervousness was obvious in Sampson's question.

Charlie turned again to look at the man. "You'll find it rough, at first," he said. "In fact, you'll find it bloody awful. But you adjust, learn to behave prison fashion. Keep your head down, until you learn the rules." Charlie paused. "And I don't mean the official ones, on the printed form." Pity he didn't practice what he preached, thought Charlie.

Sampson had his back to Charlie, trying to arrange the blankets in some proper shape over the bed and failing. Charlie thought kids made their own beds at public school: or did they still have fags to do it for them? Sampson would get a bollocking at cell inspection. After several moments Sampson turned and sat down, squatting forward toward Charlie.

"I want you to know," he announced.

"Know what?"

"What I did."

"I'm not interested."

"It's important," insisted Sampson. "I've been operating for them for eight years: I was on station in Beirut, so I was able to monitor all the Middle East activities of the British. Then I was liaison in Washington. Made some good friends there, not just in the CIA but in the FBI as well. Managed to let Moscow have a hell of a lot of personnel and biographical stuff; you know how they like that, for the personality index they keep. For two years I was in European Planning, with access to the NATO desk. I suppose that was the most productive time . . ."

"I said I didn't want to know," said Charlie, not looking at the man. Sampson was a bastard, to have done all that. Even his arrest would have worked in Moscow's favor: disclosure of what Sampson had leaked would make America as well as NATO suspicious about cooperating with British intelligence for a long time. Mean a lot of agent and schedule changes would be necessary, too.

"I've got rank, in the Russian service," said Sampson. "I'm a major." He sounded proud. "I warned them they could face a disaster."

"Good for you," said Charlie, uninterested in what the man meant. Bastard, he thought again.

"You don't understand why that's important, do you?" said Sampson impatiently.

"Yes," said Charlie, with equal impatience. "For your sake I hope you're not disappointed."

"I won't be," said Sampson with confidence. "The great difference between the Russian service and every other one is that they'll never let their people rot in jail. They always arrange an exchange. They will, for me, certainly, after all I've done." He started up, suddenly encouraged. "I won't spend thirty years in here," he said. "Maybe a year: perhaps two. That's all." The man had been moving jerkily between the bunks. Caught by the thought, he stopped and said, "How long have you been in?"

Charlie hesitated. He wouldn't let the other man know about the daily count. "Nearly a year and a half," he said.

"Oh." Sampson's confident excitement leaked away.

"Don't use that as any sort of criterion," said Charlie. "Moscow wouldn't regard me as they do you. I'm not one of theirs." That was the biggest illogicality of all; the people for whom he was supposed to have been an operative knew he wasn't a traitor and couldn't give a sod about him.

"That's not true," said Sampson, more to reassure himself than Charlie.

"Yes it is," said Charlie. "Don't get any half-assed idea that you and I are the same."

"Why are you so fucking belligerent?" demanded Sampson, in sudden, surprising anger.

Fuck: the ultimate defiance, thought Charlie. "Can't seem to help it," he said.

"We're stuck together," said Sampson, the anger growing. "Whether you like it or not, that's a fact. From what I've seen thus far, I don't like you. I think you're scruffy and you smell and I think you go out of your way to be unpleasant. And all the stories I ever heard, about your stupid social attitudes, they seem to be true, as well. If I had a choice, I wouldn't touch you with a long, disinfected pole. But I haven't. I've got to live just five feet away from you. I hope to Christ for the shortest amount of time possible. But still live with you. I know all about this crap that you did what you did because the Director set you up to be sacrificed: that you're still loyal. It's all bullshit, something you cling to like a child clings to a comfort blanket. You know the Russian way is best, just like I do. I know what's going to happen to me. I've just got to tolerate you until my release is arranged. So what do you say? Are we going to be friends? Or fools?"

"Go fuck yourself," said Charlie, turning determinedly against the wall, with his back to the man.

Behind he heard Sampson laugh at him. It was a fitting reaction, decided Charlie. He was being a prick.

"Chekhov," identified Wilson.

"Yes," agreed Harkness. "It's from *Three Sisters.*"

The British Director looked down at the chosen identification message. "If I lived in Moscow," he quoted, "I don't think I'd care what the weather was like."

"The preceding lines provide the response," said Harkness. " 'People don't notice whether it's winter or summer when they're happy.' "

"Good," judged Wilson. "Innocent enough."

"Do you know the other play of Chekhov's, *The Seagull?*" asked Harkness.

Wilson shook his head.

"There are two characters in it, Medvedenko and Masha," reminded the deputy. "There's a scene in which Medvedenko asks Masha, 'Why do you wear black all the time?' And Masha replies, 'I'm in mourning for my life. I'm unhappy.'"

"Maybe that'll be appropriate," agreed Wilson.

4

It was a tenet of his early training always to remain objective, irrespective of whatever stress or pressure, because the ability to consider everything objectively was essential for that absolute necessity, survival.

Within a month of Sampson's arrival Charlie decided, with that long-practiced objectivity, that the man was bloody good at making the world rotate in exactly the direction in which he decreed it should turn. Better than bloody good: practically a fucking genius.

It shouldn't have been that way, of course. Not according to the unofficial prison lore. Prison rule dictated that the lowest common denominator was the governing factor, everything and everybody dragged down to the bottom. Anything contrary— like Charlie was contrary—was a worrying challenge to the system, something that had to be attacked and defeated.

Except in the case of Sampson.

Charlie watched Sampson swan around with the languid public-school demeanor of inherent superiority with every bugger—the very same buggers giving him a hard time for being different—appearing happy, eager even, to accord the man the rank.

Hickley, who thought spies should be shot, behaved toward Sampson with an attitude that Charlie considered practically respect, and Butterworth, as dutiful as ever, did the same. While Charlie had to have his boots laced and be ready and waiting at the cell door for the push-and-shove slop-out, Sampson was allowed to take his time, a place always available for him in the unhurried, ready-when-you-are procession.

With the boarding-school and university expertise of recognizing the dormitory leader, Sampson marked Prudell as the landing boss. Sampson wasn't gay and Prudell knew it but they established a relationship nevertheless, a compact of understanding that in no way impinged upon Sampson's inherent superiority or Prudell's unquestioned rule, the sort of reliance that exists between the owner of the manor and his trusted butler.

There was always a good piece of meat for Sampson in the canteen—not the shitty sort of gristle that always got dumped on Charlie's plate—and the vegetables were always hot and there was a seat readily available, wherever he wanted to sit. Just as there was, always, in the recreation room, right in front of the television set, where Prudell and his boyfriend of the moment and the other landing chiefs had their reserved places, not where Charlie was always heaved and shunted, if he bothered to go at all, at the back, usually against the wall. If he hadn't wanted it that way—for the protection—there wouldn't have been a bloody seat anyway.

Sampson's uniform jacket was altered, to fit, in the prison tailoring shop, and in the second month he got one of the better jobs, in the prison hospital, not as cushy as the library but a damned sight better than the workrooms where they made the mail sacks and the street-name signs and car-registration plates.

Between them, in the cell, the first-day hostility worsened, the attitude so obvious that Hickley and Butterworth were aware of it and spread the story along the landing, which enhanced Sampson further because it meant further harassment of Charlie.

Charlie was aware of the bulge beneath Sampson's tunic as

the man entered the cell, only a token effort made at concealment. Directly inside the door, the man took the bottle from the waistband of his trousers and put it openly on the table between them. It was whiskey, single malt, in a proper bottle with the cap still sealed.

"It is whiskey, isn't it?" said Sampson.

"Looks like it," said Charlie.

"That's not what I meant," said Sampson. "Whiskey's your drink, isn't it?"

Charlie stared up at the man suspiciously. "Who said?"

"Prudell," replied the other man. "Told me that's what got you put on restrictions, for having whiskey here in the cell."

"So what?"

Sampson's face tightened momentarily, but only momentarily. The smile that came was patronizing. "So I thought you might like a drink."

"Why?" demanded Charlie.

"Why not?"

"Because it might be a setup, that's why not. Because it's been six weeks since I've been on restrictions and the bastards haven't been able to get me for any infringement and if they caught me again, with whiskey in a mug, then this time the governor wouldn't give me the benefit of any doubt."

"Which would make me a grass," said Sampson.

"Isn't that what you got thirty years for?"

"I'm trying to cross bridges, Charlie. Like I tried to cross bridges the first day."

"Why?"

"Because it's bloody stupid not to," said Sampson. "Okay, so outside you and I wouldn't even be aware of each other's existence. Want to be aware of it, even. But we're not outside. We're in a box, fourteen feet by fourteen feet, and we're going to be forced to live together for a long time. So why don't we face the reality of the situation? I don't like you any more than you like me but I'm prepared to make the effort, for life to be minimally tolerable."

The man was right of course, Charlie realized, always objective. Like Hargrave had been right. They weren't outside, with a choice. And he wasn't able to sit in judgment, in his own individual idea of judgment, and despise this man for being a traitor, any more than he could despise Hargrave for being a murderer or Prudell for being a vicious homosexual thug who beat up old ladies and stole their purses. Trouble was, Sampson was the smarmy, self-assured sort of sod who'd always got right up his nose. "You've been pretty successful at adjusting to the reality of the situation, haven't you?"

Sampson refused to react to the constant challenge and went on winning because of it. "Right!" he said. "On that first day you told me to adjust and learn to conform. And you said I'd find it bloody awful. And you're right, it is bloody awful. It's the most awful situation in which I've ever been and because it is I've adjusted and learned to conform as fast as I can, to make it as bearable as I can. I've made my peace and my arrangements with the people who matter. No one bothers me, Charlie. Because I don't bother them. I don't practice dumb insolence to little men like Hickley and Butterworth because that's what it would be, in a place like this. Dumb. And I acknowledge that people like Prudell are masters of their territory, just like my father acknowledged that our gamekeeper knew the grouse moors better than he did."

Sampson broke the metal seal on the bottle top, poured whiskey into his mug, and held the bottle out in invitation toward Charlie, who stared at it, hoping the longing wasn't obvious on his face. He made no effort to accept it.

"What is it with you, Charlie?" said Sampson, putting the bottle back on the table. "Pride? Arrogance? Where do you get this attitude that you can fight the world and win?"

"I always have," said Charlie carelessly.

Sampson laughed outright at him. "Have you?" he jeered, gesturing around the claustrophobic cell. "Have you? You call this winning! You might have been good once, Charlie. I know you were good once. I've had the lectures about your expertise more times than I can remember. But you lost it. I don't care whether you consider yourself a traitor or what you think you are. It doesn't matter. Okay, so maybe you were set up. It happens, in the business. Our business. And maybe you taught them a lesson. Which doesn't often happen in the business. But they won in the end, Charlie. The establishment always does. That's why it's called the establishment."

"Bollocks," said Charlie, unable to think of anything better but wishing he could.

"It isn't bollocks. It's reality. That's one of the things they used to say about you: that you were a realist, able to adjust and maneuver faster than anyone else. What's happened to the reality now?"

Right again, Charlie accepted, not wanting but having to. He knew it and everyone else knew it so why the hell couldn't he accept it? Because it meant giving in! he told himself desperately. He knew all the prison rules—the written and the unwritten—and all the dodges and all the shortcuts: like objectivity, it was a necessity for survival. And he could play the part—if they'd only let him—but if it stopped being that, becoming unthinking obedience and conformity instead of an act, then it would mean he had given up. "I'll settle it my way," he said, still careless.

"Jesus!" exclaimed Sampson, jeering still. "I thought you were good! I really did. I listened to all the stories and somehow you became a legend and when I learned I was coming here and that you were here I actually *wanted* to meet you! But you're not clever or smart, not anymore. You go through this bullshit routine about refusing to become institutionalized, but that's exactly what you've become, just like those gray-faced, shuffling zombies who've been here for more years than they can remember. You know what prison has made you, Charlie Muffin? It's made you fucking stupid."

He even swore better, the word natural and easy now, not forced, thought Charlie. He said, "You want a boyfriend, why not go and live with Prudell? You've got enough pull with the screws to make the change." Charlie swung away from the direct confrontation, in the familiar avoidance pose of lying out on his bunk with his hands behind his head, staring toward the noughts-and-crosses window pattern and hoping the movement would appear what he intended it to be, a nonchalant dismissal of boredom.

"Twelve years, four months, and four days," said Sampson, from the other bunk. "Three days if you subtract today, even though it isn't fully over."

Charlie swallowed, refusing to respond.

"I know all about the calendar," said Sampson, "I know about the regime you've tried to establish. How you count every day off. Seen you do it, when you didn't think I'd notice. The instructors would be proud, if they knew how well you'd remembered."

Still Charlie gave no reaction.

"I'm going to have another drink," said Sampson. "Sure you won't join me?"

"Go fuck yourself," said Charlie, gripped by a feeling of helplessness. The feeling worsened when he remembered that was how he had ended their last big argument.

It was a week later when Hickley came to the library, fifteen minutes before it closed. The doorway was blocked from Charlie's view by a shelf; he was aware of some conversation and of some halfhearted, flustered warning from Hargrave, but didn't realize what it was until the prison officer appeared at the opening into the book-lined corridor.

"Cozy here," said Hickley.

"Can I help you, Mr. Hickley?" said Charlie cautiously. He'd done nothing so they couldn't put him on restriction. Not unless it was a phony charge.

"I don't think you can help me," said the prison officer. "I don't think you can help anyone, Muffin. You can't even help yourself."

Charlie avoided looking directly at the man, careful of any

accusation of unspoken insolence. There was nothing he could say to that, so not replying wouldn't be insubordination.

"Cozy," said Hickley again. "You like it here, Muffin?"

"Yes, thank you, Mr. Hickley," said Charlie. The enforced politeness was like a sour-tasting lump, in that part of his throat from which he couldn't swallow to lose it.

"Pity," said the officer, with lead-footed sarcasm. "Terrible pity."

Nothing to say to that, either, Charlie realized. Just as he realized something else. Bastards, he thought: absolute bastards.

"Time you were transferred," said Hickley. "Bad policy to keep someone in the same job for too long. Can even be dangerous. And you didn't come here for a rest cure, after all, did you, Muffin? You came here because you're a shitty little spy who's got to be punished. You know what we did to spies in the war, Muffin?"

"Yes, Mr. Hickley," said Charlie.

"Tell me what we did to spies in the war."

"Shot them," said Charlie.

"Shot them what?" pounced the bully at once.

"Shot them, Mr. Hickley," said Charlie.

"Still should," said the man. "Don't you think spies should still be shot, Muffin?"

Sampson included? wondered Charlie. He said, "Yes, Mr. Hickley."

"Vacancy in the registration plant workshop just right for you," said Hickley. "You're transferring tomorrow."

The most dangerous place, thought Charlie: there was a small furnace and an indentation press and hammers and files and chisels and caustic solutions used in the spraying and the painting. A hundred different ways he could be attacked and hurt.

To the hovering Hargrave, Hickley said, for no other reason than to prolong his goading of Charlie, "Taking him away isn't going to wreck the administration of the library, is it?"

"No, Mr. Hickley," said the prison librarian.

"You'll get on well with the new man," promised Hickley. He began talking directly to Hargrave but finished turning back to Charlie, to savor the moment fully. "Everyone does," he said. "Sampson's a good man. Knows the way things are supposed to work."

"Bastard!" shouted Charlie, thirty minutes later, standing over Sampson in their shared cell.

The other man smiled up from his bedspace, appearing unconcerned at Charlie's fury. "I didn't fix it."

"Fucking liar!"

"A state-registered male nurse got sentenced for gross indecency: the hospital was the obvious place for him. So I had to be moved on."

"I could hurt you," said Charlie, striving for control. "I could knock shit out of you and put you in so much pain you'd wish you'd never been born."

Sampson frowned up at Charlie's bulged, sagging figure and then down at himself. Sampson never appeared to do any proper physical exercise but he was tautly thin, his body hard and muscle-ridged, and Charlie wondered if it were a threat he could carry out.

"Maybe you could and there again, maybe you couldn't," said Sampson, stretching back challengingly to expose himself to any attack Charlie might make. "But I've made friends here. Friends who might decide that if I get hurt they have to try to even the score for me. You thought about that?"

Defeated, Charlie slumped back onto his own bunk. "Bastard," he said emptily.

"A lot of institutionalized prisoners do that," said Sampson. "Talk to themselves, I mean."

General Valery Kalenin was a career intelligence officer, a man who entered the Soviet system—although fortunately from the safely protected distance in the early years from Georgia— when it was known as the NKVD and under the direction of

Lavrenti Pavlovich Beria, and risen to the rank of chairman of what is now known as the Komitet Gosudarstvennoy Bezopasnosti, the KGB, by the combination of outstanding ability and unfailing political awareness. Kalenin was a man who enjoyed his job and the power and privileges it gave him and more than any previous chairman personally involved himself in the workings and running of the agency's myriad divisions. Kalenin, whose devotion to the service precluded marriage, even casual, passing affairs, all hobbies except the history of tank warfare and the enjoyment of a wide circle of friends, recognized that his refusal to delegate could be construed as a fault. But it was a fault he could not—despite some halfhearted efforts—correct. He was the controller and he needed completely to feel that he was in control.

Which was why the monitoring of the messages from the British embassy had come so early to his attention, rather than be filtered and relayed through a deputy, who might have waited for their cryptologists to break the code before bringing it forward. That might, Kalenin reflected, have been better anyway, because at the moment all he had was an unintelligible jumble that he knew to be a coded message, was obviously therefore important but without the slightest indication of what it might be. Or what the dangers were that it might represent.

Kalenin stood at the window of his sparse office, gazing down upon the memorial to the network's founder in Dzerzhinsky Square. First, months before, the warning that there was a spy within their service. Now this, a new code, so far defying all attempts at deciphering. Kalenin didn't need it to be deciphered to know it was confirmation of the earlier intelligence.

He turned back to his desk and the telephone. The conversation with the code-breaking department was sharp and demanding, no instructions further than he'd already given, the call simply to let them know the transmissions had the personal attention of the chairman himself and were therefore important.

"I don't think that man's human at all," protested the head of the analysts' department, a mathematician named Malik. "I think he was made by a team of engineers and scientists in a damned laboratory somewhere."

"Then they made a mistake," said his assistant, not looking up from the message they were unsuccessfully trying to understand. "They overtuned his engine."

5

They didn't hurry. They didn't have to. They knew and Charlie knew they could play with him as long as they liked, a communal cat with a captive mouse: a mouse, reflected Charlie bitterly, that didn't have a hole to run to.

The workshop in which the registration plates were made was a hot, chemical-smelling, metal-clattering shell of a place, L-shaped, with the furnace that caused the heat and made the metal malleable at one end, feeding out onto a conveyor belt lined either side by the indentation punches and continuing on to the bend in the L, where the spraying was done before the final sequence, the baking on of the paint in a small series of ovens almost as hot as the furnace at the other end. And every step of the process and cranny of the workshop a potential for attack, Charlie recognized, professionally. He drew on that professionalism, desperate to remember every trick and hint, trying to get a workspot on the outer section of the conveyor, where the wall was to his back, and not in the middle corridor, the main walkway where people would always be behind him, straining to identify the main danger points in a roomful of danger. The furnace was the most obvious. It was gas-heated and the protection doors were always being opened and closed, for temperature checks, with frequent opportunities for him to be pushed forward, so the outstretched hand to save himself would go instead into the flames. And directly beyond, as well. The plates came out glowing, soft and ready for the numbered imprint, hot enough to take the skin off if they came into contact with an unprotected part of his body. The tidy-up section was the safest, Charlie decided: the plates were cool enough to handle here, beyond the impression stamp that could have crushed his hand from his arm if it were suddenly thrust into it. In the tidy-up section two banks of men, either side of the belt, honed off with rough chisels the unnecessary metal chips and edges from the stamping process and rejected any plate that had been badly printed, clipping it back into the return half of the belt for recycling. Charlie's apprehension rose, further on. Here the plates were sprayed, undercoat first, then top coat, men encased in protective clothing and helmeted and masked by filtering headgear, armed with spray guns that only needed the slightest redirection not to cover the intended plate but squirt instead a blinding stream into his eyes. And the apprehension remained at the drying ovens, where the danger of being thrust into the flames was even greater than at the furnace because they were open-ended, the plates in continuous and slow-moving procession through the banks of fire.

Although they didn't hurry, they did play. The first day, when Charlie was assigned to direct the dangerously hot metal toward the stamp and was concentrating on not getting burned and caught in the press, one of the chiselers, someone Charlie didn't know, feigned a mistake, carrying the rasp on from the edge of a plate so that it grooved across the back of Charlie's hand, stripping the skin. And at the end of that week, when he was posted by the drying ovens, vents which should always have been positioned to throw the heat away from the benches were suddenly reversed, blasting a searing gust toward him. It was obviously fixed and timed, because when it happened only Charlie was where the blast came, everyone else miraculously clear at the precise moment.

Charlie didn't protest or complain to the screws, about the chisel attack or the burning, because he knew they wanted him to do that—and that he would have made it worse for himself—

and because he was bloody sure the screws were aware of what was going on, so any complaint would have been a waste of time anyway. Charlie tried to keep the nervousness from showing, to deny them the satisfaction, and was successful at the very beginning, but there was nothing he could do, no self-control he could impose, to halt the tic that started to pull near his left eye toward the end of the second week, and around that time the hand-shaking got bad, so bad that at an evening meal he actually spilled tea from his mug. Prudell saw it happen and laughed and everyone at Prudell's table laughed with him. Butterworth was on mess duty that night and shouted for him to clear up the mess, so that others in the hall would know it too.

It happened during the third week and at the very section that Charlie had determined to be the safest, where the plates were tidied. He'd been grateful to be assigned there, actually getting on the outside with the wall behind him, and was only worried about the chisels being used as they had been that first day, which was the mistake, because he hadn't properly isolated the danger from the overhead belt. It was constructed in a loop here, an inner revolving system so that rejected plates could be returned without having to cover the full room-encompassing circuit. Every three feet along the belt there were grips, sprung jaws into which the plates could be clamped, several at a time. There were six in the grip that collapsed directly over where Charlie worked, an intentionally practiced overload designed to fail exactly as it did. Despite the unremitting noise of the workshop, Charlie heard the sound as they broke away, a snap as the suddenly freed jaws came together. There was even a warning shout, too late to have helped but a shout nevertheless because for the injury that was intended there would have to be a later inquiry and everything had to be answerable. The injury wasn't as bad as they intended. It would have been, if Charlie's reactions had been slower, the whole pile coming down on top of him: maybe even a skull fracture. It was instinctive professionalism to jerk away at the overhead jaw snap, a sound different from every other one he identified, and with in-finitesimally more time—a fraction of a second—the falling load would have missed him completely. But it didn't, not quite. The plates had been wired together, to form the crushing weight, and they came down solidly over Charlie's left forearm. He felt it break, an excruciating crack, but he only screamed once, at that initial pain, still determined to deny them as much as he could.

The skin was torn as well, because the metal was sharp, and although the wound was cleaned almost immediately, an infection developed—from the air laden with paint and solvent spray, the doctor thought—which meant Charlie was detained in the infirmary. Safe again, thought Charlie; like he had been on restrictions, when Sampson first arrived. The relief, at that awareness of safety, was a physical thing; the muscles of his body ached at the tenseness with which he'd held himself, and now he relaxed, he felt that ache—the discomfort almost as much as that from his arm, dulled by local anesthetic. Was Hargrave right? Now it had happened, now that he'd taken his punishment, would things get better? Dear God, he hoped so. He knew—always objective—that he couldn't go on as he had these last few weeks. He wanted to continue defying them. And the system. Christ, how he wanted to! But like Hargrave said and like Sampson said, it wouldn't work. Couldn't work. He had to adjust. Not conforming: not giving in. Just adjusting. Just being realistic. Was it true, what Sampson had said, about his still having a reputation within the department for realism? He liked to think so. Be good, to be remembered in the department. To be admired. Abruptly Charlie stopped the reverie. If it were admiration, it would be begrudging, after what he'd done.

Miller, the state-registered nurse who replaced Sampson as the hospital orderly, made the approach to Charlie after supper the first night. He was a flaking-skinned, nervously smiling man: Charlie thought he looked capable of indecency but hardly of making it gross.

"Sampson said he's sorry you got hurt."

"Tell him thanks," said Charlie.

"Want anything for the arm? I could give you some painkillers."

"It'll be all right."

"Sampson sent you this," said the man, offering his hand palm down, his body shielding the gesture from the doctor and the duty prison officer in the ward cubicle. Charlie cupped his hand beneath Miller's and looked down at the small container.

"It's whiskey," identified Miller.

Another medicine bottle, Charlie saw. Would it be watered like last time? "Thank him for this, too," he said.

"He said to say if there was anything else you wanted."

"Tell him this will be fine. That I'm grateful."

Charlie waited until long after lights-out, the bottle hidden within the pillow cover, his fingers against its hard edge. Set up, like he'd feared before? Or the bridge that Sampson said he was offering? Adjust, remembered Charlie; he'd decided to adjust. And it would, after all, be a way to discover if the pressure were still on. Easily able to conceal the movement from the ward cubicle, Charlie eased the small bottle from its hiding place, unscrewed the cap, and drank. It wasn't watered this time. It was malt and smooth and although the bottle had seemed small there seemed to be a lot of it and Charlie took it all. If it were a setup then Charlie decided he couldn't give a damn; it was worth it.

But it wasn't a setup. There was no search and no discovery and two nights later Miller brought in more and Charlie got away with that as well.

Charlie's arm was still strapped when he was released from the hospital, which meant he didn't return to the registration-plate workshop. He thought he might have got kitchen duties but instead was seconded back to the library, a temporary assignment because they were restocking and needed someone who knew the system. Charlie went direct from the hospital to the library the first day, so it was not until the evening that he returned to his cell and felt able to talk openly to Sampson.

"Appreciated the whiskey," he said. "Thanks."

"Glad you felt able to drink it this time," said Sampson.

Charlie hesitated at the moment of commitment, finding it difficult. Sampson was still a snotty little sod who got up his nose. At last he said, "There doesn't seem a lot of point in fighting running battles."

There was no obvious triumph in Sampson's smile and Charlie was glad of it. "No point at all," agreed the other man.

Charlie sat down on his bunk and gazed around the tiny cell. "Forgotten how small it was, after the space of the hospital," he said.

"Notice anything new?" demanded Sampson.

Charlie did, as the man spoke, standing and going over to the small table, better able to see the radio. "How the hell did you get this?"

"Applied for it," said Sampson simply. He came beside Charlie and indicated a coiled aerial wire. "I can run that up to the cell window," he said. "The reception is terrific."

"This will make life much more pleasant," said Charlie.

Sampson smiled at him again and said, "You'd be surprised."

Alexei Berenkov had been repatriated from British imprisonment to Moscow, aware of his *in absentia* promotion to general as a recognition of a lifetime of spying in the West, expecting a dacha at Sochi and maybe a sinecure lecturing at one of the spy colleges. He wondered, initially, if his appointment instead to the planning department of the KGB, attached to the Dzerzhinsky Square headquarters itself, was nepotism, the visible indication of the friendship that existed between himself and Kalenin. There were obviously some who felt the same thing and clearly the relationship between himself and the chairman was an important factor but Berenkov knew he would not have got the posting if Kalenin hadn't thought he was capable of performing the function of division director—officially designated a deputy—because Kalenin was too adroit to do anything that might cause him personal difficulty. And Berenkov was pragmatic enough to know that he hadn't caused the man any difficulty. The reverse, in fact. There hadn't been a single important mistake since Berenkov's appointment, and two— one in Tokyo, the other in Iran—impressive successes.

Berenkov was glad to be home. He missed the comparable freedom of the West—a freedom he was sufficiently personally confident enough to talk about openly and discuss—and the *bon viveur* life he'd been able to enjoy in London under his cover as a wine importer. But in Moscow he had a wife he loved—but from whom he'd spent too long apart—and a son he adored. And secretly—a secret he'd confessed to no one, not even Valentina and certainly not to Kalenin, friendly though they might be— Berenkov knew that after so long in the West, constantly living a pretense, constantly expecting the arrest that finally came, his nerve had begun to go. Now no one would know. So now he could savor the unaccustomed domesticity, which he did, and enjoy the unexpected and important job, which he did also, and consider himself a lucky man, fulfilled and content and safe.

Kalenin summoned him—officially instead of socially— before the cryptologists had broken the code, needing the benefit of Berenkov's experience in England, an experience no one else in the ministry possessed. The chairman showed Berenkov the meaningless interceptions, but because they were meaningless, Berenkov merely glanced at them, putting them aside on his friend's desk.

"Not a code we know?" he said.

Kalenin shook his head. "And one that's being difficult: it's even defying computer analysis at the moment."

"Then it's important," judged Berenkov, confirming the opinion Kalenin had already reached.

"How good are the British?" demanded Kalenin.

Berenkov shrugged. "Don't forget I've been away for a long time," he reminded. "Almost two years in prison and then back here for two years. Cuthbertson was the Director, during the end of my time. A fool, and shown up to be one."

"Sir Alistair Wilson is the successor," said Kalenin.

Berenkov shook his head. "Don't know of him," he said. "I've always felt that Cuthbertson and his crowd were an aberration, a mistake that occasionally arises in any service, because it can't after all be avoided. For all the supposed expertise of the CIA, I've always had more respect for the British service."

Kalenin shuffled through the intercepted messages. "Twenty," he said.

"Important," repeated Berenkov. "There's someone here in Moscow, a spy we don't know about, shifting an enormous amount of information to which the British attach the utmost priority and importance."

"Where?" demanded Kalenin simply.

"We'll break the code, of course. Eventually," said Berenkov.

"Of course," agreed Kalenin.

"Then we need to work backward," said Berenkov, the superb professional. "Knowing what the messages contain will only give us some indication of the damage. It won't—unless we're very lucky—quickly identify the source, and that's what we need: a way of stopping the flow quickly."

"We don't have anyone in place in British intelligence, not anymore?"

"It was Sampson who warned us," remembered Berenkov. "Said he suspected there was someone here. I was making arrangements anyway to get him out. This makes his release even more important. Once there's a transcription, he might be able to indicate a direction."

"Get him out as soon as possible," ordered Kalenin. He paused. "Try to embarrass the British doing it, too."

6

The pressure stopped. Not immediately, because the hostile screws like Hickley and Butterworth were initially suspicious, and Prudell and the other landing bosses were uncertain, too, at Charlie's adjustment. And Charlie didn't find it easy, not at first. Or even later. It was difficult not to show, by unspoken insolence, what assholes he thought some of the screws were. And let Prudell and the other bullies know he still wasn't scared of them. The adjustment was a conscious, forced effort, something he was not able to forget, not for a moment, in case in that moment his real attitude came to the surface and they saw through the charade that it was. But the relief was terrific, so good that he had to remain aware of that, as well, to prevent himself slipping into the institutionalized demeanor of acceptance. The library job was bigger than Charlie thought it to be, upon his arrival from the hospital, the actual transfer from the limited room in which it had been housed into a bigger area, further along the corridor. Although Hargrave retained the nominal title of librarian it was soon obvious that Sampson had taken over, and because of Sampson's relationship with the prison officers, even the bastards, they were able to work at their own pace, provided books were available, and by maintaining the service, which wasn't really difficult, Sampson was able to convince any officer who did query the work rate that keeping the library open slowed the move. Although Charlie made and rigidly maintained the adjustment, he was also aware that the changed response of others to him was in some measure due to his obviously changed relationship with Sampson. Which was as difficult for him as everything else. It made sense for them to behave toward each other as they were, but the thought of existing under Sampson's protection and patronage was one that really pissed Charlie off. He accepted it though—with gut-churning reluctance—because there was nothing else he could do. Another helplessness of where he was, doing what he was. And he could never forget that. Because Sampson knew anyway, Charlie openly kept the daily record of his imprisonment, the morning ritual before every day began, even slop-out.

Sampson's radio became very important, as important as the calendar count. It was a positive, tangible link with outside, something through which Charlie was able to feel that he was not completely cut off and isolated. Sampson was as generous with it as he had been with the hospital whiskey—and he still supplied that, too, although Charlie bought his share—rarely imposing his preference for radio programs over Charlie's choice, appearing as eager as Charlie for the current-affairs and talk series. They even found they liked the same music.

It took six weeks to move the library because Sampson evolved a way of even further delaying the work by insisting upon a complete reindexing. But after six weeks even the most gullible of the prison officers were becoming impatient.

"Heard where you're going?" Sampson asked. It was a Thursday and they knew that the following day was the very last that Charlie could expect to remain on library secondment.

Charlie shook his head. "Maybe administration." By lying about a nonexistent pain in his broken arm and saying he still found difficulty in gripping with his hand, Charlie had managed to get a hospital report insisting he should be excused from any heavy work, so he hoped to avoid the workshops, even though they would probably be safe now.

Sampson, who was lying on his bunk and looking up at the ceiling, said, "I tried to stop you coming back here, you know?"

Charlie frowned across the cell. "What?"

"Tried to stop you coming back here," repeated Sampson. "After your release from the hospital."

"What the hell for?" demanded Charlie. He felt a stomach lurch of uncertainty at the thought of the collapse of their fragile relationship, and the physical reaction angered him because he recognized that despite all his efforts to remain aware of what was happening, he had come to rely upon it and didn't want it to end and go back like it had been before.

Sampson did not immediately respond. Instead he swung up into a sitting position on his bunk, groped to the supports beneath where he hid the whiskey, and poured into both their mugs. Then he said, "Because of the risk."

"What risk?"

"My risk," said Sampson.

"You're not making sense."

"You weren't, before you went into hospital," said the other man. "Now you are."

Charlie sipped the drink, looking warily over the mug at Sampson. "I still don't understand."

Sampson jerked his head toward the table and Charlie's carefully annotated calendar. "Twelve years, three weeks, and two days," he said. "You think you can last another twelve years, three weeks, and two days in here, Charlie?"

Charlie drank more deeply this time, not wanting to confront the question. Another indication of becoming institutionalized, he thought. "I don't know," he said.

"I do," said Sampson. "I think you'll go mad. Or try to kill yourself, to get it all over."

Charlie couldn't imagine attempting suicide because nothing had ever got that bad. But he wasn't sure. "There's parole," he said.

Sampson made a dismissive gesture. "Not for people like us," he said. "Not for spies and child molesters."

"What's the point you're trying to make?" said Charlie. "Do you want out?" asked Sampson simply. "Out with me?" *"Out!"*

Sampson made another gesture toward the table, to the radio this time. "You didn't think I got that to listen to the London Philharmonic and *Letter from America,* did you?"

Charlie stared at the radio, then back to Sampson.

"It was always established this way, if I got caught," said Sampson. "I knew the radio to get and the long-wave frequency to which to tune and how to recognize the messages when they started to be transmitted. And they have started. Along with other things."

Charlie felt a tingling numbness, the sort of sensation he'd sometimes known during a heavy boozing session outside, when he'd been celebrating or relaxing. But this wasn't drunkenness. This was excitement, exhilarating excitement. Careful, it was the most important thing that had ever happened in his life, so he couldn't afford a single minor, minuscule mistake.

"That's why I had to get into the library," continued Sampson. "I got that instruction even before the radio, from a small ad in the personal column of the *Daily Telegraph.* Every third Tuesday in the month is my contact day, the day I have to look to see if there's a message for me. I didn't know why the library was important, not at first, but I do now: that's why everything has been moved."

"Why?" said Charlie.

"Outside construction," said Sampson. "Extension to the wing. Which means scaffolding and ladders and ropes."

"How do you know?"

"Got that from the radio," said Sampson. "Amazing how easy it is to learn of the outside contracts given by the Public Works Department if you know the right way to go about it. And the Soviet embassy do. Work is going to start in a fortnight. And it will actually involve removing the bars from the windows . . . " Sampson grinned, self-satisfied. "From the window of a room that I now know intimately, along a corridor where I'm an accepted figure, someone with every right to be there . . ." He nodded toward the radio yet again. "I'll be told when the bars are coming out: when to run. Everything will be ready, outside."

"That's how George Blake got out," remembered Charlie, looking at the black set in the center of the table.

"Exactly!" said Sampson triumphantly. "Got away from a forty-two-year sentence and is now in contented and happy retirement in Moscow. Can you imagine the embarrassment when it happens again! It'll make the British look so stupid that no other service in the world will think of telling them the time of day."

Sampson was right, Charlie thought: the embarrassment would be incredible. The numbness came again, in anticipation this time.

"Which is why I tried to keep you out of the cell," said Sampson. "You were a complication I didn't want. But when I started making moves, through Hickley, I learned that to get you transferred I'd have to have someone else. And I wanted that even less . . ." Sampson put his head to one side. "You realize what I'm saying, don't you?" he said.

"Yes," said Charlie quietly. "I realize what you're saying."

"I'll take you with me," said Sampson. "I'll get you out of this place and safely to Russia . . ." He laughed suddenly, unable to contain his euphoria. "And we'll live happily ever after."

Out, thought Charlie. Dear God, the thought of being out.

Sampson came forward on his bunk, narrowing the distance between them. "But understand something," warned the man. "I'm taking you because I haven't any choice. And I'm telling you about it because I haven't got any choice about that, either. And because I know how you feel about being in here, because I've seen the way you go on with that calendar, every bloody day. But if you do anything to fuck it up, anything at all, then I'll have you killed."

Charlie just stared back at him.

"I could do that, you know? Have you killed, I mean. It really wouldn't be at all difficult, with the contacts I've got either inside or out. Nothing, nothing at all, is going to stop me getting out. You understand?"

"Yes," said Charlie. "I understand."

I'm getting out, thought Charlie. But not your way, bastard. You're going to stay in jail forever.

The following day, Charlie was posted to the administration block, where the governor's office was and where the clerical staff worked. The prison officer caught him trying to slip a paper knife into the waistband of his trousers on the Tuesday.

The rose in Sir Alistair Wilson's buttonhole matched those in the vase on his desk, pervading the room with their perfume. The messages that had been transmitted from Moscow, from the very beginning, were attached to a master file, indexed in the order of their receipt. The British Director rippled his finger along the edge and said, "There's a hell of a lot here."

"Let's hope it isn't too much," said the always cautious Harkness.

"They haven't changed the Baikonur code," said Wilson, referring to the uppermost message, the one that had come in overnight.

"Which means they haven't broken ours yet," said the deputy. He seemed surprised. Or disappointed.

"It's taking longer than I anticipated."

"We've got to assume they've intercepted the transmission by now," said Harkness. "They'll be going mad not knowing what it is."

"They're never properly going to know that," said Wilson.

"We hope," said the restrained Harkness. "This is only the beginning, after all. The very beginning."

"Still uncertain about the sacrifice?"

"It'll be a hell of a sacrifice if it doesn't work," said Harkness.

"It'll work," said Wilson confidently. He stretched his hand out toward his beloved roses and said, "Know what these are called?"

"What?" said Harkness.

"Seven Sisters," disclosed the Director. "Appropriate, don't you think?"

"The identification comes from *Three Sisters*," reminded Harkness.

"Near enough," said Wilson. "Near enough."

7

Charlie knew he was taking a terrible risk; of the governor dismissing what he was going to say as nonsense or of Sampson finding out, because of gossip among the screws. But there wasn't any other way: certainly not one he had been able to think of since Sampson had told him what he intended doing. The sweat was banded around Charlie's waist, and his hands were damp, clasped obediently behind his back. He couldn't remember being as nervous as this, not even on a job when things looked as if they were going wrong.

Armitrage sighed up at him, a man of perpetual hope disappointed yet again. "This is serious," he said. "Far more serious than the last occasion."

"There's a reason, sir," said Charlie.

The governor picked the knife up from the desk, as if he were weighing it, and said, "There can only be one obvious reason for attempting to steal a knife, Muffin."

Commitment time, realized Charlie. He knew very slightly one of the escorting officers, a man named Dailey, but not the other one. What if Sampson did too, like he seemed to know everything and everybody else? Charlie didn't intend naming Sampson, of course: that was his bargaining counter. But it would make a hell of a story to boast about having heard, to other officers. And other officers would repeat it, even though to disclose what he intended saying outside of this room would be an appalling breach of security. Charlie knew enough about security to know how little of it really existed. He said, "I took the knife intending that I should be seen doing it . . . intending that I would be put on a charge."

Armitrage came up to him again, frowning. "What!"

"I wanted to be brought before you, sir," said Charlie.

"Definitely trying to conceal the knife, sir," insisted Dailey.

"But I wasn't trying to hide myself doing it, was I?" demanded Charlie. "I was facing you when I did it, for Christ's sake!" Regulations didn't allow him to question the warders: even behave like this in front of the governor. But he didn't give a damn about regulations. Only one thing mattered: that they eventually believe him, and even if they didn't fully believe him, become frightened enough to react properly.

Dailey waited for the correction to come from the governor, and when it didn't, he said, "It was a clumsy attempt at concealment."

"Intentionally clumsy," insisted Charlie. He paused and then he said, "There is an escape being planned from this jail, an escape the embarrassment of which will cause repercussions sufficient to bring about your dismissal. Demands for your resignation, certainly."

Probably too strong, conceded Charlie. But he had to bestir the silly old bugger somehow. On each side of him, Dailey and the warder he didn't know shifted and actually moved closer, as if they expected Charlie to make a run for it there and then.

Armitrage's demeanor of vague distraction slipped away. He came tight-faced to Charlie and said, "What is it? I want to know all about it. Everything."

"No," said Charlie.

The governor's face reddened, the anger obvious. "I want to know all about it," he repeated. "And you will tell me."

"No," said Charlie again. "Not now. I will tell you, but only in the presence of Sir Alistair Wilson."

"Sir Alistair Wilson?"

"The Director."

"Don't be preposterous!" said Armitrage.

"Tell him that it's important . . . vitally important," Charlie bulldozed on. They might have welshed on the earlier deal but they weren't going to on this one. This time Charlie intended getting his freedom.

"I have no intention of making any approach to any outside person," said Armitrage. "This is a prison matter which will be settled by me. And it will be settled. Here. Now."

Charlie stared at the man across his desk, saying nothing.

"I'm waiting," said Armitrage.

"In the presence of the Director," said Charlie. "Then I'll tell you everything."

Armitrage looked to the prison officers on either side of Charlie. "Any suggestions of unrest, worse than normal?" he demanded. "There's usually an atmosphere, just before an intended break."

"Nothing, sir," said Dailey.

"I'd better get the deputy governor in on this," said Armitrage. "And the chief prison officer."

Which would be how the story spread, thought Charlie, desperately. He said, "There's no concerted plan: you'll not discover anything, tightening security."

To Dailey, Armitrage said, "Take him to solitary."

As the order to turn and leave the office was snapped out militarily, Charlie said, "I'll say nothing, only in the presence of Sir Alistair Wilson. If it goes ahead, it'll be the biggest embarrassment of your life."

"Out!" said Dailey, thrusting him forward.

In the solitary cell, which was internal, without any window and smaller than that he occupied with Sampson, Charlie slumped forward on the bunk, head forward in his hands. Bad, he thought, judging his effort. Bloody awful, in fact. Word that he was before the governor would have already circulated through the prison, because the trusties who worked in administration had seen him marched in and out. They'd know he'd gone to solitary, too. And the silly old fart would convene his conference with the deputy and the chief screw because he was too damned ineffectual to make up his own mind without the advice of as many people as possible. Shit! thought Charlie. He'd been better than this once. A long time ago; too long. Sampson would have him killed. Charlie didn't have any doubt about that. Any more than he had any doubt that the man would learn that he'd grassed. He could apply for permanent solitary, he supposed. There was a regulation that permitted it, usually invoked for bastards who'd sexually assaulted kids and needed protection from other prisoners, forming an enclave within an enclave, permanently frightened like he was frightened now. People went mad in solitary: Sampson said he would go mad. What was better, mad or dead? Jesus! What a fucking choice!

Without a watch or a window to judge from the changing light, Charlie found it difficult to calculate the time but he guessed it was three hours before anyone came. Maybe longer, he thought, as he was marched back through the administration wing, where there were windows, through which he could see that it was dark. Did it really matter, whether it was day or night? Did anything matter anymore?

Charlie's depression—his fear—was absolute, so the stretch of euphoria was a physical reaction when he got to the governor's office and saw, among the assembled people, the man who'd looked blank-faced at him in the dock of the Old Bailey on the day he got his sentence. Charlie stopped, so that the escorting officer following actually collided with him, and he said "Thank Christ" aloud, careless of their knowing of his relief.

Sir Alistair Wilson stood—because it was more comfortable for him to stand, although Charlie didn't know that—to the left of the governor, right against the window, half-perched upon the radiator. To Armitrage's right was the deputy governor, Collis, and deferentially next to him was the chief prison officer, whose name was Dexter. One of the bastards.

Armitrage had made a concession by approaching Wilson and he knew it and everyone else in the room knew it and he tried to cover the weakness by immediately imposing his control over the meeting, nodding curtly toward Charlie as if it were an order to stop. He said, "I don't think you can have any idea what has been involved in creating this meeting. Other departments, apart from the Home Office, have had to be involved, and Sir Alistair here . . ." The man paused, turning his head toward the Director. "Sir Alistair has shown a very great public attitude by coming here at such short notice. His attendance was your condition, Muffin. And it is one that I have deferred to. If, having heard what you have to say, I conclude that this whole episode was the farcical invention I fear it to be, I shall have you charged before visiting magistrates with secreting a weapon, with intent to facilitate an escape, and make a prosecution plea that an additional sentence is imposed upon you. Further, I shall endorse your file against any parole consideration, for as long as regulations permit such suspension."

Fuck you, thought Charlie. He was home. Home and dry. Steady, he thought, in immediate warning. He'd considered he had a deal before with Wilson and the bastard had reneged upon it.

"All right," said Armitrage, still attempting to appear forceful. "What is it?"

Charlie talked not to the governor but to Wilson. "What about our deal?" he demanded.

"What deal?"

Charlie looked around the other assembled men. "You want me to talk about it here, like this?"

"What deal?" repeated Wilson.

"I could have run, in Italy," reminded Charlie. "I knew you'd found me but I could still have run. But I didn't. Because I knew our own ambassador there had gone over to the Russians I stayed and did everything you wanted me to, so you could not only stop it but reverse it, to try to create as much harm as you could—"

"Which was all set out at your trial," interrupted the Director.

"Bullshit!" rejected Charlie. "It wasn't set out, like you say it was. It was mentioned, almost in bloody passing. But the deal was that you'd make sure the judge understood. That there would be a consideration, not the maximum sodding sentence possible. And that after the sentence, you'd see I got out!" Charlie's anger grew, as he remembered the promises Wilson had made to him. "Didn't you?" he said, careless of the rise in his voice. *"Didn't* you?"

"I will not have Sir Alistair interrogated!" broke in Armitrage. "Any more than I will tolerate any longer this ridiculous charade."

"It's all right," placated Wilson, from behind the governor. To Charlie he said, "Approaches were made to the judge. I could only give you undertakings, not guarantees. He decided that what you did in Italy was a very small mitigation against the damage you did. There was no way I could prevent that."

"What about getting me out afterward?" persisted Charlie.

It was Armitrage, not the Director, who responded. "Sir Alistair has been in contact both with the Home Office and myself, long before today, seeking the earliest parole opportunity for you," said the governor. "It was because of that earlier contact that I was able to get into touch so quickly. And why Sir Alistair responded, with matching speed."

"Oh," said Charlie, momentarily deflated.

"There's only so much I can do to circumvent the existing system," said Wilson. "There's a consideration hearing in six months' time. I've already indicated I'll support any parole application you make, even though, of course, you'll have to serve the required minimum, even if that parole is granted."

"I didn't know," said Charlie.

"There's no way you could," said Wilson. He added, "Or should."

"Whatever Sir Alistair intended doing, I shall still block it if all this is a nonsense," repeated Armitrage.

He only had their word—Wilson's word—Charlie realized, recovering. It could all be a bunch of lies. "I want another deal," he said. "This time an absolute guarantee that in exchange for what I'm going to tell you I get out. Get out immediately, and I don't care about existing systems or regulations or parole boards or whatever. I just want to get out."

"I won't bargain with you," refused Wilson, quietly calm in face of Charlie's uncertain control. "Certainly not blind. If what you've got to tell me is genuine then I'll make sure it is brought fully before the parole application."

"Like you did before the judge!"

"I told you I couldn't anticipate his reaction."

"Any more than you can anticipate that of the parole committee," said Charlie. He decided he had nothing to lose and that he'd never get such an opportunity again. "A deal," he insisted. "Otherwise you're all going to look bloody fools. And that's something I can guarantee."

Armitrage half-turned, so that he could see Wilson. He indicated with his finger something written on a file sheet that Charlie had been unaware of, on the desk in front of the governor.

"I will guarantee you a transfer to an open prison," said the Director. "Further, I will guarantee a personal intervention when the parole is considered in six months' time, and I know the governor will support me in that intervention . . ." Wilson hesitated. "But let's get one thing straight," he went on. "So far I haven't got the slightest indication why I've bothered to come all the way here, apart from my interest, of which, until today, you were unaware. And that interest is rapidly diminishing. If, as the governor has said, it's all been a wild-goose chase, then any help I might have considered giving you ends. You can stay here and rot, like the judge decided you should."

He was boxed in, Charlie realized. And they realized it too. Belatedly invoking his objectivity, Charlie supposed he was lucky to have got this far. Wilson had made a concession, bothering to come. So maybe the interest was genuine. An open prison would be like heaven, after this. And he'd get parole, for the information he had.

"All right," conceded Charlie. And then he told them, in detail, gaining a passing satisfaction from the reaction from

Dexter, one of the stupid sods who'd been impressed by Sampson.

There were several moments of silence after Charlie finished. It was Wilson who spoke first. "What luck," said the Director. "What incredible, fortuitous luck."

Wilson took complete charge, appearing reluctant even for Armitrage to remain in the room, finally relenting only after going into the deputy governor's office to make a series of telephone calls. He told the prison officers escorting Charlie to remain unseen in an anteroom, so that stories would not spread throughout the prison that Charlie was unaccompanied in the governor's office, apart from some outside stranger, but lectured them as well as the deputy governor and the chief prison officer before dismissing them that as government employees they were bound by the Official Secrets Act. He added the heavy warning that if anything were to leak of what they had heard that evening in the office he would personally ensure a prosecution and press for a term of imprisonment. Charlie wondered where the Director had learned that becoming a prisoner, once having been a screw, was a prison officer's biggest fear.

"You've proved your loyalty," Wilson announced to Charlie, in the now cleared office. "I was satisfied after Italy, which is why I have been trying to help. But coming forward like this is the absolute proof."

"So we've got a deal?" said Charlie.

"Yes," said Wilson. "But not the sort you thought."

"What the hell . . . !" started Charlie, the anger returning, but Wilson raised his hand in a stopping gesture. "I'll reinstate you," said the Director. "Not on active duty, perhaps. I guess you've probably had enough of that. Or will have. But I'll bring you back into the department, restore all your allowance and pension rights. Wipe the slate clean."

Charlie stood head to one side, trying to disguise the bewilderment. "What for?" he demanded presciently. "What do I have to do?"

Wilson did not reply directly. Instead he looked down to the still-seated governor and said, "A little while ago I warned your officers that what they heard in this room was governed by the official-secrets legislation."

Two patches of red burned on Armitrage's cheeks. "I heard," he said tightly.

"I'm going to repeat that warning to you. About what you are now going to hear."

"Which is insulting and offensive," protested Armitrage. "I don't need reminding of my duty. Perhaps you need reminding that so far the only person whom you haven't cautioned is serving a fourteen-year sentence for being a traitor."

"No," said Wilson. "I don't need reminding. It's an involved story that isn't worth repeating, in the time available to us, but as I said a few moments ago, I am completely and absolutely sure of Charlie Muffin's loyalty. If I weren't, I wouldn't be about to do what I am going to do now."

"What?" asked Charlie, trying to force himself to think beyond Wilson's offer. Reinstated! With a cushy job in headquarters, where the central heating kept you warm and the roof stopped the rain making you wet. Back doing a job he could do better than anybody else—well, as good as the best, anyway—and which he'd missed like hell for every minute of every day of every year, ever since he'd set them up for trying to set him up. There had to be a catch. There had to be the biggest catch in the history of catches, some utterly impossible demand to match the utterly impossible offer.

"I want you to· go," said Wilson quietly.

"Go?" said Charlie.

"Over the wall, with Sampson. And all the way back to Russia."

Charlie was speechless. He actually opened his mouth to speak, but his thoughts were too jumbled to form a coherent sentence and so he stood in front of the Director with his mouth gaping.

It was the governor who spoke. "Are you telling me—expecting me—to agree to this!" he said, outraged. "Do you think I am going to allow an escape from this jail of two men serving sentence for treason? You're insane. Absolutely insane."

Wilson nodded in the direction of the deputy governor's office, from which he'd made the telephone calls, and said, "You will get a summons from the Home Office tomorrow. You'll meet the Foreign Secretary. The Prime Minister, as well. Your instructions will be to cooperate fully."

"Just a minute," said Charlie, at last. "Now please, just a minute. You expect me to go along with Sampson, break out and go to Russia!"

Wilson turned to him. "If you won't, then I shall have you transferred from here tonight, to a maximum-security prison. Where I shall personally see to it that you serve every last day of your sentence, never qualifying for parole. Further, I shall allow it to be known that the transfer was for your own protection because you'd grassed on other prisoners. Actually foiled an escape."

"Bastard!" shouted Charlie. The biggest catch in the history of catches, he thought.

"Yes," agreed Wilson mildly. "Because I have to be. Because the prize is worth every sort of venality and pressure I'm capable of showing."

"What is it?" said Charlie.

"You'll do it?"

"I haven't any choice, have I?"

"Yes, you have," pointed out the Director.

Twelve years, two weeks, and three days, remembered Charlie. "Acceptable choice," he qualified.

"So you'll do it?"

"I'll try. I don't know if I can do it until I know fully what it is."

Wilson smiled, appreciating the professionalism. "There'll only be this one chance for any sort of briefing," he warned. "So make sure you understand everything completely. About three months ago there was an approach to the embassy in Moscow. A first secretary retrieved his coat from the cloakroom at the

Bolshoi and in the inside pocket there was a letter. Unsigned. Offering intelligence. And there was something else, part of a memorandum of a Politburo meeting that no one in the West had even suspected of being held, discussing the normalization of relations with China. We were able, later, to establish through Peking that such approaches were being made."

"So it's reliable stuff?" probed Charlie. Christ, it was good to be involved again; to be working.

"Every time," said Wilson. "We've had three more messages concerning that meeting, plus some material from the space-exploration center at Baikonur. And there've been crop-yield figures confirmed from aerial satellite and details of improved SS20 silo construction around Moscow."

"I don't understand what you want me to do," said Charlie.

"We don't know the source," admitted Wilson. "The letter, on that occasion at the Bolshoi, identified a drop. That first time it was a telephone kiosk near the Lenina metro station. That pickup designated a subsequent drop. And that's how it's gone on, ever since."

"Blind drops," said Charlie. "Cautious."

"The last message said whoever it was wanted defection. For himself—and we're assuming it's male, although we don't know—and his family," disclosed Wilson. "The message said that everything we'd got so far was to prove his value. And we think that value is something like the most accurate intelligence we've managed to get out for years. The message also said that what he'd bring out with him would show everything he had provided thus far to be practically inconsequential."

"So help him across," said Charlie simply.

"I told you we don't know who he is," said Wilson. "And like you said, he's cautious. One of the most frightening pieces of information was the extent and the degree that our own embassy is under observation. And of the identification of our people. He won't make a direct approach, for fear of interception. We've got to make contact with him. And with someone the Russians don't know. Or suspect."

"Me?" said Charlie emptily.

"You," said Wilson.

"But how, for Christ's sake!" said Charlie. "That's impossible."

Wilson shook his head in refusal. "You'd be well received, after what you did," he said. "Accepted. Berenkov's back, you know. Attached to Dzerzhinsky Square itself, according to our information. Maybe you'd even get to him."

"So what?"

"The contact instructions are quite explicit," said Wilson. "The west door of the GUM department store, on the third Thursday of any month. Your identification has to be a guidebook and a copy of *Pravda,* the paper inside the book, carried always in your left hand. There won't be any open approach, not until he's absolutely sure."

"And how will I be sure?"

"If I lived in Moscow, I don't think I'd care what the weather was like," quoted Wilson. "It's Chekhov. Your response is 'People don't notice whether it's winter or summer when they're happy.'"

"Berenkov used Chekhov," remembered Charlie at once. "Took his codes from *The Cherry Orchard* and *Uncle Vanya.*"

"Yes," said Wilson. "We had it personally carried out—together with the message saying he wanted to defect—to prevent any monitor interception."

"Could it be Berenkov?"

"I don't know."

"It's practically impossible."

"But not completely," said Wilson.

"There'll have to be a time limit."

"Six months," suggested Wilson.

"Then what?"

"Just walk into the British embassy and demand repatriation."

"What if there's been no contact?"

"He'll be blown, I'd guess."

"There must be something else!" insisted Charlie desperately.

"We think it's headquarters," said the Director.

"Why?" seized Charlie, eager for anything.

"The range," said Wilson. "Politburo meetings, Baikonur, crop yields. That's the sort of stuff that would be compartmented, except at headquarters."

"And even there not coordinated at a low level," said Charlie.

Wilson smiled again, in further appreciation. "Exactly," he said. "I think it's Dzerzhinsky Square itself, and I think it's high level. Very high level."

"What if I make contact?" said Charlie. "What then?"

"See what he wants, how he wants it. And agree to anything. This is too good to let go. Tell him we'll guarantee safety, homes, schools for any kids . . . whatever."

Charlie looked around the office of the prison governor. "What if I'm caught?" he said.

"You've been caught, Charlie," reminded Wilson. "Don't be again."

"It took long enough," said Berenkov, looking down at the transcribed messages laid out on Kalenin's desk.

"Too long," said the chairman. "Look at it!"

For an hour Berenkov was silent, reading through the information. At last he said, "It's got to be from inside here."

"I'd already decided that," said Kalenin.

8

Wilson evolved the cover story, anticipating that in any nervousness preceding the break Sampson might become suspicious. The prison records—to which the administration trusties might have access—were endorsed with a not proven verdict on the accusation of attempting to steal the knife, but with a sentence of a week in solitary confinement for insubordination to prison officials, particularly the governor. Isolating Charlie gave the opportunity for a further short briefing. Wilson had Charlie relate back to him all the contact procedures, to ensure Charlie fully understood, and actually provided a copy of *Three Sisters* for Charlie to read.

"I still think you're screwing me," protested Charlie as the Director prepared to leave.

"What would you do, if the circumstances were reversed?" demanded Wilson.

"The same," conceded Charlie.

Wilson nodded. "This is a heaven-sent opportunity," he said. "I'll fulfill every undertaking and promise, when it comes off."

"If it comes off," qualified Charlie.

"Everyone says you were good, Charlie. The best," said the Director.

When he returned to the cell at the end of the week Charlie

realized it was a reputation he was going to have to live up to. Sampson's attitude was predominantly one of anger, but Charlie detected an uncertainty, too, an uncertainty that easily could have become the suspicion the Director feared.

"What the hell did you think you were doing?" demanded the man.

"Nothing was proven," said Charlie defensively.

"I know nothing was proven," said Sampson with sighing impatience. "That isn't the point. Why draw attention to yourself?"

"Thought the knife might come in useful," said Charlie, feigning sullenness. So Sampson had checked it out, through a trusty. Wilson was clever to have foreseen that.

"So you did try to get a knife?"

Charlie grinned, as if welcoming the chance to prove himself. "Course I bloody did."

"Fool!" said Sampson. "Stupid, idiotic fool." His voice menacingly soft, Sampson said, "I warned you what would happen if you did anything to endanger the attempt. And you did endanger it. Okay, so you got away with it, but you're still a stupid bastard to have tried it in the first place. From now on you'll do exactly as I say, when I say, and how I say. You understand?"

If everything were for real and he'd got the knife, Charlie thought how much he would have liked to shove it right up the ass of this cocky little sod. "Yes," he said humbly. "I understand. I'm sorry."

"Good!" said Sampson, savoring the bully's control. "So from now on you're going to be the model prisoner. From now on you do everything by the book and you don't even let an insolent thought enter your thick head. I don't want any screw or any instructor to be aware of your existence even."

"A knife might have come in useful," said Charlie, exploring.

"I'll decide any protection we might need," said Sampson. "And arrange it."

So there was a possibility, somehow, of weapons. Charlie

realized he'd have to be careful of that, like he had to be careful of everything else. "You heard anything?" he said, nodding to the radio.

Sampson nodded, the anger slipping away at the opportunity of boasting about a favorite toy. "All fixed," he said. "Practically all, anyway."

"So what is it?" demanded Charlie. "When? How?"

Sampson smiled at Charlie's urgency. "What's the rule about information? Our sort of rule?" he prompted.

"A need-to-know basis," recited Charlie.

"Good to know you haven't forgotten everything you were ever taught," said Sampson. "For the moment, you've no need to know."

"I thought you trusted me," said Charlie, knowing he had to make the protest.

"I never said anything about trusting you," corrected Sampson. "I said I was glad that after so long you were becoming sensible, that I knew you couldn't stand to stay in here, and that I was taking you along because there isn't any alternative and I know bloody well that because of how you feel you'd shop me if I tried to go without you. That isn't trusting you: that's knowing you."

"I know I risked cocking everything up, over that damned knife. That it was a mistake," said Charlie. "But there's the danger of an even bigger mistake—a disastrous mistake—if you leave me blind. I've got to know something."

"I won't leave you blind," assured Sampson. "You'll be told, every step of the way."

He'd forced it as far as he could—as far as Sampson would professionally expect him to force it and become unsettled if he didn't—but Charlie recognized it was now time to stop. He said, "Christ, I can't wait to get out of this bloody place!"

"You won't have to, not much longer," promised Sampson.

The corridor leading into the administration block to which he was still assigned passed the former library and as he filed along it to work the following morning, Charlie was aware of the partially erected scaffolding through the window. It was a

restricted view and he only looked fleetingly in the direction
because he didn't want to attract the interest of any prison
officer, but Charlie's impression was that there appeared a lot of
it. Charlie assumed, obviously, that the break would be at night;
wouldn't be easy, negotiating all that planking and tubing in the
dark. Certainly not in these pinching, constricting bloody prison
boots. He didn't expect there would be Hush Puppies in
Moscow. What would there be? he wondered. Difficulty, he
decided. A hell of a lot of difficulty. With no choice—indeed,
confronting a positive threat as an alternative—he'd had to
agree to everything that Wilson had demanded, but with the
opportunity of proper, sensible examination that had been
possible during his period of solitary confinement, Charlie
recognized it was a near-impossible mission. He'd made blind
contacts in the past, several of them, but then the authorities
hadn't been able to monitor or suspect his doing it. He didn't
know but he very much doubted that they'd let him wander
around Moscow, going where he liked and doing what he liked.
Not at first, anyway. And he didn't intend staying a day over the
agreed six months. Or did he? Back in the department, Wilson
had promised. Past misdeeds forgotten and everything reinstated. Be nice to go back to a place where it appeared, from
what everyone said, he still had a name and some sort of
reputation, with a brand-new coup under his belt. Be like going
back with a reference, a testimonial that he was as good as he'd
ever been. Be showing he could win, too. That was how Charlie
always thought of any operation in which he was successful.
Winning. Charlie Muffin liked to win.

Charlie had been conscious at breakfast that two prisoners
from his landing were missing but had not thought overly about
it because there could have been many reasons for it, so it was
not until he got into administration, where one of them worked,
and saw he was absent from there as well, that he asked around
and heard of the sickness outbreak on his landing. It had
started, according to the gossip, on the second day he was in
solitary, sudden attacks of convulsive vomiting that the doctor
had diagnosed as food poisoning. Almost a dozen men, five from

Charlie's landing alone, had gone down with it. There had been a cleanliness check in the kitchens, and before he'd been released from solitary, special disinfecting of the slop-out rooms. He mentioned it to Sampson, because in the cut-off society of prison anything, no matter how inconsequential, is a talking point and this was hardly inconsequential anyway, aware as he did so of the man's smile and not understanding the assurance that they wouldn't go down with the complaint. It was not until the end of the week when they spoke about it again, and this time it was Sampson who raised it, smiling as he had on the first occasion.

"Doctor can't seem to get to the bottom of this food poisoning," he said.

"We've been lucky," said Charlie.

"No, we haven't," said Sampson.

What was the self-satisfied bugger talking about now? wondered Charlie. "What do you mean?" he asked.

"Know what an emetic is, Charlie?"

"Of course I do," said Charlie.

"Apomorphine is an emetic," said Sampson.

Charlie was fully attentive now, knowing this wasn't a meaningless conversation. "Where did you get it?" he said.

Sampson sniggered. "From the very hospital where the poor victims are being treated! Isn't that classic?"

"How?"

"Miller, the pederast who took the booze to you when your arm was being treated. Supplied him, too, of course. Until he became dependent and I was able to make the demands."

"How did you introduce it into the food?"

"Easiest thing in the world, in those canteen lines," said Sampson.

"What's the purpose?"

"It's already been achieved," said Sampson. "Officially there's a salmonella outbreak they can't control. They're used to it and our going down with it will be just another indication of how ineffective they are being in finding the cause."

The corridor leading to the now abandoned library linked

with the hospital, just one landing higher, realized Charlie. And wasn't separated by the heavy dividing steel doors that partitioned off the individual landings in the main section. "When?" he said.

"Tonight," announced Sampson, enjoying the role as master of ceremonies.

"Sick tonight or out tonight?" persisted Charlie.

Sampson hesitated. "Both," he said.

Charlie felt a tingle, of expectation and excitement. Apprehension, too. What if he wasn't as good as he'd once been? It had, after all, been a long time. Four years, nearer five.

"Frightened?" demanded Sampson.

"Yes," admitted Charlie, because there wasn't any danger in the confession.

"Everything is going to be okay," assured Sampson.

"I'd still like to know more," said Charlie.

Instead of replying, Sampson extended his hand. In the palm lay two small white pills, unmarked.

"Both?" asked Charlie.

Sampson shook his head. "Just one. And now, before lock-up. I want us to be ill in the sluices, where everyone can see. Where it'll be obvious we're the latest victims."

The effect of the expectorant was far quicker than Charlie imagined it would be. The sweep of nausea engulfed him within minutes of his swallowing the drug and although he ran, which was officially against the regulations, he still failed to reach the sinks in time, vomiting at first over the floor and then heaving, his body racked by retching, over the huge receptacle. Beyond the sound of his own discomfort, he heard Sampson being violently ill in an adjoining basin.

There had been shouts at their running, demands to stop which they ignored, and the arrival of prison officers, backed by others who feared some sort of trouble, was immediate.

"Christ," said a voice from behind Charlie. "When the hell is this going to stop? Fucking doctors!"

The assembled warders dispersed, sure from the condition of the two men that no danger existed, but Butterworth remained at the entrance, disdainfully watching while Charlie and Sampson hawked and groaned. It took a long time before the convulsions were over, and Butterworth waited even longer, unwilling to risk the walk to the hospital with men who might suddenly become ill again and foul a landing. Charlie clung to the rim of the sink, uncaring of its usual purpose and his closeness to it, feeling awful. His whole body was slimed with perspiration but it was icy cold, making him shiver. His head ached and he felt physically hollowed, which he was. The worst ache, of course, was his ribs and stomach, stressed and strained by the retching.

"Jesus!" he groaned. "Oh Jesus."

"Ready to go?" asked Butterworth cautiously.

Charlie nodded, even that movement difficult.

"I need a doctor," said Sampson, from beside him, playing the part, which wasn't difficult for the man to do.

"Out," said Butterworth. The prison officer stood back, as if he feared contamination, as Charlie and Sampson walked unsteadily from the sluice room. The officer gestured them immediately along the corridor toward the hospital, where the doctor who had set Charlie's arm did not bother to attempt any sort of proper examination, satisfied from their condition that they were suffering the same mysterious food poisoning as the earlier victims.

"Just when I thought the damned thing was disappearing," said the doctor.

Charlie didn't understand the remark until he undressed and got into bed and then realized that he and Sampson were the only two people in the infirmary. Sampson was organizing everything superbly well, Charlie conceded.

The doctor gave them both medication and put a pail beside their beds and told them to be bloody careful if they were ill again not to mess the floor or the bed. Sampson was sick, but not much. Charlie lay gratefully in the bed, feeling the ache gradually diminish. By early evening he felt quite well again. There was more medication before the doctor went off duty for the night. He took their pulse and temperature as well and as he left said, "You'll be all right by tomorrow. Be out of here, with luck."

"That would be good," said Sampson heavily.

Charlie recognized Miller as the night-duty orderly. The duty prison officer was one of the good blokes, a fat, easily pleased screw called Taylor. He had two kids of whom he was very proud and sometimes showed their pictures. Directly above the small office in which they sat was a wall-mounted clock and Sampson and Charlie lay watching the slow progress of the hands.

"When?" demanded Charlie, voice hardly more than a hiss.

Sampson eased himself slightly from the pillow, to ensure that Miller and the officer were beyond hearing, and whispered back, "Ten-thirty. They'll be waiting for us outside at midnight but I don't know how long it'll take for us to get over the scaffolding. If we're not out by twelve-thirty it'll be off."

The first uncertainty, thought Charlie. There were going to be a hell of a lot more. Charlie felt the tension build up, a physical impression like the earlier aching had been, as the leisurely clock approached ten. On the hour, Sampson began to groan and move in his bed, attracting Miller's attention. The orderly began moving, to come from the office, but Sampson moved first, getting with apparent awkwardness from the bed and setting out toward the lavatories, bent as if pulled over by stomach cramps. As he passed Charlie's bed the man whispered, "Move as soon as I get the screw."

Taylor was at the door of the office as Sampson approached, shaking his head sympathetically. "Poor bugger," he said as Sampson reached him.

Sampson turned as if to enter the lavatory, hand outstretched against the doorjamb for support. Taylor was actually going toward him, offering support, when Sampson attacked. He drove his knee up viciously into the groin of the completely unsuspecting officer, driving the breath from him in a contorted squeak of agony. Charlie started to move, as Sampson had told him, and as he ran forward saw Sampson bending over the man, kneeing and punching him. By the time Charlie got to the office door Taylor was completely unconscious, blood pouring from his nose and mouth. Sampson was still kicking at the man's body and Charlie said, "Okay, for Christ's sake. That's enough. He's out."

"And got to stay that way," gasped Sampson.

Charlie got the impression the man liked inflicting pain.

Miller was pressed back against the wall of the office, eyes pebbled in surprised fear. "What's happening?" he said in a little-boy voice. "Dear God, what's happening?"

Instead of replying, Sampson entered the room and with the same viciousness as before kicked barefoot at the orderly, in the groin again, bringing the man down with another muted scream of bewilderment and pain. As Miller fell, Sampson clubbed the man on the back of the head and then kneed him, just as he had kneed the prison officer, as the man lay on the ground. "Stop it!" shouted Charlie again. "You'll kill him."

Sampson looked up from the prostrate figure and Charlie saw the man was smiling. "If he's dead, he can't do anything to stop us, can he?"

"There's nothing he can do now," said Charlie. "Fucking psychopath."

"Tie his hands and legs and gag him," ordered Sampson, gesturing to the unconscious officer.

Charlie bent, easing the man's belt from his trousers and looping it around Taylor's wrists. The man's breath was snorting from him, an indication Charlie remembered from training as one of deep unconsciousness. He thought there was a danger of the man choking from the inhalation of his own blood and used the act of securing his hands to turn him on his side, to prevent it happening. Charlie wondered how much damage he was doing if Taylor's skull were fractured.

"Hurry!" urged Sampson, from behind.

Charlie used surgical bandage to secure the warder's legs and hesitated at gagging the man, aware again of the breathing difficulty. If he didn't do it, then Sampson would, he realized.

And less carefully. Charlie wrapped the bandage as gently as possible around the warder's mouth, trying to arrange it so Sampson would think it sufficiently tight but in reality leaving it quite loose, to enable the man as much air as possible.

"Get the keys," said Sampson.

They were at Taylor's waist, locked into the securing chain. Charlie unfastened the whole affair from the prison officer's waist and gave them to the impatient Sampson, who was standing by the door making irritated, beckoning gestures with his outstretched hand. Sampson studied the bunch briefly and failed to pick the correct key in his first attempt to unlock the hospital door. He succeeded on the second attempt. He relocked it, leaving the key and the chain hanging, glanced briefly up at the clock, which still only showed ten-twenty-five, and said, "Okay. Let's get dressed."

At the door of the office Charlie paused, looking down regretfully at the two unconscious men, then hurried after Sampson. The man was a bastard, thought Charlie. A psychopath, like he'd said.

Sampson was ready before he was, whispering "Come on! Come on!" from the doorway. He unlocked it a second time as Charlie approached, easing it back from the frame and staring out. He nodded, indicating that it was clear, leading out into the corridor with Charlie directly behind. There were no cells on this landing, which formed the beginning of the administration section. It was illuminated by the dull green night-lights. The two men still moved cautiously, hesitating every few steps for any noise of approaching officers. The longest pause was at the steps leading to the lower landing, where the empty library room was: the cells began at the far end, and if a prisoner were standing against the bars of his cell there was a possibility of their being seen. Sampson mimed a treading motion with his hands, warning Charlie to walk softly, then slowly began his descent. When they reached the bottom of the stairway they stopped again, pulled into the concealing cover of the well. From the far end came the murmur of conversation from the cells. From where they were, it was impossible for Charlie to see if anyone were against the cell door: it was a very common place for prisoners to stand, particularly if they were attempting some sort of contact with a neighboring cell.

Sampson led again, keeping to the left of the corridor, to bring himself to the library door. Charlie crept behind him, nerves tight for some shout of discovery. What happened if they got caught now? wondered Charlie. If everything was cocked up before it even had a chance to start and Wilson lost his chance, would the man come forward and admit to a deal, with a prison officer suffering Christ knows what injuries? And another man as well? Government departments didn't do that, when things went wrong. They put up the barricades and denied everything. Jesus! thought Charlie.

But they reached the door unchallenged. Sampson held the connecting chain in his left hand, to prevent it vibrating and sounding against the door, and tried to locate the correct key with his right. What if the officer didn't have the library key on his chain? The fresh fear surged through Charlie. Taylor was attached to the section, so he supposed there should have been a key, but the room was disused now and in any case there might be the system of limiting keys, to apply only to the necessary duty. Charlie strained forward, feeling the sweat run in irritating, itching paths down his back.

Sampson opened the door on his fifth attempt, with only two more keys to try. Charlie was aware of Sampson's shoulders sagging, a moment of abrupt relief, and realized the other man had had the same fear as himself. The click, as the lock moved, seemed to reverberate along the corridor and they both stared in the direction of the occupied cells, for any sign that it had been heard. There was nothing. Still Sampson was carefully easing the door open to guard against any squeaking sound and only creating the minimum gap for them to slip through. Sampson went first, then Charlie. Sampson was as careful closing it as he had been opening. The lock clicked shut with another loud-sounding noise and again, momentarily, they tensed. Again, nothing.

The corridor lights and that which came in through the window were sufficient for them to move across the room, which was cleared anyway of everything except the skeletal shelves to be restocked when the outside extension work was completed. Charlie set out immediately for the window, aware as he got closer that the bars had been removed, but his attention was more fully upon Sampson. The man wasn't going to the windows, as he should have done, but standing instead against the shelving by a far wall, legs apart and gazing up, as if trying to orientate himself. As the impression came to Charlie he realized that was exactly what Sampson was doing. The man paced off two divided sections in the shelving and reached up and even from where he stood Charlie detected the grunt of satisfaction.

"What is it?" whispered Charlie, when Sampson came to the window.

The other man held out his hand, palm uppermost. Charlie felt the sensation of sickness, like he'd known earlier in the day after ingesting the drug. Cupped easily in Sampson's hand was a short-barreled gun. In the poor light Charlie couldn't positively identify it but it looked like a .38, maybe a Smith and Wesson.

"Where the hell did you get that?"

"Get anything, with the right contacts," said Sampson. "And I didn't bugger about, remember? Arranged for my bank to transfer two thousand pounds into Prudell's account, a month ago. Prudell's sister brought it in, inside a radio just like mine. Idiots didn't check the inside of the case, just that it played when they turned the knobs. Didn't think that a small transistor inside a big case left lots of room for something to be hidden."

"What do you want it for?"

"Don't be ridiculous!"

"Why's it so bloody necessary to hurt people?"

Sampson leveled the gun, so that the muzzle was only inches from Charlie's chest. "I told you nothing was going to stop me," he said. "Just like I said I'd kill you if you got in the way. You thinking of getting in the way?"

"The sound of that would bring every screw in the place here in about thirty seconds," said Charlie.

"But you wouldn't be alive to see it," said Sampson.

The bastard was mad enough to do it, Charlie thought. He said, "No, I'm not going to get in the way. Let's get the hell out of here."

Without bars at the windows, some attempt had been made at security by meshing barbed wire against the scaffolding frame. Sampson adopted his customary role as leader, squatting on the window ledge and carefully trying to ease the strands aside, to create a sufficient gap, but even when he moved, his clothes were snagged on barbs, and Charlie was caught when he tried to follow, and in twisting to try to free himself, he drove a point deeply into his hand, wincing at the sudden pain. He felt the warm stickiness of blood on his hand as he crawled forward through the wire and onto the planking that had been set up, as a walkway, between the metal struts. Sampson was just beyond, hunched impatiently, not talking through the fear of discovery but making his familiar snatching, beckoning movements. Despite Sampson's demand for speed, they could not move fast. The floodlights were on in the yard, but there were canvas sheets hung like a wall along the edge of the scaffolding, and while that sheeting provided them with perfect protection against any outside patrol, it meant no lights penetrated their narrow, uneven walkway. They shuffled along, one behind the other, using the metal tubing as both a guide and support. The wind was comparatively strong, occasionally lifting the canvas in a snapping, crackling way, and Charlie supposed it was quite cold: he was sweating so much, through nervousness, that he was unaware of it. At each intersection there was more barbed wire. There had been some light by the library window, when they first encountered the obstruction, but now there was none and they had to grope and bend in a tunnel of complete darkness. Ahead Charlie heard the other man grunt in what could have been pain, and hoped he'd impaled himself. Hoped it hurt, too.

After about two hundred yards the scaffolding broke away from the main prison building, jutting to the left over some lower buildings where the main extension work was being carried out, raising them in extra stories to provide additional accommodation. Without the protection of an adjoining wall the wind was stronger here, lifting the canvas more easily. Once it snagged, for several seconds, and through the gap Charlie could see the yellow streetlights of Shepherds Bush and actually hear traffic moving along the streets outside. And in a brief burst of excitement at the thought of freedom—any freedom—forgot what had just happened back at the prison and what might happen in the future. The wall was very close, close enough for him to see the outline of the bricks and the backward-pointing metal bars that would make it difficult for anyone to get over, even if they reached the top and the black threads of the floodlight wire. Reality flooded back very soon—too soon—but Charlie knew that as much as he hated and despised Sampson and as much as he feared whatever faced him in Moscow—if he ever got to Moscow—freedom from the life he had known inside prison was going to make a lot worthwhile. Why the hell had it been so necessary for Sampson, whose tight ass was jerking only inches from his face in the sudden infusion of outside light, to be as brutal as he had been? In Charlie's time in the service there had been regular, mandatory assessments, psychiatric as well as psychoanalytical, specifically to identify the sort of mental illness he suspected Sampson to be suffering. But was it mental illness? He had a deal, a setup. If he'd been facing thirty years and had the chance, just one desperate, possible chance, of getting out, wouldn't he have done everything possible to have prevented that chance being taken from him, even if it meant pummeling the shit out of a fat man who tried to be kind doing a bloody awful job, and some eye-twitching sexual misfit? He didn't know, Charlie acknowledged. He didn't think so—didn't want to think so—but truthfully he didn't know. There had been a lot of times in the service when he'd set people up, either to escape himself or create a situation of advantage, and because he hadn't actually pulled the trigger or inflicted the punch or made the arrest that would lead to God knows how many years in prison, he'd still done, by proxy, what Sampson had done back there in the hospital office. So maybe he wasn't a psychopath. Maybe with a different accent and a different background and different breeding Sampson was what he always proudly regarded himself as being: a survivor.

The scaffolding ended abruptly, and not as they expected, fifty yards from the outer wall—for it to finish at the wall would have been too much to expect—with another bundle of wire and with the access ladders removed, another security precaution.

"Shit!" Charlie heard the man in front of him exclaim.

Charlie drew up beside the man, gazing beyond the wire and through the now open end of the scaffolding tunnel even closer to freedom. "Ignore the wire," he said. He pushed at the canvas, which gave sufficiently for them to get between it, the scaffolding, and the planking and use its protection to scramble, arms and legs wrapped round the tubing, downward. They did not, however, go right to the ground because the scaffolding was erected at the very end on top of the flat roofs of some outbuildings. Unsure of what was below and apprehensive of the sound they might make, they walked as carefully across the roof as they had earlier inched along the occupied corridor toward the library.

They were lucky. It was still an appalling breach of security and one which Charlie, in passing, guessed would be seized upon in the inquiry that was inevitable after their escape, but the ladders were laid, neatly one atop the other, beneath the protective parapet. But unsecured, by any chain or locking device. It was obvious, Charlie recognized, that the workers and the prison authorities imagined any danger to be from ladders stored in the yards and that because they were on inaccessible roofs the danger was minimal, but it was still a lapse that would earn justifiable criticism.

At Sampson's hand-gesturing sign language, they did not immediately try to move the ladders, instead creeping light-footed the full length of the roof on which they found themselves, reconnoitering for the best advantage. And they were lucky again. The building upon which they stood ran almost to the outer wall, only a narrow passageway separating the two. And what formed the roof of that was covered by a supporting structure and then mesh, once again to prevent any upward escape attempt, with no consideration of the advantage it created for someone from above. Without the elevation of the preventative mesh, one ladder length would have been insufficient to reach the top of the wall, but by carefully and quietly selecting the longest from the untethered pile, stepping delicately upon the mesh-support bars and not the mesh itself, and using one of those same support bars as the center base beneath the ladder, they were able to reach right to the very top, actually beneath the protruding spikes, and use the ladder steps as footholds easily to maneuver over what was supposed to be an escape preventative. On top—once again—rather than below the spikes they actually provided a convenient platform upon which to crouch and stare over the outer rim, into the side street below. There were the regulated lights and there were lights, too, in several of the opposite houses, which Charlie presumed to be prison-officer accommodation, but the road itself was deserted.

"Where's the car?" said Charlie urgently.

"We're early."

"We'll never be able to get the ladder over that metal lip," said Charlie, gesturing behind him. "Too much risk of losing our grip and letting it fall back and wake up every bastard in the nick."

"We'll have to jump," agreed Sampson. "Let ourselves down as far as possible from the edge and then drop the rest."

Charlie looked down again, concentrating upon the distance this time. "Bloody long way," he said.

"You got a better idea?"

After several moments Charlie said, "No."

"You first."

"Why?" protested Charlie.

"Why not?"

It didn't make any difference, Charlie supposed. He twisted over, onto his stomach, and wriggled himself backward, so that first his feet and then gradually the rest of his body first stuck out and then hung over the edge. Charlie clung, at the very point of release and the plunge down to the unseen road beneath, frightened of letting go. And then he did, pushing himself out slightly at the moment of release, away from the rough wall, trying to keep himself loose and ready to roll at the first intimation of contact, as he had been taught during the physical survival courses. He'd never got it right, on the course, when he had been fitter and younger. The ground came sooner than he anticipated and he wasn't able to roll properly, jarring sideways instead. The pain, as his ankle twisted, felt like someone thrusting a hot prod throughout the length of his leg.

"Fuck!" said Charlie. It didn't do anything to ease the pain.

He supported himself against the wall, looking upward to Sampson. There was the briefest outline against the night sky as the man came over the edge, and then Charlie had an impression rather than saw him falling. Sampson landed as Charlie had intended to, a fluid sideways movement at the moment he reached the ground, the classic parachute drop.

"Fuck," said Charlie again, disappointed.

"What's the matter?"

"Hurt my ankle."

"Just don't become a burden. Or an obstruction," warned Sampson.

"Get off my back," said Charlie. He wouldn't let the antagonism interfere if they got to Moscow, because that would be stupid as well as unprofessional, but if it were at all possible, Charlie determined that he was going to teach Sampson the sort of lesson that old ladies used to embroider on cloth and frame over bedheads, as reminding clichés.

The main road, where the main gate and the prison forecourt were, was to their right. Sampson moved off in the opposite direction, close against the wall now, wanting its black-shadowed protection. Charlie followed, trying to control the limp as much as possible, the pain burning up through his leg at every step. He swore again, but mentally, not aloud, not wanting Sampson to know his difficulty. Just before they reached the end of the wall they were following, getting actually to the rear of the prison, a faraway clock began to strike and Sampson stopped, bringing Charlie to a halt, while he counted. It was a clock that chimed the quarter-hours. They both counted three and Sampson said unnecessarily, "Quarter to twelve."

Charlie stood with his foot lifted slightly off the ground, like a lame animal, trying to ease the discomfort. "We can't stay out here in the open for fifteen minutes," he said.

"I didn't intend to," said Sampson.

Just before the very end of the wall, Sampson darted across the road to the bordering houses, holding himself briefly in the protective cover of an unkempt hedge and then, bent double, actually entering the garden in which it grew. Charlie was directly behind, accepting as he finally crouched that the concealment was perfect. The house in whose garden they hid was in darkness but there was light on in the front of the immediate neighbor and Charlie could just detect the sound of a television show. It could, he supposed, have been a radio but he didn't think so: there were too many breaks for applause.

"Know what I wish?" whispered Sampson.

"What?"

"That this were the garden of that prick Hickley."

Despite everything, Charlie wished it too.

It seemed a very long fifteen minutes, so long that once Sampson risked raising himself, very carefully, to look over the hedge, imagining as Charlie imagined that they'd failed to hear the hour strike. But then it did strike, easily audible, and Sampson said, "Come on," getting up again and scurrying around to the front of the house, still shielded by the hedge but in the road where there was no possibility of their missing the pickup car.

It came, precisely on time, some indistinguishable black

limousine turning the corner from the rear of the prison, going neither too fast nor too slowly.

"How do we know if it's the right one?" demanded Charlie.

"Wait," cautioned Sampson.

About fifty yards down the road, approaching them, the vehicle stopped. The driver got out, came forward, and kicked the front offside wheel as if testing for a puncture, then went to the boot, lifted it, appeared to gaze inside, and then closed it again, softly.

"That's the right one," said Sampson. "That's the identification."

He thrust out from their concealment, leading as he had throughout. Charlie hobbled behind, trying to keep up. They were very near, Sampson actually against the front of the car, when the figure rounded the corner. There was a streetlight there and in its perfect illumination Charlie registered the bell-helmeted shape of a policeman.

The policeman began walking down the road and then hesitated and Charlie realized they would be completely visible in the light and that the light would show perfectly prison uniforms that the policeman would instantly recognize.

"What the . . ." he actually heard the man start and then there was a fumbled movement as he groped for something in his pocket, a truncheon or whistle maybe.

Sampson's reaction was quicker. He ran across the road, directly at the policeman. Charlie saw his arm come out, not at once realizing what was happening, and then there was the muffled explosion of a shot, too muffled because the gun was held directly against the policeman's body for the sound even to reach the late-night television viewers in the opposite houses. The policeman staggered back, arms thrust out in a physical reaction of surprise, and then his legs buckled and he fell, in a stumbling collapse. Sampson did not step back immediately. Instead he stood over the body and Charlie saw him lean down, put his arm out again, and then heard another muffled explosion. Charlie was against the edge of the door, leaning weakly against it, when Sampson ran back.

"A copper," said Charlie. "You shot a copper!"

"You knew nothing was going to stop me," said Sampson.

"A copper!" repeated Charlie.

Sampson's arm came up, the muzzle against Charlie's chest like it had been against the policeman's. "Get into that fucking car," ordered Sampson.

Berenkov stared down at the brief freedom signal that had been transmitted from the prison pickup car to the embassy and sent from London an hour before, trying to think and digest clearly through a swamp of conflicting emotions. It wasn't easy, because his mind kept being blocked by the name he often— almost daily—thought about but which he never thought he would again professionally confront. Charlie Muffin. Would the man have changed, over the years? Maybe not: only four, maybe five, after all. Shambling, untidy man, suit buttons strained and shirt collar frayed, spread-apart shoes for feet that were always causing him discomfort. The sort of man people dismissed as some object of fun, which was a terrible mistake and why he dressed like that anyway, like a chameleon alters its colors to match its surroundings and stay safe. Berenkov knew the Russian service regarded him as their foremost agent, which was why he occupied the position he did today, despite Kalenin's friendship. Yet despite that expertise, Charlie Muffin had got him. Got him brilliantly and professionally and debriefed him with matching expertise, without any hostile stupidity that the others had shown, imagining they were different people just because they were on different sides. Charlie had admired him as a professional and Berenkov had admired Charlie as an equal—no, better—professional. Just as he had admired Charlie's brilliant retribution against his own service, when it decided to dump him. And admired it for its brilliance, not because he was a lucky part of it, the prisoner upon whose release Kalenin insisted after the KGB arrest of Cuthbertson and Wilberforce in Vienna, an arrest to which Charlie had led them, like innocent lambs to the slaughter. Except they hadn't been slaughtered. Just rightly exposed as the incompetent, overpromoted fools they were, incompetent first for imagining that Charlie was disposable and secondly for falling into the Viennese trap anyway. Berenkov had often wondered, during the frequent reflections, how Charlie was withstanding imprisonment. Now, it seemed, he could ask him personally when he arrived.

Because of the special relationship that existed between them and because Kalenin was anxious for Sampson's release in their search for the internal spy, Berenkov's request for a meeting with the chairman was immediately granted.

"With Sampson?" queried Kalenin, when Berenkov made the announcement.

"That's what the message said," repeated Berenkov. "It's very brief, just the first confirmation of the escape."

"Wasn't it planned?"

Berenkov shook his head. "I knew Charlie was in the same jail as Sampson, obviously. Just as it was obvious that they would meet before I could get Sampson out. I actually intended to ask Sampson as much about him as possible, when Sampson got here. I liked Charlie."

"I liked him too," said Kalenin, who had personally met Charlie and led the Austrian arrests. "But he isn't a traitor, not like Sampson and the rest."

"I know," said Berenkov, conscious of his superior's caution.

"I felt sorry for him, after his capture."

"I feel sorry for anyone in jail," said Berenkov. "Even though I knew I'd get out, just like Sampson knew he'd get out, there were times when I felt so depressed that I thought of suicide . . ." Berenkov smiled, embarrassed at the confession. "Difficult to believe that now."

"Charlie will find it difficult, adjusting here," predicted Kalenin.

"Not if he adjusted to jail," said Berenkov.

"Sampson is the important one," said Kalenin, hurrying on. "When are they due?"

"Two days . . . three at the most."

"I've blanketed the embassy here," confided Kalenin. "A squad for anyone who leaves."

"We've had that embassy in a net from the moment of the first transmission, weeks before there was any transcription even," said Berenkov. "We should have established the contact procedure by now."

"We should have done a lot of things by now," said Kalenin bitterly.

9

Charlie sat pressed into the corner of the car furthest from Sampson, physically wanting to distance himself from the man: from what he'd done and from everything about him. Charlie decided he was buggered; buggered in every way. A difficult but maybe just possible operation in the comparative orderliness of the governor's office was right out the window now, if they got caught. And they would get caught. There had been occasions, during his time in intelligence, when Charlie had been on the periphery of a cop killing and he knew the effect it had among the police. Within an hour of the finding of that poor, face-blasted bastard back there behind the prison there'd be alarms sounding throughout every southern constabulary, and an hour after that roadblocks and policemen everywhere. Armed. And ready—wanting—to shoot at two on-the-run spies who were now killers as well. Cop killers. Buggered, thought Charlie again.

He looked with contempt at Sampson, belatedly conscious of the argument that had erupted between Sampson and the front-seat passenger, a bulky, bull-shouldered man twisted round to face them both. Charlie hadn't recognized the row being in Russian, engrossed in his own thoughts, but he isolated the language now. But didn't understand it. He'd had a passing ability, a long time ago, but this was too fast; Sampson appeared as fluent as the man whose natural language it was. Not that Charlie needed to understand, even with the driver joining in with matching anger. The demanding gestures from the front-seat passenger were indication enough, beckoning insistence on being given the gun, matching with Sampson's head-shaking refusal to surrender it. It was the driver who resolved the row, pulling the car into the side of the road, stopping the engine and turning to shout "Out!" in English.

For several moments there was complete silence in the vehicle. Then Charlie said, "For Christ's sake, give him the bloody thing. You've caused enough trouble with it already. We're just asking to be caught, stuck here like this!"

If he got to Russia and managed to achieve what Wilson wanted, the deal might just stick. But not if they got picked up now. If, if, if, thought Charlie; every consideration was ruled by a doubtful if.

Reluctantly, actually halting the movement in the middle of making it, Sampson offered the Russian the gun. In the sudden illumination of an outside streetlamp Charlie saw it was a Smith and Wesson. Sampson handed it over butt-first, so that the Russian took it with the barrel directed toward Sampson.

"Why not shoot the stupid bastard!" said Charlie bitterly.

As the car started again the Russian in the passenger seat said, "Why the gun? Everything was already difficult, before this."

"Ask him, not me," said Charlie. He was glad the conversation had reverted to English.

Sampson looked despisingly across the car at Charlie and then said to the Russian, "Because it was necessary. And you damned well know it. If I hadn't been able to silence the policeman as I did, we'd have been caught, which would have been an embarrassment to Russia. And worst, the vehicle would have been linked to the escape and to the Soviet embassy and been an even greater embarrassment. I didn't want to kill the damned man. It was his misfortune to be in the wrong place. I didn't have any alternative and every one of you knows it. Just as I know you were bluffing back there. You wouldn't have forced me out of the car."

"Maybe it was a good thing for everyone that the challenge wasn't put to the test," said the Russian, appearing unimpressed at Sampson's bombast.

Charlie turned away from the ridiculous dispute. Through the car window he saw a direction sign to Tower Hamlets. They were traveling east. Where? he wondered. The London streets about which he'd reminisced all the long days and nights in the cell were eerily deserted, the actual City of London always quieter than the rest of the capital. He thought he heard the wail of a police siren and tensed, but didn't detect it again, so guessed he must have been mistaken. How long would it be before they found the man crumpled back there by the prison wall?

From inside the car he heard Sampson say, "Where are the clothes? Surely you thought of clothes?"

The arrogant sod was trying the position of command even here, Charlie recognized. From the front the passenger handed back two grips.

"Me first," insisted Sampson, twisting and turning in the confined rear space. After he had changed and stuffed the prison uniform into the grip, Charlie switched, aware of the good quality of the clothing as he put it on and aware, too, that the pockets had things in them, as they would have done if they were normally worn suits. What he thought was gray worsted and definitely a well-laundered white shirt. The shoes pinched but with his feet Charlie was used to that. He left them half on and half off, for comfort.

"There," said the Russian in front, an order.

Obediently the driver stopped and the other man stuffed the refilled hold-alls into a refuse bin at the pavement edge, carefully ensuring the covering flap came back concealingly into position.

"We are returning from a dinner in London," dictated the Russian as the car moved again. "There are counterfoils of the tickets in your left-hand jacket pocket. Tombola tickets, too . . ." He smiled back at them, holding up a crystal decanter with a ticket still attached. "I was the lucky one."

Very good, decided Charlie, realizing as he did so that they were clearing London. Any roadblock would be hurried, particularly out of the capital. Photographs certainly wouldn't be available, not this quickly. It was the sort of cover story that might get them through, if the need arose. The ever-present if, he thought once more.

"It's fortunate we made the departure arrangements that we did," said the man in front. "Let's hope they'll still be possible." Heavily he added to Sampson, "And this car is not traceable to our embassy in London."

Charlie was caught by the disclaimer as the man came to him. "You are called Muffin?"

"Yes." Charlie nodded.

"I am Letsov."

Charlie frowned at the introduction. There shouldn't have been identities if the man were attached to London. The frown deepened, in self-irritation. It had taken him too long to realize that the Russians would never have risked anyone actually from the embassy. He looked with renewed interest at the two in front. They were called *spetnaz*, he remembered; an elite and highly secret commando group within the KGB, the equivalent, he supposed, of the British SAS or the American Special Forces. Moscow must regard Sampson as very important indeed to go to all this trouble. The other Englishman appeared relaxed and comfortable in the opposite corner, hand casually looped through an assistance strap near the door, as if he were actually being chauffeured back from some mundane late-night outing.

To Letsov Charlie said, "We're getting out tonight?"

"Of course," said the Russian, as if he were surprised at the question.

Outside Charlie caught brief sight of a signpost to Braintree. "And you're coming all the way?"

"No further reason to stay," said Letsov, confirming Charlie's guess at their being *spetnaz*.

⌐ The driver said something that Charlie didn't catch, in Russian, and he didn't hear Letsov's reply, either, but from the way the man stared through both the front and the rear windows at the remark Charlie guessed it was a reference to there being no obvious police presence.

"Thank you," said Charlie, to Letsov. "For all this."

The Russian shrugged. "There were orders," he said.

"Which I initiated," Sampson reminded.

Fuck you, thought Charlie.

They even risked the motorway when it came, traveling almost completely along its full length before a warning from Letsov at a sign that took them off on an obviously reconnoitered route through minor roads. There were two darkened, sleeping villages and then a bigger place, a small town, which they entered without Charlie being aware of any name. They parked once more to an obviously prepared plan, in a covered, multistory car park. Letsov turned back toward them, hefted the decanter, and said, "It seems my luck is holding."

Almost at once, the smile went. "The car was a cover. It isn't any longer," he warned.

Reluctantly Charlie put his feet fully into the shoes, feeling his ankle as he did so. There wasn't any swelling from his clumsy landing and he was glad: he didn't want any indication of weakness in front of Sampson. Or the other two men, either.

As they emerged onto the deserted street Charlie saw, about fifty yards in the opposite direction from which Letsov led them, the telltale blue sign of the police station. They really meant to rub it in, thought Charlie.

Letsov and the driver led familiarly but cautiously, almost at once leaving the main road for smaller, bordering ones. Charlie smelled the smell of sea and heard an early shrill of seagulls. Dawn was tentatively on the horizon when they reached the estuary, already forming the buildings in black-and-gray outlines. Boats, too. It was hardly a proper marina, more a parking place for weekend sailors avid for the pastime without the money truly to enjoy it. Charlie guessed the boats, if he could have seen them more clearly, would be run-down, like the mooring.

Their boat was at the end of a small slipway, isolated from the other craft and cowled in a protective covering which the two Russians expertly and silently unclipped and stowed, gesturing Sampson and Charlie into the cramped cabin. The odor was of damp and leaked fuel and in the light which Letsov snapped on, behind curtained windows, Charlie saw most of the inside varnish had peeled whitely away from the timbers.

There was another hold-all on a single bunk to the left. Letsov opened it and tossed heavy blue Guernsey sweaters at them and said, "Now we're enthusiastic amateur sailors, leaving early. But you two stay below until we've cleared."

Charlie and Sampson swapped the jackets for the sweaters and sat unspeaking on either side of the cabin. Above, Charlie heard the muted, careful sounds of the other men preparing their departure. They must have left only one securing line at the end because directly the engine fired, overloudly in the morning stillness, they cast off, without waiting for it to warm up. They proceeded downriver at the lowest throttle, but from the note Charlie guessed that unlike the rest of the boat, the engine wasn't old or disused. At full throttle it would probably have torn itself from its mountings.

"So everyone shit themselves for nothing," sneered Sampson triumphantly from across the cabin. "We made it."

Charlie said nothing.

After about half an hour there was a change in the motion of the boat, as it encountered the sea swell. The engine increased its note and the smell of diesel permeated the cabin.

"How much longer before we can go on deck?" demanded Sampson, of no one.

Charlie looked at the man and realized he was suffering seasickness, and was glad. "Be slop-out time back at the nick," he said, wanting to encourage it. "All that smell of piss."

"Shut up, for Christ's sake," said Sampson.

Charlie did, not to spare Sampson but because the baiting

was pointless and if he made the bastard sick for the rest of his life it wouldn't be retribution for what he'd done.

It was another hour before Letsov opened the hatch, and by then Sampson was heaving. The man fled to the stern of the boat, retching into the wake, and momentarily Charlie thought how easy it would have been to have seized his legs and tipped him over the gunwale. The temptation receded as quickly as it came. They could loop easily, to pick him up. Pointless, like encouraging the sickness.

It was fully light now, a dull gray day with the clouds stubbornly against the sea, as if they didn't want night to go. Far to port Charlie detected a duck line of fishing boats heading back to harbor and wondered which one it would be. He stepped up into the cockpit. The car driver retained his role, as helmsman. Letsov stood with a chart spread between them, minutely focusing a radio. Charlie became aware that the man was concentrating upon a heavy wristwatch and at some clearly prearranged time pressed a relay button on the set. It would be short-burst transmission, Charlie knew, expertly: a full message electronically reduced to a meaningless blip to any accidental interception, decipherable only to those properly listening for it.

"We were lucky," said Letsov, speaking to Charlie but looking beyond, to the still-retching Sampson. "I guess it took a long time to find the body."

"He didn't have to die," insisted Charlie.

Letsov came fully to him, smiling wearily. "I know of you; of your street experience," said the Russian. "And I agree. The policeman could have been immobilized." He looked back to Sampson. "He never worked the streets. Always liaison or administration. A good agent to have in place, but a bad one to be trapped with."

There was a low shout from the helmsman behind them and as they turned Charlie saw the outline of a vessel forming on the horizon. As they got closer he discerned the oddly shaped radar bubble and the stiff-haired antennae of what the Russians called trawlers and the rest of the world spy ships.

Letsov depressed the transmission button once again, positive identification Charlie supposed, and then turned as Sampson forced himself to join them, whey-faced.

"How long to reach Russia in that?" he asked, strained-voiced.

"Murmansk," said Letsov. "A couple of days."

Sampson made a grunting sound of despair.

The helmsman maneuvered the motorboat into the lee of the larger vessel. They exchanged loose linklines, which meant they had to jump for the rope ladder thrown down from the trawler. Charlie went first, easily, looking back hopefully to Sampson. At first it looked as if the man might actually balk at jumping across the narrow channel of heaving sea, but then he did, misholding at the first attempt and hanging one-handed for a brief moment between the two vessels before snatching out a second time, getting a grip, and hauling himself upward. He stood shaking at the rail break, almost appearing unaware of where he was. Around them seamen bustled, going through what was still a well-planned exercise. There were shouted, relayed messages from the bridge wing to the sailors to the two still in the boat and then Charlie saw charges being handed down. It took minutes to place them and then the two who had rescued them made the crossing and climbed aboard. At once the trawler cast off and moved away. Letsov remained at the rail. When they were about fifty yards away, Letsov said, with professional pride and without consulting his watch to get the time, "Now!" and precisely on cue the explosion came, in a dull crump, tearing the bottom completely from the cabin cruiser. It jumped, surprised, in the water, then sank at once.

"Welcome," said a voice behind them, and Charlie turned to face the captain. "Welcome," the man said again. "To a new life."

Christ, thought Charlie.

With the murder of the policeman it had not achieved the humiliating propaganda success that had been intended and Berenkov knew it, just as he knew their personal friendship would not prevent Kalenin delivering the necessary and deserved rebuke.

"I'm sorry," he said sincerely. "I had no idea they would have a gun."

"Charlie Muffin?" queried Kalenin.

Berenkov shook his head. "Letsov radioed a full report. It was Sampson. He panicked. Charlie doesn't panic: I know that too well."

"How are they?"

"Letsov says there's ill feeling between them."

Kalenin indicated the intercepted messages from the British embassy: there were four more since they had last discussed it. He said, "We planned for Sampson, even before all these. And the help he might be able to give. What about Charlie? Can he be of any use?"

"I wouldn't imagine about these," said Berenkov, making his own indication toward the messages. "He was on the run for three years, don't forget. Out of touch. But if he wanted to he could teach agents we intend introducing into the West more about the business—and survival—in a month than they could learn from our instructors in a year."

Kalenin pulled down the corners of his mouth at the unqualified admiration and at the reservation. "Wanted to!" he said.

"I was considered the best, wasn't I?" asked Berenkov. There was no boastfulness in the question.

"Yes," agreed Kalenin.

"He caught me," reminded Berenkov. "Just like he caught those idiots in his own department who considered him expendable."

"I don't understand the point you're making," complained the KGB chairman.

"Charlie's brilliant," said Berenkov simply. "He's also the most awkward bastard imaginable."

10

Charlie was handcuffed for the return to England after his Italian arrest and there had been an escort of at least two warders for every remand appearance and then the eventual taking to Wormwood Scrubs, and there was the impress of *déjà vu* during the journey to Moscow, another guarded trip to another sort of imprisonment. Sampson was ill throughout the voyage to Murmansk, rarely leaving the cabin—for which Charlie was grateful—but recovered dramatically when they got ashore. Almost at once he started behaving like a deprived child on its first outing, using his Russian wherever he could, pointlessly reading out signs and posters and staring around excitedly at buildings and streets. Letsov and the other Russian, whose name emerged as Orlov, remained with them throughout, right to Moscow, but increasingly during the voyage and more so once they reached the Russian mainland, their attitude grew into one of undisguised boredom and disinterest, men whose task had been completed now burdened with the irksome task of baby-sitting.

It was dark when the plane from Murmansk arrived at Sheremetyevo airport, which seemed larger and more brightly lit than when Charlie had last landed there, ten years earlier on secondment to the embassy. And the journey into Moscow appeared to take longer than he remembered. It was difficult, because of the darkness, to recognize any landmarks. He thought he isolated the river but wasn't sure. He definitely located one of the red stars illuminated above the Kremlin, and using that as a marker, realized they were being driven far out into the suburbs of the city.

Orlov, who was driving as usual, had difficulty finding their destination, twice having to stop and ask directions. It was an apartment block, a vast, anonymous pile of a place, seeming to stretch the entire block and rise blackly up into the night sky. Only a few windows were lighted and the impression was of abandonment, which Charlie decided was fitting.

Orlov didn't bother to get out of the car, leaving Letsov to complete the final part of the assignment. The bulky Russian led the way into the building and up a flight of chipped and smelling stairs to an apartment at the far end of an unlighted corridor. From behind the closed doorways they passed came the scuffing and murmur of occupation and once the louder sound of a radio; a woman was singing a melancholy Slavic dirge and Charlie decided he knew how she felt. The pervading smell was of cabbage.

Letsov entered the apartment peremptorily, snapping on the lights and indicating the place with a take-it-or-leave-it gesture with his hand.

"You must stay here," he said. "You will be contacted."

"Together?" demanded Charlie at once.

"Stay here," repeated Letsov. He pointed toward the telephone. "Tomorrow."

Charlie looked around the room. It was a Spartan place, just a couch and two chairs, with a table and two more chairs against the far wall. Beside the table an opening, without a door or curtaining, led into a kitchen. To the left was a short corridor. As he watched, Sampson, still with his little-boy excitement, discovered the bathroom and two separate bedrooms.

"Good-bye," said Letsov, at the doorway.

"Thanks again," said Charlie. During the voyage he had attempted some approach to the man, whom he recognized as a complete professional, but like a complete professional, Letsov had rejected anything more than the most necessary conversation. Charlie regretted it. He thought Letsov was the sort of man he could have liked; understood at least.

"Good luck," said the Russian, making a last-minute concession.

"Thanks for that, too," said Charlie.

Sampson emerged from the further bedroom as the Russian left and announced, with his predictable command of every situation, "I'll have this one. You take the other."

Charlie shrugged, uninterested in arguing about it. He hoped to Christ they weren't together for much longer. "Where did you get your Russian?" he said.

"I got my degree in modern languages at Oxford," said Sampson. "Got an aptitude for it. And for almost the last two years I was number three on the Russian desk."

"You were in the Russian section?" said Charlie. He wondered why the man hadn't boasted about that earlier, like he had about almost everything else.

"I was ordered to penetrate it, from here, when I was on station in Beirut."

"So for two years Moscow had an open door into everything we knew or thought about them!" demanded Charlie. What a bastard, he thought.

"And a lot of what NATO thought: Washington too," reminded the other man. "I told you I was important, didn't I?"

"Yes," said Charlie emptily. He went to the uncurtained window, staring out. There appeared to be a matching apartment block on the opposite side of the street, picked out with as few lights as theirs. He wondered if that smelled of overcooked cabbage as well. Six months, he thought. Six months was bearable. But was it time to achieve what Wilson demanded? And would the deal still stand, either way, after the murder? There was, of course, another alternative. The one he had been deliberately shunting aside in his mind. What if the Russians came to suspect what he was really doing? And that's all they would need to do, just suspect. Another prison, if they let him live at all. And no limit on the sentence this time. Compared to the *gulags*, Wormwood Scrubs would have been a village in the sun. Charlie shuddered, a physical reaction, and from his side Sampson said, "It's not cold."

"No," said Charlie, who hadn't been aware of the man's approach. If I lived in Moscow, the weather would not matter, he thought.

"This is it, Charlie," said Sampson, with his undiminished enthusiasm. "Like the captain said, a new life."

"Yeah," said Charlie, unimpressed.

"Aren't you excited?"

"No."

"You're going to have to do it, you know," said Sampson. "Just like in the nick."

"What?" said Charlie.

"Adjust. Stop being a bloody fool and adjust."

He wasn't going to be a bloody fool, Charlie decided. Sampson thought he was the clever one, the expert; but that wasn't how it was going to be. Charlie determined that no matter how difficult or impossible it seemed, he was going to find whoever the unknown defector was and arrange his escape and show this arrogant, conceited smart-ass—and Moscow and the department in London—that he was still what he always had been. Better than any of them.

"You're right," he said. "I am being a bloody fool. It's going to be great, when I get used to it."

"That's better," said Sampson, actually throwing his arm around Charlie's shoulders.

Charlie managed to resist pulling away at the touch. If Sampson was as important as he claimed—and appeared to be, from the rescue—the man might actually be the way to get to people in Dzerzhinsky Square. And he'd need shortcuts. Only six months, after all. "I wonder how long the debriefing will take?" he said.

"Longer for me than for you; you've been away from things for too long."

Jesus! thought Charlie. "You're right," he said, actually

managing to intrude the impression of admiration into his voice. "You're the one they really rescued, after all."

It was Sampson, of course, who answered the telephone when it rang the following morning, the expectant greeting fading into a frown of annoyed incomprehension when he replaced the receiver. "You," he said to Charlie. "They're sending a car for you first. I'm to wait."

Satisfaction warmed through Charlie, the feeling remaining as he left the apartment building thirty minutes later. He didn't look up but hoped Sampson was at the window. The unspeaking chauffeur drove quickly, using the center lane reserved exclusively for government vehicles, but not, Charlie realized, back into the center of the capital but still further out, toward the peripheral road. The KGB had extensive offices in the suburbs, Charlie remembered; but Dzerzhinsky Square was the headquarters he had to penetrate, and he was going in the opposite direction.

It was a huge, modern building—American in style almost—actually bordering the ring road. From the rear he saw the driver radio their approach, so a man was waiting when the vehicle pulled up, not at the main entrance but at a side door. The man, who was slight and bespectacled and wore a civilian suit, not any kind of uniform, opened the door from the outside and said, in English, "You are to come with me."

At an inner desk the escort produced an identity pass and led Charlie, unspeaking like the driver, along an encircling corridor to a bank of elevators, selecting the sixth floor.

"If I lived in Moscow, the weather would not matter," Charlie said to the man, just for the hell of it.

The man looked back expressionless, without replying. He led out onto the upper floor and produced his pass again, twice, to get them through two more checkpoints.

The door at which he stopped was unmarked, either by name or number. He knocked, opened the door immediately, but just sufficient for him to look around, for fuller permission to enter, and then stood back, ushering Charlie through.

Charlie started to enter the room and then stopped, in

abrupt surprise. It was quite a spacious office, with a view of the circular highway outside. There were flowers on a low table and one wall was lined with books. His debriefer sat at an uncluttered desk, smiling a greeting. And was a woman.

The escape and the shooting created an outcry in England. After three days of persistent demands the Prime Minister agreed to a commission of inquiry. The dead policeman was identified as a single man, a probationary constable, without parents, any immediate family, or even close girlfriends, and the human-interest coverage in the newspapers switched to the battered prison officer, who posed for photographs at the urging of the Prison Officers' Association, demanding better protection for its members from his hospital bed, surrounded by his worried-looking family. Wilson was twice summoned to Downing Street, personally to brief the Prime Minister before House of Commons question time.

Harkness was waiting when the Director returned after the second visit, conscious at once of the anger in the usually urbane man.

"Judged a disaster," said Wilson. "A ridiculous disaster."

"We expected that," reminded Harkness.

"But not quite the degree of public reaction," said Wilson. He sat at his desk, leg out stiffly before him.

"What about the governor?" said Harkness.

"No positive commitment, but I managed to get a stay of execution," said the Director. "Until after the inquiry, at least. But not to have the damned thing in camera, which I wanted. Newspapers wouldn't stand for it, I was told."

"Who runs the country, the Government or newspapers?" said Harkness in unaccustomed bitterness.

"Sometimes I wonder," said Wilson.

"Do you think the Russians will make them available in Moscow? They have with defectors in the past."

The Director pursed his lips doubtfully. "Not with the shooting," he said. "If they'd simply escaped, yes. But they'd be parading murderers and admitting to harboring them. So no, I don't expect any press conferences."

"So we sit the storm out and wait upon Charlie Muffin," said Harkness.

"Yes," agreed Wilson. "For the moment, everything depends upon Charlie Muffin."

11

About thirty-five, guessed Charlie; maybe younger, but he doubted it. Black hair, without any attempt at style, loose to her shoulders, and no makeup that he could discern. Freckles around her nose and practical, sensible spectacles, heavy-rimmed. Nice teeth, shown by the smile. Gray dress, tunic fashion but not a uniform; because she was sitting behind the desk, he could only see the top half, but the dress was quite tight and the top half would definitely be worth seeing. Women—and sex—had been of necessity rigidly excluded from any thoughts in prison and he'd hardly had time since. Charlie decided he'd very much like to break the celibacy of the last few years with her. And then he remembered where he was and what he was doing—or supposed to be doing—and realized prison rules still applied.

"Please," she said, still smiling and holding her hand out in invitation toward the chair slightly to the side of her neat, orderly desk. As he sat, she said, "Welcome to Moscow."

"People keep saying things like that," said Charlie. There was hardly any accent in her voice, which was quite deep. He tried to make casual the look around the office, to locate the likely positioning of the cameras and recording devices. Some would unquestionably be in place and the seat to which he'd

107

been directed was clearly positioned for a reason. There were too many possible positions and he decided the examination was pointless.

"This is only a formality, you understand?"

Liar, thought Charlie. He said, "I understand."

She took up a pen, looked down at an open folder, and said, "I don't know anything about you, other than your name."

Liar again, thought Charlie. The KGB index was a legend, a computerized record far more detailed than any comparable system in any Western service. He'd have been on it for years and his file would have been heavily annotated after the affair with the English Director. It wouldn't have been erased after his capture and imprisonment, either; nothing was ever removed from the Moscow index. She might be attractive but she wasn't much good. She should have known he'd be aware of the Soviet system.

"I don't even know yours," he said. If they were debriefing him with someone as inexperienced as this, he wasn't regarded as anyone of importance. Which meant what he was supposed to do was going to be bloody difficult. Charlie didn't like being regarded as someone past importance. Careful, he thought; he was beginning to think like Sampson.

The woman frowned momentarily at the clumsy flirtation, then smiled again. "Fedova," she said. "Natalia Nikandrova Fedova."

"Do I call you Comrade or Natalia?"

"I don't think you call me anything, but rather remember this is an official meeting," she said.

Charlie thought she had to force the stiffness into her voice. He said, "But only a formality."

"I have a file to complete," she said, tapping the paper in front of her.

Like he'd already decided, a clerk, thought Charlie. He said, "Charles Edward Muffin—Charlie to friends. Born Elstree, England. Mother Joan, a cook. Father unknown. Entered British service from grammar school through immediate postwar exigency, when they were short and recruitment was easy. Active field agent until five years ago. Realized I was being set up by my own service as a decoy during an entrapment operation involving your own General Berenkov, who for many years ran an active cell in London and whose arrest I led. So I taught the bastards a lesson and made it possible for your people to seize the British Director—who should never have been Director anyway—and arrange an exchange for Berenkov . . ." Charlie paused, aware of the carelessness of the recital. He said, "Most—if not all—of which should be in that folder in front of you because I know the sort of records you keep and I was, after all, personally involved with Berenkov and with your current chairman, General Kalenin . . ."

Natalia showed no reaction whatever to his impatience. She said, "What happened then?"

Then I had four miserable years on the run and never a day went by without my realizing what a bloody fool I'd been, thought Charlie. He said, "At first I stayed in England, because I knew there would be a hunt and they wouldn't have expected me to do that. Seaside towns, where there are always lots of visitors, so strangers aren't unusual. Then Europe, holiday places again, never staying anywhere too long . . ."

"What about your wife?" demanded the woman.

It was several moments before Charlie replied, confronting the deepest and bitterest regret of all. Then he said, "I was almost caught, after the first year. A combined operation by my own service and the CIA, because I exposed their Director, too, and the Americans wanted me as well. I got away. She was killed." Dear Edith, he thought. Neglected and cheated on and forced by what he did into the life of a fugitive, which she'd hated. And never a moment of complaint or criticism. Why the hell had it taken her death to make him realize how much he'd loved her?

"And then?" persisted the woman, bent over the papers in front of her.

"The British service was by tradition one of university

graduates," remembered Charlie. "I never did fit. I was kept on by a marvelous man, one of the best Directors ever. He had a son, a Lloyds underwriter. He let me work for him—it had never been made public, what I did, because of the embarrassment it would have caused, so he didn't know."

"You were working for him when you were caught?"

Charlie nodded. "In Italy," he started. The pause was momentary and he didn't think she would have noticed it before he finished—differently from the way he intended—by saying, "Two and a half years ago." Part of the original deal—the deal he believed Wilson had reneged on—had been to say nothing at the trial, even though it was held in camera, about the entrapment in Italy of the British ambassador as a Soviet spy because Wilson wanted to keep the conduits open to feed as much disinformation as he could to Moscow. Dismissive of this meaningless encounter with the woman, Charlie realized he'd allowed himself to become careless, unthinking about the answers. Unthinking! The word stayed with him, an accusation. He was being unthinking. And stupid and arrogant and the worst—unprofessional—in imagining the meeting was meaningless. She'd made the mistake and he'd almost missed it. Natalia Nikandrova Fedova had said she knew nothing about him and then interposed the question about Edith: about whom she was supposed to have no knowledge. So the clerk demeanor was a trick, a trick that had worked to achieve precisely the effect it had, lulling him into carelessness by the time they reached the point of the meeting, their need to know if the Italian ambassador had been uncovered. Charlie remembered the beaten prison officer and the murdered policeman and supposed Sampson would be absorbed into the Soviet service. Maybe it was a convoluted way of getting back at the man—misleading the KGB Sampson would undoubtedly join—but at the moment it was the only opportunity he had. He'd have to be careful to maintain his earlier attitude.

"What were you doing for Willoughby's son?"

Another mistake, isolated Charlie. He hadn't named Willoughby as the Director for whom he'd worked all those years and ended practically idolizing. Charlie said, "He was an underwriter, like I said. Sometimes some of the claims seemed suspicious. I'd investigate them."

"What was suspicious about Italy?" pressed the woman.

"It was a huge jewel robbery, involving the wife of the British ambassador," said Charlie, lounged in the chair physically to convey the uncaring attitude he wanted her to go on believing; the hidden cameras, too. "It coincided with the renewal at a vastly increased valuation of the policy and it looked a bit doubtful. People sometimes overinsure and then conveniently lose things if they're short of money."

She smiled disarmingly across the desk and said, "Even British ambassadors?"

"Even British ambassadors," said Charlie, trying to recapture the earlier flirtation.

"Was there?"

"Was there what?" said Charlie, knowing the question but maintaining the pretense.

"Anything suspicious about the robbery?"

Charlie shrugged. "Never had time to find out. The station officer at the embassy for British intelligence was someone who had been in the department with me. He recognized me and sounded the alarm. And I got caught."

The basic lesson of every interrogation course Charlie had ever undergone—and reinforced during countless actual sessions when he was operating—was that a good liar tells as few lies as possible, to minimize the chance of being caught out. He'd been as vague and as flippant about Italy as he had about everything else and he knew damned well they couldn't trap him upon what he had said so far.

"Was America involved in your capture?" asked Natalia, approaching from another direction. "You said they tried in an earlier operation; the one in which Edith was killed."

He hadn't mentioned Edith by name, remembered Charlie: another slip. He said, "No, just the British."

"Still a large operation, though?"

The ambassador would have warned Moscow of the influx and the personal danger, Charlie supposed. He said, "I caused the disgrace of both the British and American directors. And they failed to get me once. They didn't take any chances the second time. They flooded the place with people." He stopped for just the right amount of time and added, "And they got me, well and truly."

"Why did you betray your country?" she demanded suddenly.

"I didn't betray my country," responded Charlie instinctively. Yet another direction surprised him and he decided definitely that she wasn't as inexperienced as he had first thought. With that realization came another; so he wasn't being dismissed as unimportant. It pleased him.

"Of course you did," she said. "You exposed two directors to arrest and enabled the repatriation of a Russian your country had jailed as a spy."

"It was a personal thing," insisted Charlie. "I told you they were prepared to screw me: I screwed them instead."

"What gave you the right to question the decision of your superiors?"

"The fact that it was my life they were making a decision about," said Charlie vehemently.

"To whom do you consider the first loyalty."

"Me," said Charlie at once. "My first loyalty is always to me." There was no danger in this philosophizing, but Charlie was cautious now, conscious how she used directional changes in attempts to off-balance.

"There must have been many times, as an active field agent, when you were engaged in an operation which put your life at risk."

"No," said Charlie, refusing the argument. "All the other operations carried the acceptable risks, which I knew and understood. This time they made an active, positive decision to sacrifice me. That wasn't acceptable."

"To you?" she said.

"To me," agreed Charlie. He thought he knew the tactic: to prod and goad until he lost his temper. *Never lose your temper:* another caution in interrogation.

"Many people would regard that attitude as arrogant," said the woman. She paused and added, "Which it is."

"And many people would regard it as an instinct for survival," said Charlie. "Which it is." He feigned annoyance, raising his voice, curious where she was leading the questioning.

"The court that sentenced you thought otherwise."

Back to Italy, recognized Charlie. Very clever. He said, "I didn't expect anything else."

She waited several moments, waiting for him to continue. When he didn't, she said, "Didn't you try to put your point of view to the court?"

It had been a secure hearing and he didn't think there could have been any way for them to learn of the evidence. He said, "Of course I did. But they didn't want to listen, did they! Made their minds up before the trial started."

"They weren't seen to get their revenge, were they?" she said. "The hearing was in secret."

Good again, admired Charlie. He said, "It's customary, under our law, in the case of security. Like I've already said, they'd have been embarrassed if the full facts had come out about their own Director being seized."

"What did come out?"

"Not much," said Charlie, hoping he sounded dismissive enough. "They made it sound as if I was a long-term Soviet agent, which I wasn't and never had been: that my whole purpose in being in intelligence was to get to the point where I could trap the Director. That wasn't true, either."

"Wasn't and never had been," echoed Natalia.

"You know that," said Charlie, anticipating another move.

"Then why have you come to Moscow?"

Charlie laughed, genuinely. "I didn't have any choice, did I? Sampson was in the same bloody cell."

"Is that all?"

"No, that's not all. I came because I couldn't stand another day in that damned prison," said Charlie, genuine still.

"But you don't think of yourself as someone subscribing to the communist way of life?"

Careful, thought Charlie. No more lies than absolutely necessary, he remembered. "No," he admitted honestly. "I don't see myself subscribing to your way of life."

"Why then should we give you sanctuary?" she asked forcefully, staring up at him. "People were hurt, killed, during your escape. Why should we harbor you to the embarrassment of ourselves?"

"I didn't hurt anyone. Or kill anyone," said Charlie.

"Something else you're not guilty of?" she said jeeringly.

She almost won. Charlie felt the burn of anger, coming close to giving way to it, and then stopped himself. He said, "Sampson is a maniac."

"What if he attests the same against you?"

"Your own people saw him shoot the policeman," said Charlie, scoring. "Ask them."

"You don't like him?"

Charlie laughed again. "Like him! I despise him. He's a traitor and he's dangerous. Not as a traitor. As a man. I think he gets pleasure from inflicting hurt."

"How was he regarded within your service?"

Another pathway, recognized Charlie. He was comfortable with the interrogation now, no longer complacent but confident he could anticipate the traps. "I don't know," he said.

"Weren't you contemporaries?"

"No."

"Not even in the same departments?"

"No."

"You don't consider yourself a traitor?"

Which way was she going now? "No," repeated Charlie.

"If you had been in the same department—knew his capabilities—would you tell me? Or would you regard that as being a traitor?"

"My dear Natalia," said Charlie, intentionally patronizing and seeing an easy escape. "If I knew anything at all about Edwin Sampson, I'd tell you."

"So what do you know about him?"

She'd refused to become irritated by his attitude, just as he had by hers, Charlie knew. He said, "About his work in the service, nothing. And about his betrayal, only what I read in the newspapers, like everyone else. In jail he was very clever, ass-crawling to everybody who mattered and getting himself trusted, which made the escape possible. And during that he delighted in causing as much physical harm as possible, as I already told you."

"Just as you already made it clear to me that you don't like him," said Natalia. "Would you trust him, professionally?"

"No," said Charlie immediately. "Sampson's first regard would be to himself, not to the operation."

"Wasn't that your attitude when you exposed your directors?" she pounced. "And isn't it still?"

Shit, thought Charlie. He said, "I never failed, in any operation in which I was ever involved. I always won."

"Was that because of loyalty to the service?" she asked presciently. "Or personal pride?"

Shit again, he thought. Charlie said, "The two made a great contribution."

"Will you cooperate with us?" asked his interrogator. "Cooperate in a full debriefing and supply us with whatever information we ask of you?"

Crunch point, decided Charlie. He'd have to give if he were going to stand any chance at all of achieving what Wilson wanted. But immediate acquiescence hadn't been the role he'd adopted that morning. Trying to maintain the established attitude, he said, "I don't know."

Natalia Fedova snapped the folder shut, staring at him

across the desk. "We'll talk further," she said. She wasn't smiling anymore.

Such a debriefing would not normally have occupied the chairman, but Kalenin wasn't any ordinary chairman in his attention to detail, and in addition, he was anxious to get through the necessary interrogation as quickly as possible, to involve Sampson in the effort to trace the spy working through the British embassy. So he saw the video recording of Charlie's interview that night, with Berenkov, who was the deputy in charge of Natalia Fedova's division and who had personal experience of the Englishman. They watched it completely once, without any halt or discussion, and then a second time, stop-starting the tape at moments they considered might be important. A written transcript had also been provided and they studied that, too, so it was several hours before they began to talk.

"Well?" said Kalenin.

Berenkov made an uncertain rocking motion with his hand. "There's not much there we didn't already know. Nothing in fact."

"I only personally met Charlie a couple of times. You knew him better. What do you think?"

"He'd have conducted a better debriefing than that," said Berenkov honestly.

"I thought he was sloppy," said Kalenin. "Careless and sloppy."

"Maybe," said Berenkov, not so convinced.

"He couldn't have cared less about the answers he gave," argued the Chairman.

Instead of replying Berenkov rewound and replayed the tape to the part of Charlie's momentary pause when Natalia reached the Italian arrest. "He changed his mind there," Berenkov judged. "And was sharper from then on."

"You sure?"

"No, I'm not sure," admitted Berenkov. "I got caught by underestimating Charlie Muffin once, remember?"

"He's not the important one," said Kalenin. "Sampson is important."

"Charlie could still be useful in many ways," insisted Berenkov. "I think they should be kept together in that apartment. It's wired and I think it might be interesting."

"To learn what?"

"I don't know, not yet," admitted Berenkov. "I know it's important to find as quickly as possible the spy for Britain. But I don't think we should cut corners."

"I don't intend cutting corners," said Kalenin stiffly. "I just think it would have been better if we'd begun the debriefing with Sampson."

Berenkov accepted it as an observation, not a criticism. He said, "We'd have to make a lot of adjustments if the British uncovered the ambassador in Italy. And it was important to establish Sampson's stability. We know from our own people how he responded, confronted with the policeman."

"What's Sampson's stability got to do with anything?" said Kalenin. "Maybe he panicked. It's understandable. And maybe he likes inflicting pain. I don't see how either thing is going to affect our use for him."

"Everything is an eagerness to please, to impress us," pointed out Berenkov. "We want to get whoever it is in contact with the British, not be misled by somebody saying anything that comes into his head, imagining it's going to be what we want to hear."

Kalenin gestured toward the now blank screen in the viewing room. "There was nothing there to give any indication that Sampson might do that." Kalenin paused. "In fact," he added, "from your assessment the person that might do that is Charlie Muffin."

Berenkov shook his head. "Charlie Muffin won't trick me again," he said.

"He made it possible for you to be repatriated," reminded the chairman.

"Because it suited his purpose, not because of me," said Berenkov. Now Berenkov indicated the screen in front of them. "My first loyalty is always to me," he quoted.

"Do you want to meet him again?" asked Kalenin.

"Very much," admitted Berenkov. "Very much indeed."

12

Not bad, judged Charlie, reviewing the debriefing. But not good, either. A stupid start, from which he'd had to make a hurried recovery, and he would never know if that recovery was obvious. And she'd backed him into a corner at the end. But they were minimal uncertainties. The biggest—and one he'd failed to realize until now because everything had been so hurried—was the possibility that Sampson knew, from his then undiscovered position in London, how Wilson had used the Italian ambassador. Would there be any trace of his own involvement? The British Director had been personally involved, keeping it a top-echelon matter, but Charlie supposed there would have had to be some headquarter discussion. And official paperwork. Sampson had been number three on the Russian desk, he recalled. If there had been paperwork, no matter how minimal, then at that clearance level Sampson would have read it. If he'd read it, then Sampson would have alerted Moscow, Charlie thought, carrying the internal discussion further. So why had she bothered to quiz him so closely? Maybe not the sort of test he'd imagined. Maybe he'd misinterpreted the whole damned thing and they'd just been checking to see whether he'd cooperate or lie. If that were the case, then he'd emerged worse than he imagined. Worse but

119

still recoverable. He'd said he wasn't sure he'd cooperate, and if he were later accused of lying about Italy, he could convincingly argue that he wasn't lying but uncertain at the time of his first debriefing about a full commitment. Could he argue it convincingly? He wouldn't know until he tried. Back in the familiar labyrinth, he recognized. Difficult to imagine that just a month earlier—five weeks at the most—he was actually missing it.

As Charlie entered the shared apartment, to find the anxious Sampson waiting directly beyond the threshold, Charlie realized a way to retrace some of his steps if he had been trapped.

"What happened?" demanded Sampson at once.

"A debriefing, that's all," said Charlie, moving further into the main room.

"What do you mean, that's all! What happened? Was it a committee? Just one man? What do they want?" He jerked his hand irritably toward the telephone. "I've been sitting in this damned box all day and there's been nothing, nothing at all."

"You keep telling me how important you are," said Charlie. "Perhaps they need time to prepare."

"Cut it out," insisted Sampson, voice quiet in his anger. "I want to know what it's like."

It had gone well, decided Charlie. "Just one person," he recounted. "A woman in my case. Natalia Fedova. Said she knew nothing about me, which had to be a lie. You know as well as I do the sort of records they keep. Went over everything, in a pretty general manner, from the time I exposed the Director. Finally asked me if I'd cooperate."

"You said yes, of course," anticipated the other man.

"No," said Charlie.

"No!"

"Depends what they want me to do."

"No it doesn't and you know it," said Sampson. "Christ, when are you going to learn?"

"I won't betray everything, not like you."

"You haven't got any choice."

Not the response he'd wanted, thought Charlie. "Maybe you haven't," he said. "You're committed."

"There was discussion about me!"

Better, thought Charlie. "Yes," he said.

"What? When?"

Perfect, decided Charlie, taking the second query. "Soon after I was questioned about my detection in Italy. You knew all about that, of course."

"About what?" asked Sampson, impatient again.

"My arrest in Italy. You were in London then?"

Sampson shook his head. "Beirut," he said. "I didn't get back for several months after. The trial hadn't happened, but you were back in the country."

So the man wouldn't have known! Safe, thought Charlie. It had been easier than he thought. Not wanting a later discernible pause he said, "They asked if I knew anything of you in the service. What sort of person you were. Whether I liked you even."

"What did you say?"

"That I never encountered you when I was working in the department, that I thought you were a shit and that I didn't like you."

"Bastard!" exploded Sampson.

"Do you think a reference from me is important?"

"Because of me you're not rotting in jail."

"Because of you a copper is dead and a prison officer is probably brain-damaged."

"Aren't you ever going to forget that?"

"No," said Charlie simply.

"You're a cunt."

"One of us is." Had he covered everything he wanted to? wondered Charlie. It had to be now. He said, "You'll cooperate, naturally? As soon as you're asked?"

Sampson frowned, surprised at the question. "This is the moment I've been working toward—waiting for—for ten years. I just can't understand why I'm being treated like this."

"It's only the first day, for Christ's sake," said Charlie. It seemed much longer.

"I don't deserve it," protested Sampson, petulantly. "After all I've done, the risks I've taken, I don't deserve to be ignored, not even on the first day."

"Perhaps you're not as important as you think you are then," jeered Charlie.

"We'll see," said Sampson. He laughed viciously and said, "And do you know what I'm going to do when I get into some position of power?"

"What?" said Charlie.

"I'm going to screw you," promised the other Englishman. "I'm going to make your existence here as miserable as I can so you'll wish in the end that you'd stayed in jail."

Can't happen, asshole, thought Charlie. "Fuck you too," he said.

Charlie made the search much later, when he was sure Sampson was asleep, using the pretext of getting water to drink from the kitchen. One listening device was concealed in the overhead light assembly in the main room, almost directly beneath which they'd argued earlier, and another was in the door handle of the bathroom. There would be more, Charlie guessed. But the transcripts from these would support the woman's examination. A field agent of his expertise would be expected to search and find them, he knew. But tonight might be a bit too obvious. Tomorrow would be soon enough. He'd spent two years in jail, after all; that would be explanation enough for not looking sooner. He'd got rusty.

Wilson stumped impatiently around the office, occasionally feeling down to his stiff leg. The pain was always worse when there was some professional pressure.

"It's the damned waiting," he said. "Waiting, and with no way of knowing what's happening."

"That's the way it always had to be," reminded the more controlled Harkness. "They'll be waiting too, don't forget. And they'll be more anxious than us."

Wilson sat at last. "And it'll be worth everything, if it all works," he rationalized. "Spectacular, in fact."

"Spectacular," agreed Harkness, who normally wasn't given to hyperbole.

13

It was a standard interrogation method when two people are involved, choosing one, then the other, before the first is completed, calculated to off-balance. Sampson responded excitedly to the summons the following day, small-boy enthusiasm returning. He sat forward on the edge of the seat as the car went along the capital peripheral, gazing around at his first proper view of the Moscow suburbs, several times asking the driver about buildings or monuments they passed but getting no reply on any occasion. He sat respectfully on the seat that Natalia Fedova indicated, leaning forward from the edge for the questions, answering crisply and concisely, a hopeful applicant for a new job. He gave a full résumé of his career within British intelligence, from the time of his university entrance, carefully listing the names of the operatives with whom he had come into working contact and actually spelling out their names when she paused uncertainly. He gave a detailed background to all the information he provided, since his recruitment by Soviet intelligence, filling out the sparseness of his earlier, cryptic messages and reminding her that one of his last communications had been the warning of a possible spy in Moscow.

"Did you find him?" he demanded.

"I ask the questions," the woman cut off abruptly. Then, confirming the questioner's role, she repeated the query she had made the previous day to Charlie, whether he would be prepared to cooperate. Sampson said at once, "But of course; that's what I've been doing all these years and what I want to continue doing."

"Why?" asked the woman.

"I don't understand," protested Sampson.

"Why do you want to adopt our way of life?"

Sampson smiled. "Because I believe it is the right way of life. I'm not naive enough to believe that there aren't faults in the communist system. Abuses, too. But I consider there are greater faults in the so-called Western democracy, which is nothing of the sort. The labor and socialist movements have tried and they've failed. Britain is controlled by vested, capitalistic interests. Capitalism destroyed any proper reforms considered by Mitterrand in France. Money, profit, and success to the already successful is the creed in America, and their CIA maintain and manipulate fascist, right-wing regimes throughout Central America and crush the first signs of liberalism. And Africa, too. The CIA put Mobutu in power in Zaire and have kept him there for more than a decade. And what's happened? He's corruptly become a billionaire—with his money safely in Switzerland—and his country is one of the most poverty-stricken and suppressed on the continent . . ." Sampson paused breathlessly and then finished. "So-called capitalism doesn't set people free. It makes rich men richer and suppresses the poor . . ."

"You seem angry," said the woman mildly.

"I am angry," agreed Sampson. "Which is why I offered myself, all those years ago. And why I am offering myself now."

"What are you prepared to do?"

"Anything," responded Sampson immediately.

"Unquestioned?"

"Unquestioned," promised the man.

"Why did you bring the other one with you?"

"Muffin?"

"Yes."

"I had no choice. We were in the same cell. I could have

created a situation to get him moved—I actually set out to do so—but then I learned I'd have to have someone else. And that wouldn't have been someone who would have considered a life here. Nor someone you would have considered admitting."

"Would Muffin have tried to prevent your escape? Raised an alarm, perhaps?"

"Who knows what he would have done?" said Sampson contemptuously. "I don't think he's aware half the time what he really is doing."

"You didn't escape from the cell, according to Muffin. You escaped from the infirmary. Muffin didn't have to be involved at all."

"Are you doubting me?" asked Sampson indignantly.

"Yes," said Natalia openly.

"Then look at your records, of all the contacts with me inside prison. Only at the very end was apomorphine proposed. Initially I thought I'd have to escape from the cell. And there was no way I could have done that without Charlie Muffin knowing about it."

"Why didn't you kill him, like you did the policeman?"

Sampson came forward even further, to reinforce what he had to say. "I didn't want to kill anyone; cause any more harm than was absolutely necessary. And like I said, I thought I had to get away from our cell. There are regular cell checks, every few hours. He would have been discovered."

"What about the prison officer you battered being discovered?"

Sampson smiled, as the points came his way. "The infirmary isn't checked during the night. There wasn't a risk of discovery."

"There was with the policeman."

"I had to make the decision on the spot. I didn't know whether the people you sent for me would drive off at the first indication of danger. Whether I could subdue the man before he had time to sound an alarm. Could subdue him, even." Sampson gave another pause. "If I created a difficulty, then I'm sorry. It seemed the only thing—the right thing—to do at the time."

"Do you like killing? Hurting people?"

"Did that bastard say I did?"

"Do you like hurting people?" repeated the woman.

"No."

"You told me you were prepared to do anything."

"Yes," remembered Sampson cautiously.

"If you were told to kill someone, would you do it?"

It was several moments before Sampson replied. Then he said, "I would argue against the order."

"Why?"

"I am not trained to kill, to be an assassin."

"Is that your objection, your lack of training? You've no moral objection?"

There was another long hesitation from the man. At last he said, "If I am properly convinced of the need, then no, I have no moral objection."

"What do you think of Charlie Muffin?" she demanded, in one of her directional changes.

Sampson sniggered, contemptuous again. "There's nothing to think about," he said.

"I don't understand that answer."

"He was probably good, once," said the man. "That's the reputation he had in the department, despite what he did. Maybe even a grudging admiration. But now he's past it. He's middle-aged, out of condition, clinging, like a drowning man to a piece of driftwood, to some ridiculous charade about not being a traitor."

"Wasn't he?"

"I don't know." Sampson shrugged carelessly. "He exposed the British and American directors, so of course he was. But it seems to have been a personal thing, not through any ideology . . ." Sampson hesitated. "I really don't think it's important. I don't think he's important."

"What is he, then?"

"A has-been," judged the man.

* * *

The conference that night between Berenkov and Kalenin did not last so long because Sampson's commitment was so obvious, but it was still later than normal when Berenkov returned to the exclusively guarded compound for the Kremlin hierarchy at Kutuzovsky Prospekt. Valentina was waiting, with the newlywed pleasure as always, despite their twenty years of marriage. Because effectively they were newlyweds. Berenkov had been posted as an illegal in the West within six months of their marriage, time sufficient for Georgi to be conceived but not for him to know what it was like to be a father, any more than to be a husband. The eventually established front in London as a wine importer—one of the capital's best for more than fifteen years—enabled wine-buying trips to Europe, where they had been able to meet for brief reunions, but that was exactly how the encounters had seemed to both of them, holiday romances each knew would end. Throughout it all, each had remained faithful to the other, despite, in Berenkov's case, frequent opportunities and frequent temptations as a London *bon viveur.* The three years in Moscow since his repatriation— three favored, even indulgent years of special accommodation among the Kremlin elite, shopping facilities in concessionary stores, a Sochi villa whenever they required it—had been for both of them the happiest in a strange, unreal life. The only blur to that happiness was the difficulty that Berenkov had in getting to know his son, and that was not a difficulty of dislike or youthful rebellion, because the boy knew enough of what his father had been doing to accept his mother's insistence that Berenkov rightfully deserved the award as a Hero of the Soviet Union. It was, rather, the difficulty of strangers becoming father and son.

Valentina kissed him and held him tightly and he held her tightly too and then she led him into the apartment and poured him the Scotch whiskey their concessionary facilities allowed them, neat, without water or ice, the way he'd taught her it was properly taken in the West.

"Dinner won't be long," she said.

"No hurry."

"Georgi is skating."

"What about the examinations?" asked Berenkov. They were preliminary, before the proper graduation tests, and if he achieved the necessary grades the boy was eligible for foreign-exchange consideration; the possibility of Georgi going to the West—that amorphous place which had robbed her for so many years of a husband—was an increasing point of dissent between Valentina and Berenkov.

"He thinks he did well," she replied. "He won't know for some time."

"How well?" persisted Berenkov.

"Top five," said Valentina unhappily. She was a petite, almost birdlike woman, neat and precise, a comparison in opposites to Berenkov's expansive, casual bulk.

"So he could qualify?"

"Yes," she said. "He could qualify."

"He'd benefit, going somewhere like America to finish his education," said Berenkov, aware of the familiar hesitation. "A lot of our people do it."

"I lost one person I love for too long to the West," she said. "I don't want to lose another."

"It wouldn't be for long; two years at the most," he said.

"Still too long," she insisted stubbornly.

"Something I never expected has happened," said Berenkov, wanting to move away from their usual disagreement.

She looked up to him, waiting. He held out the glass and she obediently refilled it, giving him the opportunity to decide what he could and could not say about Charlie Muffin. He should not have told her at all, of course, but Berenkov never conformed to any set of rules. When he finished telling her of Charlie's Moscow arrival she said, "Will I meet him? Will he come here, perhaps?"

"I don't know," said Berenkov. "Maybe."

"He gave you back to me," said Valentina simply. "I'd so much like to thank him."

"Maybe," repeated Berenkov, savoring the whiskey and wishing it were the single malt he'd enjoyed in London.

"Alexei?"

"What?" he said.

"Do you miss it?"

"Miss what?"

"The West?" asked the woman anxiously. "The life you led there."

Berenkov looked back at the whiskey he had been contemplating. "Yes," he said honestly, because one of the understandings of their relationship was that they were always honest with each other. "There are many things that I miss about it . . ." He looked up at her, smiling. "But there are many things about living in Moscow that I prefer. And the most important of those is you."

She didn't answer his smile, remaining serious-faced. "You'd never do it again, would you?" she said. "You'd never go away and leave me again?"

"Never," assured Berenkov, seeing her need. "For the rest of our lives, we're going to be together."

On the other side of Moscow, Charlie Muffin managed to complete his sweep of the apartment before Sampson returned. He located six listening devices. Nosy lot of buggers, he thought.

14

Natalia wore a severely tailored black suit and a white shirt open at the throat, and she seemed to have taken more trouble with her hair, straining it back into a chignon. Charlie decided it suited her. The outfit, too. Definitely nice tits. There was no welcoming smile and the gesture to the carefully positioned chair was curt.

"We will talk today in much more detail," she announced, making it sound an order.

New approach, thought Charlie: today was aggression day, putting him firmly into his place. He'd determined upon his demeanor, too. It was going to clash. He leaned forward, so that he could reach the edge of her desk, and counted out the devices he found in the apartment. As he did so he recited ". . . tinker, tailor, soldier, sailor, rich man, poor man . . ."

Natalia pursed her lips, an expression of strained irritation.

Charlie grinned at her and said, "It's a game we play in England, with kids, counting out the fruit pips. Supposed to forecast the future."

"You didn't finish it," she reminded him. "It ends 'beggar man, thief.' What role do you think you're going to play in the future?"

"Not sure, not yet," said Charlie. He couldn't be certain if he were off-balancing her, which was the intention.

131

"No," said Natalia pointedly. "I'm not sure either."

Charlie recognized that she was fighting back but thought the remark had been too heavy. Nodding toward the lined-up devices, he said, "How many did Sampson bring you?"

"Perhaps he was more trusting than you. Or doesn't like kids' games."

"If he's more trusting than me then he's stupid, isn't he?"

"Am I supposed to be impressed?" said Natalia, trying for contempt.

"Yes," said Charlie. He'd have to be cautious, about appearing overconfident. Which he wasn't.

"You don't seem to be taking anything very seriously," she said.

"Believe me, I am," said Charlie. "For the first time I'm beginning to realize what it's like to be out of prison."

Her face relaxed, very slightly, at her acceptance of the explanation. "Is that all you've realized?"

It was going very well, Charlie decided. "No," he said.

This time there was an actual smile. "So you're going to cooperate?"

"No," said Charlie again. "I'm going to listen to all the questions and I'll answer all that I feel able to." To concede more than that would be wrong, he knew.

Natalia's face hardened. "That's not cooperation."

"How do you know, until you've tried it?" Charlie wondered what her rank was in the service.

She appeared about to argue further and then to change her mind, going back again to the folder. "All right," she said. "Let's try it. Start from the very beginning, from your moment of entry. Tell me all about the examinations you took and the tests you underwent. Tell me about the instructional schools you attended and where they were. Tell me about the departments in which you've worked and the places where you've worked and the people with whom you've worked. Tell me about your promotions and demotions . . ." She looked up at him, waiting.

"All that!" said Charlie, trying for mockery.

"All that," she said, refusing him. "For a beginning."

Charlie had determined his reaction. He knew he had to impress her and whoever else was involved, assessing the interviews, and that meant convincing them that although he'd made the effort in attempting to retain some little portion of integrity, at the end they would believe they'd got all they wanted. And in fact there was a lot he could tell them that wouldn't endanger anyone or anything. From the beginning, she'd said. Which was easy, because the training facilities through which he'd gone, in Hertfordshire, no longer existed. Charlie was extremely careful, overdetailing what no longer mattered, avoiding what did. Some of the early operations were as extinct as the Hertfordshire training school and so he had no hesitation about them. It was the period when he established the reputation that was to last and he actually enjoyed the telling, realizing as he did so that he wanted to impress Natalia in a way different from anyone else who might study the inevitable tapes and transcripts, that he wanted her to admire him. He was passingly intrigued and even amused. She was, after all, the first woman with whom he'd had any contact for a very long time, so he supposed it was a natural reaction. What, he wondered, would hers be if she knew what he was thinking? Was she married? There was no ring but that didn't necessarily mean anything. Charlie tried to push the intrusive reflection away, hurrying on with the account, anxious to submerge her in as much peripheral detail as possible. The headquarters of MI-6 weren't in Mayfair anymore, so he felt no hesitation about speaking at length about them, bothering with floor layout and office apportionment. He didn't stop at listing the directors under whom he'd worked, either. Apart from Cuthbertson— who didn't matter because they knew what he had done to him—none of the directors whom Charlie had known were still alive, and although their identities were supposed to be a secret, even after retirement and death, Charlie knew damned well that it was a nonsense and that the KGB had a complete record. Cuthbertson brought him to Berenkov and Charlie gave every detail of that operation, well knowing that upon his return

Berenkov would have been even more fully debriefed and that therefore he was giving nothing away that the Russians didn't already know. The woman let Charlie make his own pace, only very rarely intruding for a point of clarification and never upon anything that Charlie didn't want to talk about. Not wanting to interrupt the account, Natalia had coffee and sandwiches brought in at midday and Charlie was conscious of the deference the woman received and wondered again at her rank. It was late when they finished, already dark outside, lights pricked around the motorway. Charlie ached physically, from the effort and the strain. It had been important to swamp her with minutiae—to make them all believe they were getting something—but he'd spoken for so long that it was difficult for him to remember precisely what he'd said. Which was dangerous because it meant if they weren't completely convinced—or if a query arose that she hadn't thought of immediately—then he might get caught out in a reexamination. He'd have to be bloody careful. But then that had always been a requirement.

"How much longer?" he said.

"Longer?"

"Sessions like these."

"Until we're satisfied," she said.

"About what?" Charlie knew but he wanted to see how far she would commit herself.

"That you're going to be of some use to us."

"Thanks for the honesty," said Charlie, trying to sound offended.

"Isn't that what we're trying to establish between us, honesty?" she said.

"Yes," agreed Charlie.

"Today was better," said Natalia. "Much better."

Was she attempting to reassure him? Deciding it would sound a perfectly natural question, Charlie said, "What happens when you're finally satisfied? What will I be required to do?"

"That's not for me to decide," said Natalia. "Not even to be finally satisfied."

Was six months sufficient time to achieve what he had to

achieve? He supposed he could always stay longer, if he thought there was a chance of succeeding and he was sure he'd evaded any suspicion. But how could he tell Wilson, to stop the man panicking? No way, Charlie realized. The moment he went through the embassy doors, there wasn't any coming out again. So he had to go in with something. If he stayed out longer than six months, then he'd have to take the chance with Wilson. They should have foreseen the possibility, rushed though the preparations had been. Another if, to go with all the others. He said, "Do you like it?"

She frowned up at him. "Like what?"

"What you do."

She hesitated and Charlie was sure she came near to blushing, which he found a strange response. She said, "Yes, I enjoy it very much. I find it challenging."

"Catching people out?"

"If there's something to catch them out upon, then yes. Is there something to catch you out upon, Charlie Muffin?"

Charlie met her look unflinchingly. "Not me, love," he said. "You get what you see."

"I hope so," she said.

Charlie wondered what she meant.

"I don't think we should wait any longer," insisted Kalenin. "I don't think we can afford to wait any longer. It was Sampson who actually warned us: mentioned it at the debriefing."

"Fedova?" queried Berenkov.

The KGB chairman shook his head. "I want you to do it."

Berenkov accepted the instructions without argument, half-expecting them anyway. "Normal procedure?"

There was another headshake. "I want this settled and I want it settled quickly."

"Sampson was very forthcoming," said Berenkov. "If he'd known more I would have expected him to offer it."

"That's what worries me," said Kalenin. "So would I."

15

Berenkov decided against confronting Sampson at Dzerzhinsky Square. It was the headquarters and the man knew it and Berenkov had listened to all the tapes—not just the debriefing records but those from the apartment, as well—and was aware of Sampson's arrogance. He didn't want the man arrogant. Although he'd criticized the attitude to Kalenin, he wanted the man still anxious to prove himself, as he had been during the encounter with Comrade Fedova. So Berenkov chose the same meeting place, the peripheral road building, even utilizing an office on the same floor. He was undecided about wearing uniform but in the end decided against it.

Sampson entered the office as eagerly as Berenkov remembered him from the video film, smiling hopefully, the expression growing when he saw that the interrogator had changed and that it was a man. Berenkov supposed Sampson would imagine the meeting more important: which it was, he conceded.

Berenkov made no effort at any introduction, determined to keep Sampson in the subservient role. And proceeded cautiously, as if the encounter was nothing more than a continuation of the earlier interview, actually reverting back to some of the things talked about with the woman, as if clarification were necessary. It was a worthwhile test. Sampson

136

responded as willingly as before and there were no variations in the answers, which was important. It was a full hour before Berenkov approached the true purpose of the meeting.

"How long were you on the Russian desk?" he asked suddenly.

"About sixteen months."

"Precisely," insisted Berenkov.

"Sixteen months and two weeks."

"An assistant?"

Sampson nodded. "There was the division director and then two of us. The other assistant had more seniority."

"Does that mean he had greater access than you?"

Sampson shook his head. "Our clearance was the same level."

"I'm aware of clearances and I'm aware of how things actually resolve, in working conditions," pressed Berenkov. "Did you have access to everything with which the other assistant dealt?"

"We worked our own cases; our own people. But I definitely had access. I've made that clear in the reports. I made a point of seeing what he was doing."

"What about the division director?"

"Officially he was cleared higher than I was. It had to be that way: there again, I got to what I could."

"But not everything?"

Sampson hesitated and Berenkov knew the man was wondering whether he could afford an overcommitment. "Of course not," said Sampson. "It was actually trying to get at something that I shouldn't that got me put under suspicion in the end."

Berenkov was glad the man hadn't tried to boast stupidly. "Give me a percentage," he demanded. "How much stuff did you have access to? Or could you reasonably expect to have had some awareness, at least?"

There was another pause and Sampson said, "Eighty percent."

That hadn't been a boast either, Berenkov decided. Kalenin wasn't going to get what he expected from this meeting, he thought. Berenkov said, "Did you have access to the cable traffic, coming into London from the embassy in Moscow?"

"Most of it," said Sampson. "It depended upon the classification at the point of transmission, of course."

Berenkov saw the point and snatched for it. "You know all the classifications?"

"I don't know," said Sampson, and Berenkov realized the man was being completely honest and was glad of it. "I know a lot of them."

Berenkov pushed some paper across the desk at the other man and said, "Give me some. From the highest classification of which you are aware and working downward."

Sampson stared back at the order, the curiosity obvious. "Is there a point to this?" he said.

"It's a debriefing," said Berenkov. "There's a point to everything."

Sampson was unconvinced and showed it. "If I knew a purpose, maybe I could help more easily."

"Just the classifications," insisted Berenkov. He was impressed by Sampson: was sure the man was telling the truth and was even curbing the tendency to overcommitment. But this was too important to allow the slightest relaxation.

There weren't that many, so it only took Sampson minutes. As he handed the list back, Sampson said, "It's an alphabetical progression. Having detected me, I'll guess they will have changed it, but it won't matter because the alphabetical designation only has dating significance anyway. I was caught in June, the sixth month. The coding that year had actually originated from A, for January. So June—the sixth month—was the sixth letter, F. The important indicators follow that on the initial grouping of transmission letters. MD is for Wilson himself. M for main; D for Director—main Director. Various division directors have the prefix, designating the station. Here for instance, the division is designated S, for Soviet. So there would be a letter for the month, then S, then D, directing it to the director of the Soviet division. I could actually set out an example, if you want me to."

Berenkov shook his head, not needing any further explanation. To show Sampson he understood completely he said, "So if from Moscow in February of the year you were detected there was sent a message prefixed B—for the second month of the year—and then M, for main, and D, for Director, Wilson himself would have been the recipient."

"Yes," said Sampson. "But not any longer. They'll have changed everything, because of my coming across. It's obvious I would tell you."

There had been ten messages before Sampson had been detected, all addressed personally to the main Director: from the changes after Sampson's detection it would be easy for the cryptologists to cross-reference and find the new British designation code. Not that Berenkov considered it necessary. "Tell me about Wilson," he said.

Sampson hesitated, composing the reply. "Aloof man, not often seen in the various divisions. Bad leg, from some accident or other. Former full-time army officer, but you'll know that from the listing in *Who's Who* or *Burke's Peerage*. Fills the bloody place with roses. Grows them. Widower. Absolute professional, admired by a lot of the old-timers . . ." The man smiled up. "Actually heard a suggestion that when he discovered what I'd done he didn't want the thing settled by trial: preferred a more direct and unpublic removal."

"What about involvement?" pressed Berenkov, wanting to achieve his point. "If Wilson considered something sufficiently important, would he become personally involved: run control himself?"

"Oh yes," said Sampson at once. "Ex regular officer, like I said. Baxter—that was my divisional chief—was always moaning that he was poking his nose in, at executive level."

Berenkov sat for several moments, uncertain. Settled as

soon as possible, Kalenin had ordered: at least he was more personally satisfied with Sampson than he had been when the meeting began. The Russian reached sideways, into the briefcase beside him and unseen behind the bulk of the desk. It didn't matter which communication it was but he glanced at it anyway, completely accustomed now to the code and able to read it as if it were ordinary Cyrillic script: it was a message about additional silo construction at Baikonur, for the protective version of the SS-20 missile, which had the highest security classification and of which they had been sure that nothing could leak out to the West. He passed it across to Sampson, like he had the paper earlier, and said, "What does that say?"

Sampson frowned down, the effort at concentration—and the need to succeed—obvious. "C," he said at once. "So it was transmitted in March, before my detection. MD, so Wilson was the recipient . . ." The man's voice trailed. "I don't understand what follows: it's a code with which I'm not familiar. Neither the actual message code. It looks like random computer choice, to me. God knows how you'd break that."

It hadn't been God, remembered Berenkov: it had been a team of twenty mathematicians working around the clock, at their own computers. Taken four and a half months. And was still incomplete. He said, "What do you know about Baikonur?"

Sampson shrugged. "Soviet space-exploration center, like Houston and Canaveral, in America. Why?"

"You didn't see any transmission, in March—three months before your detection—concerning Baikonur?"

The Englishman looked back to the meaningless collection of letters and figures, then back up at Berenkov. "You know everything I saw in March," he said slowly. "I transmitted it. In March I wasn't suspected."

"Nothing about Baikonur passed through the Soviet division?" persisted Berenkov.

"I was right about the spy!" said Sampson, in belated, excited awareness. "The one I warned you about. But you haven't caught him!"

Berenkov supposed it was hardly the elucidation of the decade, after the way he'd conducted the meeting. Still sharp enough, though. He said, "A spy operating for some of the period when you were still clear, for us."

"I told you," said Sampson impatiently. In reflection he said, "I knew Wilson and Harkness were up to something. I just knew it."

"They ran it themselves?" queried Berenkov.

"Definitely," assured Sampson. "I'd have known, otherwise." He fluttered between them the piece of paper bearing the code he could not comprehend. "Baikonur?" he asked.

"Yes."

"So you've broken the code?"

"Part," agreed Berenkov. Deciding the man deserved the acknowledgment, he added, "And it was computer choice, although not quite random. We don't understand the clearance line."

"I'll be able to help," said Sampson confidently. "If you make the transcripts available to me, I'll be able to decide the echelon at which they're being considered: maybe even determine the sender, from here in Moscow."

Berenkov realized Kalenin had been right in forcing the pace. And that he had been wrong in arguing caution. He wondered if that would be Kalenin's feeling when he considered the films and the transcripts of the encounter. To Sampson he said, "That's what we want: we want your help in finding the sender."

"Conditions," insisted Sampson, with continuing confidence.

"Conditions?" queried Berenkov, surprised.

"You know I'm genuine: you've never had any reason to doubt me. And if you doubted me now, we wouldn't be having this conversation. I'll do everything I can to help, over these messages. But in return I want to be split up from that dreadful man Charlie Muffin. I want a respectable apartment. And to be treated properly, as a colleague. Not like some doubtful suspect."

He'd talked to Kalenin about keeping them together, remembered Berenkov. He said, "All right."

"Immediately?" pressed Sampson, a man aware of a moment of power and determined to get everything from it.

"Immediately," agreed Berenkov.

"This is what I came here to do," said Sampson. "To help."

"We haven't caught him yet," said Berenkov.

"We will," said Sampson confidently.

I hope, thought Berenkov. Having spent time with both men, Berenkov could understand easily how Charlie had offended every one of Sampson's sensibilities. To someone like Sampson, Charlie would be anathema.

There is the closest cooperation between the radio intercept installation maintained by the British at Cheltenham— officially called the Government Communication Center—and America's National Security Agency at Fort Meade. With slight variations dictated by geographical needs, the world is divided between the two monitoring stations and their impressively equipped substations so effectively that they confidently expect to intercept and have the ability to transcribe—once they know the code—at least ninety percent of the Soviet and Eastern-bloc radio communications.

With ironic coincidence—considering the chance message that Berenkov had chosen to show Sampson—it was the change of code from Baikonur that was first detected, by America, who did not understand the significance. Sir Alistair Wilson did, as soon as the information was relayed from the liaison officer at Cheltenham, because the British Director had made a special request to be informed immediately something like that happened. Within twenty-four hours there was confirmation, from changes of code being used along Soviet-embassy microwave channels and its sea, air, and land forces.

"Took them longer to break than I thought it would," said Wilson.

"But now they have," said Harkness. "I'm surprised they

think it might be from something as simple as intercept, but it means they are reading the messages coming to us and are taking every precaution they can think of: even changing their codes."

"Christ, they'll be worried," said Wilson, expressing the familiar attitude.

"So am I," admitted Harkness.

16

Sampson was tight with excitement and self-satisfaction, actually strutting around the apartment: Charlie was reminded of the proud pigeons who used to parade around Whitehall and Trafalgar Square. How long ago had it been since he'd seen proud pigeons in Whitehall and Trafalgar Square? A million years? Two million?

"Told you how important I was, didn't I?"

"Yes," said Charlie. What was the silly bugger on about now?

"I suppose you saw the woman again?"

"Didn't you?"

Sampson smiled smugly. "Gone beyond her now."

Strut and boast, thought Charlie; strut and boast. He said, "Who then?"

"There wasn't any identification," said Sampson. "Clearly someone important."

"A man?"

"Of course it was a man," said Sampson irritably. "Important, too. A senior officer."

"How do you know that, if there wasn't identification?"

"Everyone in the building was practically shitting themselves."

144

Charlie's outward attitude hadn't changed but he was fully attentive now. "What was he like?" he coaxed gently.

"Big man: very big," said Sampson. "High liver, by the look of him."

That had been one of the first assessments of Berenkov, in the very early stages, long before the man was suspect: before they even knew his name, remembered Charlie. And Berenkov was back here: Wilson had made the point during their meeting in the governor's office. *Maybe you'd even get to him,* the Director had said. Surely it wouldn't have been Berenkov! Wilson had hoped for contact because of what had happened before; their involvement. Sampson had never been involved. And then Charlie remembered something else. The Russian desk. Sampson had been number three on the Russian desk. Careful, he thought, halting the slide. Of course Sampson would be important, because of the Russian desk. But not this important, this quickly. Not days after they'd arrived. Unless there was a panic, making it necessary to abandon all the usual rules of procedure. What could cause a panic that big? The answer was obvious but Charlie didn't at first want to confront it. Which he realized was stupid, and so he did. If the Russians suspected a spy, they'd abandon all rules of procedure; a spy as important as Wilson had made out the unknown man to be. For someone that important they'd rewrite the whole bloody regulation book. Still desperately circumstantial, Charlie attempted to rationalize. "High liver?" he said, as if he hadn't understood.

"Florid-faced, that sort of thing," said Sampson, impatient again.

Berenkov had had a florid face; until jail, that is. Then he'd got the pallor that they all developed. Charlie hesitated, unsure how to proceed with the man. His conceit, he decided. He said, "Wonder if I'll see him?"

Sampson gave a dismissive laugh, as if the idea were amusing. "You! Why should you see him?"

"Just a thought," said Charlie, pushing ever so gently.

"I told you," lectured Sampson. "This is important."

"But still only debriefing?" said Charlie.

Sampson laughed again. "No, Charlie. This isn't debriefing. This is me being fully and absolutely accepted . . ." He held out his hand, a cupping gesture. "Right there," he said. "Right in the middle."

Charlie wondered if he'd located all the bugs during his search. If he hadn't, then those listening were going to be pissed off with Sampson's boastful indiscretion. But still not indiscreet enough. "Bullshit," he jeered in open challenge. "What reason would there be to do something like that?"

A look of wariness came into Sampson's face. Shit, thought Charlie.

Sampson said, "There's reason enough, believe me."

"What?" said Charlie, with no alternative.

There was another dismissive laugh from the man. "Do you expect me to tell you that?"

"Why not?"

"Don't be bloody stupid!"

He had been stupid, Charlie realized in self-recrimination: he'd tried to push too hard too quickly. Still believing that Sampson's conceit was the man's weakness, he said, "I don't believe you. I think you're full of crap."

It didn't work. There was yet a further jeering laugh and Sampson said, "Full of crap, eh!" He gestured around the ugly apartment. "You like it here?"

Charlie frowned, uncertain where the conversation was going. "No," he said. "I don't like it here. I think it stinks. Literally."

"Neither do I," said Sampson. "So I'm not staying. I'm going somewhere else—somewhere better—away from the smell of cooking . . ." He paused, to make the point. "And away from you. It's taken me long enough, maybe too long, but at last I'm getting away from you, you downtrodden, scruffy, backward-looking little snob. I told them that's what I wanted, and that's what I'm getting. That seem crap to you?"

If Sampson had got that sort of concession agreed so quickly—and there was no reason for the man to be lying, because he'd be seen to be a liar at once—then whatever he was involved in was important. Surely it could only be the would-be defector whom Wilson wanted him to find! Sampson's so recent posting on the Russian desk dictated that it had to be. Would the bastard know enough to uncover whoever it was, before him? Always objective, Charlie recognized that from the simple chronology of how long he'd been away from the department, compared to Sampson, then Sampson had to have an advantage. If his surmise were correct—and he still wanted more, to be absolutely sure—it meant he and Sampson were working against each other. He'd like that, Charlie decided. He'd wanted to teach the snotty little sod a lesson, and what better way than snatch a defector whom the man was seeking right out from under his nose? Almost at once came the balance. The chronology, remembered Charlie again. And not just the chronology. Official Soviet backing and resources, too. The bastard had all the advantages. And more. Son of a bitch, thought Charlie. He said, "No, that doesn't seem like crap. That seems like a two-way deal in which I gain as much as you. I can stand the cabbage smells."

"Go to hell, Charlie," said the other man. "Go to hell and stay there."

"Up yours," said Charlie.

Kalenin listened patiently while Berenkov outlined the arrangements he had made with the Englishman, his face showing no reaction, so that it was impossible to gauge whether the KGB chairman approved or not. Finally he said, "You appear to have changed your mind about the man?"

"Absolutely," admitted Berenkov at once. "He was completely honest—making no effort to exaggerate and impress me. I think we should use him, and use him to the utmost."

"But he was excluded!" protested Kalenin, driving a fist into the palm of his other hand in an unusual show of emotion.

"It would certainly seem that way," said Berenkov. "But I think if we make everything available to him, then he might be able to find some intelligent assessments of something . . .

transmission source, at least. At the moment we've got nothing."

"I don't need reminding what we haven't got," said Kalenin. Rarely at any time since his chairmanship—or even before—could he remember feeling so impotent. The feeling extended beyond impotence, to an uncertainty he couldn't even define.

"Then it's certainly worth trying," insisted Berenkov.

"Yes," agreed Kalenin. "It's certainly worth trying . . ." He hesitated and said, "If we make everything available to Sampson—and I accept that we must, to give the effort any point in the first place—then he's going to become a very knowledgeable man, isn't he?" There was an even further pause. "Many might say too knowledgeable."

"I don't have any doubt about him," repeated Berenkov.

"It's unusual, utilizing a defector like this."

"The circumstances are unusual," reminded Berenkov. "And we'd have complete control over him at all times."

"Yes," agreed Kalenin, the doubt still obvious. "We haven't any alternative."

"There's something else," said Berenkov.

The KGB chairman looked across his desk at the other man, waiting.

"Do you have any official objection to my seeing Charlie?"

"Officially seeing him?" queried Kalenin.

"No," said Berenkov at once. "I was never able to thank him for what happened before."

"You said that was for his benefit, not yours," remembered Kalenin.

"I was the person who won," said Berenkov. "Charlie lost."

Kalenin was silent for several moments. Then he said, "No, I don't see any reason why you shouldn't meet him . . ." He smiled up. "I wouldn't mind seeing him again myself. I liked him."

17

Sampson's transfer was more of a leap than a move. The new apartment was directly off Pushkinskaya Ulitza, a smaller but far more modern and complete place than that he shared with Charlie. And without smell or neighbor intrusion, a special place for special people. The furnishings were modern—mostly from Finland, he discovered, by turning them over and seeing their country of origin—and the decoration unmarked anywhere, so that he knew everything had been redone before his occupation. There was a modern refrigerator and stove in the kitchen— where the previous ones had been antiquated and barely running—and a disposal unit and a television in the lounge, neither of which had been available before. Sampson surveyed everything with smiling satisfaction. A special place for special people, he thought again. They'd even thought of providing alcohol, the inevitable vodka and imported whiskey and gin. The initial satisfaction increased with every day. He was allocated a car—a Lada and comparatively small, but still a car—and before the end of the first week was officially informed that he was being placed on salary, four thousand rubles a month, which he recognized—even without a gauge with which to compare—as being high. By some standards exceptionally so. And even higher if equated against the additional grant of access to the special concessionary stores. No day passed without there being for Sampson some reminder of the accepted and adjusted change in his importance, but the most indicative was the selection of his place of work. Dzerzhinsky Square itself. There was a practical reason for the choice—Kalenin was there and Berenkov was there and the specially selected cryptologists were there—but for Sampson to gain admission to the KGB headquarters was for the man the most positive—and the most dramatic—evidence of what he was required to do. Sampson responded fittingly and properly, accepting the elevation but not becoming overconfident because of it.

Everything was provided for him: the raw, originally incomprehensible interceptions and then the increasing decipherment, and from them he was able to distinguish that his original assessment—during the meeting with Berenkov—that the code was random computer choice was wrong. It was computer. But not random. It was a mathematical alternative, and then with an alternative built in. Within intelligence it was called a ripple code. A denominator figure was decided upon, from base—in this case London—and from it letters accorded to figures. The letter against figure numbers rippled twice, once from the origin of the original message and then upon a factor of two, to quadruple—two times two—the transmitted message. An additional precaution that the British had imposed—a precaution that had delayed the final translation for a month, even though with hindsight the protection was obvious—was that even from the dispatch from Moscow the receiving message had to be multiplied by a factor of two to be intelligible.

Sampson's influence did not end with the apartment allocation or by the admission into Dzerzhinsky Square. There was an office staff—secretaries and two aides—and he utilized them completely, ordering easels and graph charts and spending days creating his own charts and maze paths, calling upon the advantage that the cryptologists and their computers did not—could not—possess. Which was his awareness of the customs of the British—and Russian desk—working pattern.

Employing their best technology—to confuse the first metaphor—the Russians had unpicked a haystack, straw by straw. And found not a pin but a needle. Without knowing what pattern the needle would knit. Further to mix the metaphor, Sampson recognized his function to be to continue the unraveling of that pattern and reverse the finished design. Metaphor was actually the word that Sampson used, in his by now regular meetings with Berenkov—of whose identity he was finally aware, a further pointer to his importance—in a continuing admission of difficulty.

"There's somebody here, within these headquarters, with access from division to division," said Sampson. "It runs right throughout the building."

"We're already aware of that," said Berenkov, disappointed. He'd swung completely behind the man: provided a guarantee almost. He'd expected more than this. And quicker.

"You're insisting that I work backward, to find source," said the Englishman. "Why can't you? The number of people who have access over that sort of range must be limited. It has to be."

Berenkov had thought of that too. It came down to six deputies and their immediate subordinates. Twelve people at most. Thirteen, if Kalenin were to be included. And he had to be included, unthinkable though it might be. Berenkov had imposed his own surveillance—and from it learned of other surveillance imposed upon himself. Kalenin, he guessed. He was not offended. It would not take long, Berenkov recognized, before the uncertainty started to become insidious and undermine the very center of their organization.

"How much longer?" demanded Berenkov, wanting the impatience to show.

"I don't know," said Sampson. "I've got everything— perhaps too much—but I can't progress beyond it: the one thing I don't have is the key they are using in London."

"We do," insisted Berenkov. "Our mathematicians worked out the multiples and the progressions."

Sampson had come prepared for the dispute, because it hadn't been the first. He threw across four of the raw messages and the transcriptions and said, "Okay, what's missing?"

Berenkov sighed, prepared also. "The complete identity line," he admitted.

"Right!" said Sampson triumphantly. "We can read the message but not anything beyond the recipient, Sir Alistair Wilson. Why haven't your cryptologists been able to get past the addressee?"

"It's a different code," said Berenkov, making a further concession.

"Which you're expecting me to crack without a computer, or even mathematical training!"

"You worked there!" came back Berenkov. "People make codes, not the computers that merely put them into practice. What code would Wilson have created, for absolutely secure and personal messages, that only he and maybe a handful of other people were handling?"

Sampson smiled, a moment of sudden and hopeful understanding. "It would smell," he said.

Berenkov looked at the other man in blank incomprehension.

"And they're a favorite in Britain," added Sampson.

It was for Charlie Muffin a suspended time, existence within some sort of capsule. Almost literally that because apart from the interrogation periods with Natalia it was spent incarcerated in the odorous apartment, a prison like the other prison he had known. Two nights after Sampson's departure he had tried to leave, to be immediately confronted outside the main entrance by a plainclothes guard who told him—in English, which meant the man was specifically assigned—that he wasn't allowed out of the building. With no other access to anyone in authority, Charlie complained to Natalia, who appeared unimpressed—even uninterested—in his protests. So he taught them all a lesson—and to prove that he could still do it—slipping out through the rear entrance and managing to avoid the obvious guard posted there. He stayed out for over two hours, just aimlessly wandering the streets—belatedly aware that he didn't possess any rubles to do anything else—before presenting himself at the front of the building through which he wasn't supposed to pass and in such a way that the concierge as well as the guard saw him, so that both had to report upon one another. He knew both had, from the next meeting with Natalia. She attempted, in her usual method of interrogation, to approach it obliquely but, completely accustomed to her now, Charlie avoided it until finally she had to ask outright and he grinned at her, like he had on the occasion presenting the listening devices, and said, "I was out spying!"

She sighed, although not unkindly. "Do you know something?" she said.

"What?"

"I've got to make a recommendation about you," she said. "I've got to assess all our conversations and all our debriefings and I've actually got to make a recommendation about what use you could be, if you stayed here."

Charlie was glad of her impatience because he was impatient also. Although it was only conjecture he was increasingly convinced he had been correct about the reason for Sampson's abrupt removal. Which had been three and a half weeks ago. Which—taking into account the period it had taken them to reach Moscow—meant one of his six months had already gone and he'd achieved absolutely fuck all except to soften the attitude—and he was sure he'd softened the attitude—of a very attractive girl with big tits. Which wasn't the point of his being there. "I haven't got any money," he said, wanting to increase her annoyance.

Natalia frowned, accustomed by now to his changes. "So what?" she said.

"So I can't invite you out to dinner. Why don't you ask me?"

It worked better than he expected.

Allowing her irritation to show—which she rarely did, despite his previous provoking—she said, "Why don't I recommend your being sent back to England as someone no use to us?"

"Is that what happened to Sampson?" demanded Charlie.

Her face became fixed, almost a pained expression. "What happened to Sampson isn't of any concern to you."

"It would be, if he'd gone back," said Charlie, refusing to give up. "I'd like to know the bastard has been sent back."

"He hasn't been," she said, exasperated. "There was a purpose for him."

"More than me?" demanded Charlie at once, not wanting to lose the momentum.

"Yes," she said, recovering quickly. "Far more than you."

"Great mistake," said Charlie.

"Prove it!" she came back, just as determined.

"Let me," he said, matching her.

That night, in the lonely, smell-steeped apartment in which nothing ever happened, the telephone rang. So unusual was it that Charlie stared at the instrument, surprised, only snatching it off the cradle when he realized the caller might ring off.

"Charlie?"

"Yes."

"Alexei," said the voice. "Alexei Berenkov."

Thank Christ, thought Charlie.

18

Having decided to meet, there was a difficulty with the venue. Berenkov knew it would be inappropriate—forbidden, in fact— for Charlie to come to Dzerzhinsky Square, and Charlie— without a proper reason for the feeling, because it was not of his choice or making—was reluctant for the Russian to come to him among the cooking smells. The decision came from Berenkov and Charlie said he would like very much to go to the Russian's home and meet his family. Until now—apart from the one rebellious walkabout—Charlie's existence had been within the apartment, the telephone-arranged pickup, and Natalia Fedova's office alongside the peripheral road, and as he left that night, emerging from the apartment block with no obvious guard in place, Charlie had the impression of escaping again. The driver was as taciturn as they all appeared to be but at least he accorded Charlie the respect of holding open the door of the car. It was a large vehicle, a Zil, opulent by Soviet standards, an official car. The driver used the government-reserved center lane, like the man who took him out for the debriefings, but Berenkov's Zil seemed to belong, whereas the debriefing transport always appeared to Charlie to be an intrusive interloper. The route was different, too, back toward the center of the city. Even the street lighting was brighter and he actually saw the illumination around the Kremlin and Red Square. He

155

made the guess and was proven right when they moved into the Kutuzovsky Prospekt complex. The government enclave, Charlie knew. Which meant Berenkov had returned in triumph. And was still held in active—and more important, working— respect. Charlie tried to curb the excitement. Even before they met he had confirmation of Berenkov being in Dzerzhinsky Square: Wilson hadn't been sure, that night in the governor's office. *Maybe you'd even get to him.* And he had. Things were suddenly looking good: better than he'd dared hope they would, in fact. Still too early to start counting chickens—the eggs weren't even laid yet, let alone hatched—but at least he was being given a look inside the henhouse.

There were the predictable security checks and as they moved forward Charlie stared up at the carefully segregated blocks, wondering what Politburo member was behind what lighted window. He made another sure guess and was right again; there wasn't any odor of cabbage.

Berenkov was in the lobby of his section, to take Charlie past the final security. For a few moments each man stood on opposing sides of the foyer, gazing at each other in silent recollection. Berenkov, always the more exuberant of the two, broke the mood, striding across with both arms outstretched and booming, "Charlie! Charlie! . . . It's good to see you!"

Charlie accepted the embrace, conscious of the attention of the driver and inner guards: Berenkov smelled as Charlie remembered from their initial, fencing encounters—before he'd made a case and was able to arrest the Russian—of expensive cologne and expensive cigars. "And you, Alexei," he said sincerely. "It's good to see you."

From a cubicle one of the security men said something Charlie didn't catch but indicating a book, a clear reference to some noted entry formality, but Berenkov waved his hand dismissively, typically refusing to conform, leading Charlie instead toward the elevators. "Clerks!" he said. "The world is full of clerks."

They stood apart in the elevator, each surveying the other

again. Berenkov shook his head and said, "You don't look good, Charlie. I've seen you look better."

"I've been better," confessed Charlie. "You look fine." The Russian did: much fatter than Charlie remembered, even from before the arrest, actually appearing physically bigger than Charlie's memory. Florid-faced, too, he saw, remembering Sampson's description. *High liver, by the look of him.* Berenkov certainly looked like a high liver. But then, he always had been.

"Things are pretty good," said the Russian as the lift stopped.

Eighth floor, Charlie noted. He wondered if degree of importance were indicated by the level of the apartment. If they were, it would make Berenkov very important.

Valentina and Georgi stood waiting, nervous and uncertain in the main room: they were overawed as much—maybe more—by Berenkov's physical presence as by encountering someone from the West, Charlie guessed. With no reason for having made any prejudgment, Charlie was surprised at how neat and diminutive Valentina was; he'd expected Berenkov to have a wife matching him in size, battleship to battleship. Georgi was about the same height as his father but without the weight, and much darker, too, darker-skinned and darker-haired. The greetings were shyly hesitant, the boy and his mother deferring to Berenkov's boisterous lead. Charlie wished he'd had the facility and money to bring Valentina a small gift. Commerce had been easier in the nick than it was here, he thought in passing. Berenkov gushed whiskey into glasses and apologized for its inferior quality, and Charlie drank it gratefully and said it was wonderful, which he thought it was. Valentina laid out pickups, tiny dishes of smoked fish and nuts and olives, and Georgi sat alertly attentive. Forcing himself to make the contribution, the boy said, "How long have you been in Moscow?"

"Not long: only three or four weeks," said Charlie. Berenkov wouldn't have told either of them, he supposed; not everything anyway.

"How long do you expect to stay?"

It didn't look as if he'd told the boy anything. "A long time," said Charlie easily. He felt no difficulty. It was business; their type of business, at which they were both expert. Berenkov would understand later.

"My father was a long time in the West."

Charlie smiled sideways at Berenkov, who was sitting contentedly listening to the boy practice his English in the conversation. "I know he was," said Charlie. "He was very successful there."

"You were a close friend of my father's?"

Charlie smiled again, aware of Berenkov's attention upon him now. "Your father and I had the same sort of job but we were competitors," said Charlie. "There was a lot of mutual respect between us."

Berenkov laughed approvingly, and echoed, "A great deal of mutual respect."

Books lined two walls of the Moscow apartment, as they had in the Eaton Square flat which Berenkov had occupied in London. The identification for the person he had to contact was Chekhov, and Berenkov had used Chekhov for his London codes. The spy was someone in headquarters, Wilson had said: Berenkov was at headquarters. As likely as it seemed, Charlie knew he could make no move whatsoever. He could be mistaken. And Berenkov was too astute to miss an approach.

"I'm very glad to be able to thank you," said Valentina: she had a predictably small voice. "I've always felt that you made it possible for Alexei to come back home."

"I suppose I did," said Charlie. She clearly knew more than the boy.

"Georgi may qualify to become an exchange student," said Berenkov, the pride obvious.

"England?" queried Charlie curiously.

"Possibly," said the boy. "Or America."

"The experience will be good for him," insisted Berenkov.

Could it be this easy! Charlie thought. He was aware of the looks that went between Berenkov and his wife. To Georgi he said, "Do you want to go?"

"I want to do what my father considers best," replied the boy dutifully.

Berenkov insisted upon refilling their glasses twice before they ate. The trouble to which Valentina had gone with the meal was obvious and Charlie complimented her on the borscht and then the veal—aware the family had extensive concessionary facilities to obtain everything on the table, another indication of Berenkov's importance—and smiled over his wineglass at the Russian. "French?" he guessed.

"A little indulgence I allow myself," confirmed Berenkov. "I always regretted not being able to teach you about wine, Charlie . . ." Berenkov paused, appearing to consider the statement. He added, "It was, I guess, the only thing that I knew better than you."

"Maybe there'll be time now," said Charlie.

"Maybe," agreed Berenkov.

After the meal Georgi excused himself to study in his room and Valentina made much of clearing the table, to leave them alone. Berenkov offered brandy—French again—which Charlie accepted, and an imported Havana cigar, which he didn't. Berenkov savored the ritual of wetting the leaf and clipping the end, lighting it in a billow of bluish smoke and said, "The greatest advantage of having Cuba as an obedient satellite."

"You've a nice family, Alexei," coaxed Charlie. "It must be good to be home?"

"Yes," agreed Berenkov reflectively. "It's good." He smiled across at the other man. "I never expected to be entertaining you here in Moscow, Charlie."

"I didn't expect to be entertained." Why didn't Berenkov come out with Chekhov's innocent remark about the weather!

"I never had the chance to thank you, either," said Berenkov. He raised his brandy bowl. "I've made the toast before, in your absence, but I'll make it again, now you're here. Thanks for making the repatriation possible."

"I'm glad somebody benefited," said Charlie.

"Was it bad?"

"I would never have done it if I'd known just how bad,"

admitted Charlie. If Berenkov were thinking of running, Charlie realized that what he was saying could actually be a disincentive, but again it would provide an opening for the identification if the Russian would accept it. He told the other man, in greater detail than he'd bothered during the debriefing with Natalia, because he knew Berenkov would understand. He talked about dragging around Europe, on the run with Edith, jumping at shadows, and of the pursuit when they were discovered and Edith's death and of the loneliness and the drinking afterward, just occasionally interrupted by doing things for Willoughby's son.

"Remember what you told me when I debriefed you in jail?" he asked Berenkov.

The Russian frowned, shaking his head.

"How glad you were, in the end, that I'd got you? That you were getting scared you couldn't go on much longer?"

"I remember," said Berenkov. He hadn't until now. He didn't think he'd admitted that to anyone: Charlie must have been a better, more insidious debriefer than he recalled.

"That's how I felt in Italy," said Charlie. "I'd have gone on running, if I'd had the chance, but I was really very tired. The feeling I remember, when I knew they had me, was of relief."

"I know that feeling," said Berenkov, fully confessional too.

"Then prison," said Charlie bitterly. "Jesus, how I hated prison!"

"I told you about that," reminded Berenkov. "When I was there. I told you never to get caught."

"I know," recalled Charlie. Openly he said, "I suppose formally being a defector is different. There's protection. Security."

Berenkov smiled but said nothing.

Valentina came from the kitchen with coffee, put the pot between them, and then—appearing aware of the depth of their talk—withdrew again.

"Still surprised you came here, Charlie," said Berenkov.

"You told me I'd go mad in prison; something like that,"

said Charlie, still in memories. "You were right. I would have done. Bloody nearly did."

"Still didn't expect you to come to Moscow," insisted Berenkov.

"I'm here now," said Charlie with obviously forced brightness.

"And?"

"Tonight's been the first good time," admitted Charlie. "The apartment stinks—literally—but I accept I can't expect anything better. The debriefings, I accept, are necessary too: part of the procedure. But they're becoming repetitive. At least I suppose I'm lucky to have got rid of that asshole Sampson."

"He's a very clever asshole, Charlie."

"Assholes often are." It would be too much to hope for an indication from Berenkov of what the man was doing, but there was something instinctive about trying, with the disparaging remark.

"What are you going to do, Charlie?" asked Berenkov, casually disregarding the lure.

It had been too much to expect, conceded Charlie: offensive almost. He said, "You tell me. What am I going to be allowed to do?"

"There could be something," said Berenkov. "Something that might not create a conflict."

So the man had studied the debriefing and knew about his refusal to Natalia that first day. Charlie carefully put the brandy bowl on the table between them, knowing the gesture wasn't overdemonstrative. Was it going to be the approach for which he'd been waiting, or the offer of a job? "What?" he said.

"I don't want to make promises I can't fulfill," withdrew Berenkov. "I wanted us to meet and to talk. To get an idea of how you felt. I need to talk to other people before I go any further."

"Will you?" urged Charlie. He was unsure about Berenkov but knew he had to maintain the link.

Berenkov hesitated, appearing to consider the question.

Then he said, "Yes. It's not a commitment, you understand: it could be rejected by other people."

"I understand," said Charlie. "I'd appreciate it. I don't want to atrophy, like I was atrophying in prison."

"I owe you a favor, Charlie," said Berenkov. "A very big favor."

Georgi emerged from his room, to bid them good night, and Charlie wished him luck with the examinations which could qualify the boy for the exchange course. And then he looked back over the table where the French wine stood and accepted some more French brandy from his hospitable host and decided he should try further. To Berenkov Charlie said, "If Georgi passes, when would he go?"

"This year, sometime," said Berenkov, rekindling his cigar. "About nine months, I suppose. Maybe sooner."

According to Wilson, whoever their mystery informant was wanted all his family out. With Georgi freed by the exchange, that would only leave Valentina. Charlie looked around the spacious apartment and at the books again. He had a delicate game to play, Charlie realized; probably a game more delicate than he'd ever played before in his life. If he made the slightest, infinitesimal mistake—and a monstrous mistake like wrongly believing it was Berenkov who wanted to cross back to the West where he'd lived for so long—then the Russian would identify it immediately. And being the absolutely dedicated professional he was, Berenkov would see him inside a *gulag* so fast there'd be scorch marks left on the ground. Remembering the look that had earlier passed between Berenkov and his wife, Charlie said, "How would Valentina feel about his going?"

"You still don't miss a lot, do you, Charlie?"

"Like you, it's automatic."

"Valentina thinks of the West as some sort of monster that swallows up people she loves."

"How do you think of it?" risked Charlie.

"I had a hell of a time," admitted Berenkov nostalgically. "I got nervous, in the end. And it was always unreal, without Valentina. Georgi, too. But it was good to me. Damned good."

Careful, decided Charlie. He was going to have to be very, very careful.

"Whatever happens—about the job, I mean—we'll have to meet some more," said Berenkov.

"I'd like that," said Charlie.

Tanks had been in the forefront of the Ardennes offensive, the last attempt in the Second World War to break through the Allied front in the West, seize Antwerp, and bottleneck supplies for the British and American armies about to invade Germany, and so the Battle of the Bulge was one frequently recreated by Kalenin. He'd had papier-mâché models created, to scale, of the contours and the geography, with towns like Charleville and Sedan and Revin picked out, and he had his tank forces to scale, as well. Kalenin admired von Rundstedt's strategy—bringing the vehicles across terrain supposedly impossible for them— and regarded Montgomery's success more due to luck than tactics. Another hour, another day, another person looking in another direction and the outcome might have been completely different, he thought. To test the theory, he moved the American tanks that Montgomery controlled just fifty kilometers from where they'd actually been, using Reims as the marker, and timed von Rundstedt's assault twenty-four hours earlier. Completely different, he thought again. Was he looking in the right direction, to find the traitor opening a window for the British to look right inside his very own headquarters? Kalenin had permanent twenty-four-hour surveillance on the deputies and their immediate subordinates—everyone with likely access—and the reports were being channeled directly to him, even here, at night. The observation reports from the British embassy, too. And discovering nothing, not the slightest squeak from an unseen, unsuspected tank track. The feeling of impotence—and that vaguer feeling of uncertainty beyond— was worsening as every day passed. When, oh when, was he going to be able to realize where the break had been made? Kalenin rearranged the tanks, in the properly recorded formations and divisions. It hadn't been necessary in the Ardennes, at the very end of 1944, but it was always possible to detect an assault by inviting one, remembered Kalenin: it had even been an earlier strategy successfully practiced by von Rundstedt.

The KGB chairman straightened from his war-games table and crossed to the desk upon which lay the latest batch of meaningless surveillance reports. Beside them lay the master list of the people under suspicion. He'd have to invite an attack, Kalenin decided, staring down at the twelve names. To each— but exclusively to each—would have to be given specific and apparently vitally sensitive material. They'd broken the key, after all. As soon as they intercepted the message, they'd know the source. Kalenin was irritated that the subterfuge hadn't occurred to him before. Commanders who took too long to think of strategies usually lost battles. Sometimes even the war.

19

Although there are many natural varieties, botanists recognize 250 distinct species of rose, which is perfectly divisible by a factor of two. Sampson summoned the mathematicians who broke the earlier code and instructed them what he was looking for—suggesting the ripple attempt which had been successful before—and had to wait a full, irritating week because there weren't the necessarily complete listings available in any Soviet textbook. Even when the books from the West were provided, there were still variations which had to be cross-computed and the initial reaction from men accustomed to working within the conforming rigidity of patterned figures was one of skepticism at the aberrations of a clearly deranged romantic. The final entry into the machines began with the hybrid Agnes and concluded with the Zephirine Drouhin, officially designated a rambling, climbing rose. The first week's failures were confirmation for the men of practical science that they were dealing with a madman. Sampson insisted upon further cross-referencing—discovering, for instance, that the hybrid tea Michele Meilland had been omitted because the programmer had considered the floribunda Michelle to be the same flower—and listing in full, instead of by general description, the spinossima species. The attitude of the mathematicians—men of patterns and design after all—changed when they realized a shape was appearing, and by the end of the second week Sampson told Berenkov he considered he had broken the hitherto unintelligible identity line. From the first indication, Berenkov spent all the time with Sampson, watching the designation of operative and sender of the secret messages gradually emerge from the morass. There was practically euphoria with the completion of the sender's name, which was Wainwright, and who, Berenkov knew immediately, from the complete Soviet awareness of the British embassy staffing, was the designated first secretary whom Sampson had already identified, from his debriefing with Natalia Fedova, as the British intelligence chief of station, the resident. Wainwright was involved in fifteen of the most immediate messages but then the control changed, the name now appearing as Richardson, whom it was equally easy to identify as someone who served as cultural attaché. The early excitement—an excitement with which the ebullient Berenkov immediately infected Kalenin, who was anxious for just this sort of breakthrough—faded within hours with the discovery that while Wainwright was still on station, Richardson had been withdrawn to London a month earlier, at the conclusion of a normal and accepted diplomatic tour of duty.

Sampson had completely deciphered the identity logo on every message by ten in the morning. The planning conference with Kalenin took place at noon. By four, Wainwright had been arrested during a late lunch return as he passed the Tropinin Museum, on his leisurely way back to the embassy, and by six the British diplomat was in jail. Lubyanka would have been more convenient, directly attached as it was to the KGB headquarters in Dzerzhinsky Square, but from the time of its notoriety as a slaughterhouse under Yagoda and Beria, the yard-bordering cells and torture chambers at the rear had been converted into minuscule office accommodation for the burgeoning intelligence organization. Convinced that Wainwright needed to be immediately frightened—and knowing the need for speed, because of the inevitable and difficult-officially-to-confront British protests when they began, and increasingly anxious to start moving against their traitor as soon as possible—Kalenin had the Briton taken instead to Lefortovo, a more modern prison still conveniently in the center of the capital and with a matching, more up-to-date notoriety from postwar dissidents.

Moscow was to have been Cecil Wainwright's swan song as an intelligence officer, the concluding grading guaranteeing him an index-linked pension of fifteen thousand pounds a year, upon which he had decided he could live comfortably in the already purchased and paid-for bungalow on the outskirts of Bognor, the darkroom already installed and equipped for the hobby of photography that he intended to pursue. Wainwright was a sparse-haired, precise man whose delight in detail made him an efficient fact gatherer and extended to always sharpened pencils and always filled fountain pens to record those details. He had begun in army intelligence in Germany, which meant he saw the bestiality of Bergen-Belsen and Dachau and learned through the interviews with the maimed and crippled survivors in preparation for the Nuremberg war-crimes tribunal of the torture ability of the Gestapo.

Wainwright was a brave man because he was a coward and tried not to be. He had been terrified by what he saw and heard in Germany and terrified further by the accounts that had leaked from Russia—long before his posting there—of precisely the same things happening under Stalin and his successors: terrified because Wainwright knew there was no way—if ever he had to confront it—that he could withstand torture. Fully aware of the fear—which he saw as cowardice—he had always rejected any idea of transferring from the service to a branch where the demand for him to find out—and worse, show—just how scared he was might never arise.

He had lived for three years in Moscow, had six months to go before the Bognor retirement, and had, as the days and weeks were ticked off from the carefully consulted calendar, begun to convince himself that it was a personal test he was never going to have to confront or an admission never to be known by anyone.

He actually squealed in fright when the car pulled up alongside him on the north side of the museum and he realized, in the initial seconds of being manhandled into the back and surrounded by a grappling mob of men, that he hadn't got away with it and that it had happened—the biggest terror—after all.

He recognized Lefortovo as they swept through the gates, and Wainwright had to sit tight-buttocked and with his legs pressed together against any immediate, personally embarrassing collapse. He knew he'd mess himself—always known it— when the pain started, the agony that would make him scream and weep—but he determined to hold out as long as possible, just like he'd refused to give in all these years.

There is a procedure about interrogation—a method of obtaining the most, quickest—and it begins by letting the victim's own fear work against him. Wainwright's high-voiced demands for an explanation or for access to the British embassy were ignored. He was put into a windowless room, a tiny metal-shuttered grille set into the steel door, without lavatory facilities and with only a boxlike table and two chairs beneath a harsh, ceiling-mounted light. Wainwright's hopeless abandonment was accentuated by the reflection of his loneliness in a large mirror set into the wall facing the door, in which he was reflected from whatever part of the room he attempted to occupy, and unseen behind which, because it was a two-way mirror, Kalenin and Berenkov sat waiting for the interrogation to begin.

They watched Wainwright sit, stand, sit, then stand again, come directly up to the mirror and stare into it, as if he suspected its proper function, and instead closely study his own face for indications of strain. He walked tight-legged, the discomfort obvious, and twice actually felt down vaguely in the direction of his bladder, as if to hold himself would suppress the need. Once, with the apparent need to reassure himself, he went intimately through everything in his pockets, examining things of which he should have already been familiar, carefully returning each item to the pocket from which he took it in the first place. He sat, stood, then sat again. The need to urinate appeared to become increasingly more urgent.

"I almost peed myself," remembered Berenkov. "Funny reaction. Nearly always happens."

"Did you?" asked Kalenin.

"Managed to stop it happening."

"Don't think he'll be able to," judged Kalenin. "This shouldn't be too protracted."

"I'm surprised the British left him on station," said Berenkov.

"Who knows how anyone will react, until the arrest actually happens?"

"It's time we had some luck," said Berenkov.

"Sampson did well," said Kalenin, in reminder.

"I was wrong," repeated Berenkov. "It was right to use him: I shouldn't have argued against it from the beginning."

The interrogation continued its defined course. The interrogator, whose name was Koblov although Wainwright was never to know it, burst suddenly into the room, an impatient man in a hurry, walking by the British diplomat without bothering to look closely at him, just nodding curtly and saying "Sit down."

Wainwright made a valiant effort. He straightened, striving for the stance of outraged importance, and said, "My name is Cecil Wainwright. I am accredited to your Government as the first secretary to the embassy of Her Britannic Majesty, Queen Elizabeth. I am covered by full protocol of the Vienna Convention. I demand a full explanation of your conduct and access immediately to the British embassy."

"Sit down," repeated Koblov.

"I said I demand an explanation," said Wainwright, still upright.

"Sit down!" shouted Koblov.

Wainwright did.

From a briefcase Koblov extracted a purposely thickened file, moving to another stage of questioning, the impression of knowing everything, so that the questioning becomes only a formality, the need for confirmation. Without bothering to look up, he dictated. "Your name is Cecil Roy Wainwright. Your accredited position as first secretary is, in fact, a cover for your true function as an agent, actively working against the free interests of the Union of Soviet Socialist Republics. You are, in fact, the resident for MI-6. Throughout your period in Moscow you have carried out your function as a spy . . ." The Russian turned the page, the attitude still one of impatience. He picked up the fifteen messages listed against Wainwright's name, which had been typed out, in English, in their entirety, including the decipherment of both the mathematician cryptologists and Sampson. Koblov offered Wainwright the first and said, "This was transmitted from the British embassy on May 6th. It is classified, restricted information concerning the governing Politburo of the Union of Soviet Socialist Republics . . ." Koblov dealt the second message. "This was transmitted on May 18th, further information about the composition and attitudes of the Soviet Government, concerning the attitude of the Soviet Government toward NATO aggression in Europe . . ." Koblov maintained the attack and the delivery, a dealer holding all the marked cards, taking Wainwright in chronological progression through the messages he had transmitted.

The British diplomat sat rigid, practically to attention, legs tightly closed again. From where Kalenin and Berenkov sat they could see the perspiration picked out in tiny bubbles on Wainwright's forehead and upper lip. As they watched, a tiny drop broke away, meandering a rivulet down the side of the man's face and creating a delta on his chin. Hurriedly, as if he thought the interrogator might not see, Wainwright scrubbed his hand over his face.

"There won't need to be any physical pressure," said Berenkov.

"That might have been difficult anyway," said Kalenin. "We'll have to let him go."

"When?"

"Only when I'm completely satisfied," insisted Kalenin, determined. "I don't give a damn about the Vienna Convention or any other convention. I've got a leak that's got to be plugged."

Would Kalenin have officially informed the Politburo? Since Khrushchev they had maintained overall control, after all.

Despite their friendship, Berenkov decided he could not openly ask Kalenin. Knowing as little as Kalenin did about how to stop it, Berenkov didn't think he would, if he had been in Kalenin's position. He didn't envy his friend.

On the other side of the screen, Koblov completed the recital. Wainwright had watched, blinking increasingly, as one piece of evidence was piled on the other, finally creating a stack in front of him but making no effort to accept the Russian's invitation personally to look at them. Koblov waited and when Wainwright still made no move, he reached forward, retrieving them, and tapped them back into a neater arrangement and returned them to the file. "Well?" Koblov demanded.

"As an accredited diplomat to your country I demand access to my embassy," insisted Wainwright. His voice was weak and wavering.

Koblov leaned forward across the small table. "You're not a diplomat," he said. "You are a spy and you will be treated as one. You will make a full admission and answer all my questions."

"I will not," fought Wainwright desperately. "I deny every accusation and demand to be released."

"Fool!" shouted Koblov in sudden anger, so unexpectedly that Wainwright visibly jumped. "I wanted to help!" Koblov stood, just as abruptly, gathered up his file, and strode from the room as quickly as he had entered, slamming the door behind him and leaving Wainwright alone once more.

For several moments the Briton did not move, remaining just as stiffly on the chair. Then he sagged, as if unseen support holding him in shape had suddenly been taken away. His teeth worried his bottom lip, and from behind the mirror Berenkov and Kalenin heard the first whimper of despair. Wainwright stood, looking to the door through which Koblov had left, and then, the increasing feeling of helplessness obvious, around the bare room. Wainwright started at the scream—as he was meant to—as if an electrical current had suddenly been charged through his body. It was a recording but there was no way of his knowing that: an actual recording, however, of physical torture, mind-destroyed, animal sounds of a human being from whom everything had been racked, sanity, shape, dignity, and almost existence. The sound of agony continued, unintelligible gibberish, and there were other sounds, muttering of men more controlled, and scraping and dragging which grew and then diminished, conveying the audible impression that the victim had actually been hauled directly outside Wainwright's cell.

Wainwright's bladder went. A deepening, dark stain began to grow and he looked down at himself and the watching Russians heard him say "Oh no . . ." Almost at once, in private conversation with himself, Wainwright said, "Knew it would happen; always knew it would happen." He slumped back in the chair again, legs apart now for a different sort of comfort.

The torture recording had been made under psychological supervision. The sounds didn't end at once. They seemed to come from a distance, fresh sounds of agony and then gradually subsiding groaning, the screams becoming sobs, then discernible, helpless crying.

Wainwright sat comparatively upright but with his head lolled forward, as if he were examining the wetness of his lap, hands together in a loose praying gesture. Despite the sensitivity of the listening devices, Wainwright's words were at first difficult for Kalenin or Berenkov to hear. They strained and at last identified it, a mantra to which he was still trying to cling.

". . . accredited as the first secretary to the embassy of Her Britannic Majesty, Queen Elizabeth . . . protected by Vienna Convention . . . accredited as the first secretary to the embassy of Her Britannic Majesty, Queen Elizabeth . . ."

Kalenin jabbed at the console in front of him, depressing the button that would send Koblov back into the room. The Russian's entry was different this time—a continuation of technique—no longer curtly abrupt, but less hurried, more sympathetic.

"They'll be here soon," he said, soft-voiced also. "Maybe fifteen minutes. I'm sorry. It's not my way."

"No!" said Wainwright, pleading.

"I'm sorry," repeated Koblov. "I don't decide."

"Please no."

"They're impatient."

"Let me tell you: let me tell you now."

Because the room was completely wired, they were ready outside. The sound at the door was not a knock but the flat-handed thump of a familiar workman demanding access to a repetitive job. Wainwright cringed from the sound. There was fresh wetness and he reached out to Koblov and said again, "Please no. Please!"

Koblov appeared to consider the plea and then shouted, in Russian, "Wait! In a moment." The response from outside was guttural, a muttered protest of impatience, and Koblov shouted, "I said wait. Give me a moment." He actually smiled at Wainwright and said, "You'll have to hurry."

"What?" said Wainwright emptily. "Tell me what you want."

"Everything," urged Koblov. "Tell me everything, from the very beginning."

Wainwright did. He started at the moment of contact, when he received the note in the pocket of a coat he retrieved from the cloakroom at the Bolshoi, and of the information that accompanied it, alerting them to the level of intelligence available. And then of the subsequent drops, every item as startling and as important as that which preceded it. Wainwright recounted London's excited, anxious response and the estab-lishment of the special code and the decision, after he had made fifteen pickups, to transfer the control to another of their station men, Brian Richardson, because London was determined against losing the source by detection.

"That's when I stopped being control," said Wainwright. "Two and a half months ago."

Koblov didn't hurry or depart from the procedure, despite the need for urgency, of which he was well aware. He took Wainwright back to the beginning again, the Bolshoi itself, and filled in the gaps that Wainwright had hurried by in his anxiety, establishing that the drops were always dictated to and never by Wainwright. He took the slips from the file again and went through them, one by one, formally establishing each in their order of transmission, and at last approached the essential of the arrest and the interrogation, the identity of the source. Koblov even did that circumlocutiously.

"What was the code cover: the name by which he was known?"

"Rose," said Wainwright, and behind the mirror Berenkov smiled wryly and shook his head.

"Always Rose? The code never altered?"

"It may have done, when Richardson took over. I would have expected it to be changed, with a new control. That is the procedure."

"What's the real name?" Koblov asked the vital question quietly, dismissively almost, continuing the impression that all he was doing anyway was confirming what they already knew.

"I don't know," said Wainwright at once.

Beside him Berenkov felt Kalenin stiffen.

Koblov, the professional questioner, showed no reaction. "The person who made contact at the Bolshoi. And then on the other fourteen occasions," he elaborated, as if he imagined Wainwright had misunderstood the initial question. "Who was he? What was his name?"

Wainwright looked back curiously at the Russian. "But I thought I made that clear," he said. "There was never a meeting, an open contact. It was a blind approach at the Bolshoi and that was the way it continued. When we picked up from each drop there would be the next one specified. He—if it is a he—was only ever Rose."

"We were wrong to pick him up," said Kalenin distantly. "We knew the other man had already gone; we should have let Wainwright run."

In the interview room, Koblov was continuing smoothly on, his outward demeanor giving no indication of his inward frustration: he was aware of being literally under the eyes of the chairman himself and wanted the interrogation to be a triumph. "After you ceased being control, Richardson took over?"

"Yes," reiterated Wainwright.

"But you're station chief: the resident?"

"Yes."

"So you were in charge of Richardson?"

Wainwright shook his head. "I told you that, too," he said. "When London realized what it had, they suspended some of the normal procedures. Richardson worked entirely independently: taking over the cipher codes. The Rose operation itself. I was actually told not to become involved, so that I wouldn't know."

"You must have talked," persisted Koblov, still gentle. "It had been your operation, to begin with. And it was a spectacular one, according to London's reaction. You must have talked about it to Richardson."

Wainwright smiled, an unusual expression for the man. "Not about the subsequent information. I was banned from that. And there wasn't anything to talk about anyway. They continued to be blind contacts."

"So you discussed the identity!" seized Koblov.

"I asked him if he'd met Rose," qualified Wainwright. "I've never known an operation like this before; neither had Richardson."

"And?" prompted Koblov.

"Richardson said it was the same for him as it had been for me: he'd never met Rose."

"Did you believe him?"

Wainwright hesitated. "I had no reason not to."

"But you'd been moved from control," reminded Koblov. "Distanced from what was happening. Richardson would have lied to you, wouldn't he, if he'd been told to?"

"Oh yes," agreed Wainwright at once. "But I didn't get the impression that he was. I think I would have known."

"Richardson's been withdrawn," reminded Koblov.

"Yes."

"So who's the new control? Richardson took over from you. Who's taken over from Richardson?"

"I don't think anyone has," said Wainwright.

"You wouldn't think," said Koblov, minutely increasing the

pressure because he felt the Briton was relaxing. "You're still the resident. You'd know."

"I'm unaware of anyone taking over control."

"Are you saying that the Rose operation is over?" demanded Koblov.

"No," said Wainwright.

"What then?"

"We didn't talk about the messages, like I said," explained Wainwright. "But from the quickness in the way things happened—and from the impression I got from Richardson, although he didn't actually say anything—I thought he'd gone back to arrange a crossing."

In the viewing room Kalenin said, "If that were to happen, it would mean disaster on top of disaster."

"Crossing?" said Koblov.

"Defection," provided Wainwright needlessly. "One of the last conversations I had with Richardson, he said, 'I wonder how much longer Rose can carry on?' It struck me as odd at the time."

"Those were the exact words? 'I wonder how much longer Rose can carry on?'"

"I don't remember exactly," said Wainwright. "That was the meaning of what he said."

"We shouldn't have openly arrested the damned man," said Kalenin, exasperated. "We should have trapped him; turned him, so that he could have told us if a new control were being imposed."

"If his inference is right, then there won't be a new control," said Berenkov. "There'll be a defection."

"They don't just happen," said Kalenin. "A crossing has to be arranged and someone has to do the arranging. And that will have to be through the embassy. Picking up Wainwright was a disaster."

"I'm sorry," apologized Berenkov. "It seemed the right thing to do, in the circumstances."

"It is as much my fault as yours," said Kalenin. "I approved the decision before it was put into operation."

Although he did not doubt the friendship, Berenkov wondered if Kalenin would share the guilt before any Politburo inquiry. And the way this was going, a Politburo inquiry looked increasingly likely.

It got worse.

Determined to strip Wainwright to the bone—in case he were a consummate professional rather than a pants-wetting man wrongly retained beyond his time—Kalenin held the diplomat far longer than was acceptable even by the usual disregarding Russian standards against the British diplomatic protests. There was no physical indication of pressure when the man was finally released into British protection from Lefortovo—because no physical pressure had been necessary—but mentally he had been reduced to admitting and confronting every weakness, fear, and cowardice in that perpetually reflecting mirror in that stark interrogation room. Moscow publicly named Wainwright and announced the smashing of a major Western-inspired spy ring—actually recalling the Soviet ambassador from London for an undisclosed period, which was unprecedented—and Whitehall responded with a contemptuous denial.

Moscow announced Wainwright's expulsion—and in another rare departure it was fully reported in *Pravda* and *Izvestia* and upon Moscow television, because Kalenin was grabbing at straws and thought the publicity might frighten whoever their spy was from defection until they found another way to locate him—and in the customary tit-for-tat response London declared a senior trade counselor at the Soviet trade delegation at Highgate *persona non grata.*

No one thought—properly thought—of Wainwright. A brave man who had known he was a coward but tried instead to be a brave man—and failed an abject coward—Wainwright on the night before his recall locked the door of the embassy residence room in which, womblike, he felt quite secure. Completely aware that courage was a quality he lacked, he consciously drank half a bottle of vodka to obtain it falsely and when that proved insufficient drank more, so that when they broke the door down the following morning, more than three-quarters of the bottle had gone. Like the defiance of his interrogation, Wainwright's attempt at suicide was a miserable, clumsy near-failure. The embassy beam was more than sufficient to support his body weight and the belt didn't break, either. But he placed the buckle wrongly, in the final, drunkenly brave seconds, and so when he kicked away the chair, he didn't die quickly, from the neck-break of hanging, but twisted and turned in the sort of agony that had always been his ultimate fear and which was confirmed by later autopsy, and died slowly, from strangulation.

It was, therefore, a month before Berenkov felt able to raise positively the suggestion he had mentioned in passing to Kalenin, and even then, from Kalenin's absentminded reaction, Berenkov knew it was premature.

"Spy school?" queried Kalenin, the distraction obvious.

"Charlie Muffin," reminded Berenkov. "The debriefing is finished now. I think he'd be an asset."

"He can be your responsibility," agreed Kalenin, distracted still. "If you think he can be of some use, put him to it."

20

It was a long month for Charlie. Frustrating, too. Increasingly
so. There was no formal announcement from Natalia Fedova
that the debriefing was ending. They had become repetitive,
certainly, but that was not infrequent with such interviews and
Charlie had come to rely upon them, his only source of outside
daily contact. He left the by now familiar building by the
peripheral one evening expecting another summons—getting
up at the regularly established time and bathing and waiting for
the telephone to ring on several subsequent days—but nothing
happened. Charlie was disorientated by the abrupt halt, recognizing that his reliance upon the encounters extended beyond
the simple fact of meeting another human being. He recognized,
too, his was a predictable response: there'd even been lectures
about it, during the instructional sessions, the attachment that a
subservient interviewee psychologically develops toward his
debriefer in situations of stress, cut off and far from home.
Knowing the attitude, Charlie was surprised it had happened to
him; the instructional sessions were, after all, warnings to
prevent it. Had it been what the psychologists had warned
about? Okay, so he was cut off and far from home, but he knew
the way back. And the stress of the unstarted mission wasn't
anything he didn't think he could handle. Charlie didn't like falling
into categories evolved by mind doctors, most of whom he

179

thought were a bloody sight dafter than the people they were supposed to treat anyway. So what was it then? Had he fancied her? She was the first woman he'd seen—been near at all—for a long time because of the circumstances. And he had, on several occasions, got the impression that she was responding to the flirtation: wasn't offended by it at least. Yes, he answered himself finally: he had fancied her. Which was dafter than he'd just considered all psychologists to be. The debriefed didn't pull their debriefers; Charlie smiled, realizing another definition for the word. Debriefers kept their briefs on, he thought. He supposed there was nothing wrong in fantasizing as long as he didn't lose sight of the fact that that was exactly what it was, a fantasy. Still a bloody attractive woman: big tits, too. And the termination meant he was imprisoned again, stuck inside the smelly flat.

He was disappointed, too—on a professional as well as a social level—that there was no further contact with Berenkov. He'd expected it—they'd arranged it that night, after all—but no calls came. After the first four empty, echoing days, Charlie decided upon another rebellion and found things different there, as well. No one tried to stop him.

Charlie had an excellent, inherent sense of direction and he had the advantage of the drive—even though it had been at night—on his way to Berenkov's apartment, so he set off confidently toward the center of the city. The excursion began as the test to see if he were still under restriction, but as he walked he realized what he'd find in the center of the city and thought: Why not? It was the only contact point he had. And it was the reason for his being in Moscow at all. Having decided actually to go to the GUM complex, Charlie wondered about clearing his trail, smiling as he had earlier in the apartment as the tradecraft expression came automatically to mind. No, he determined. Not on this, the first outing. He didn't have any doubt that there was surveillance, but if he evaded it they'd become suspicious and that was the last thing he wanted. It was better to make the journey just that, an apparently aimless outing of someone trying to relieve his boredom—and he genuinely felt that, after all—by visiting the most obvious tourist spots in the city. Which naturally—unsuspiciously—included the largest department store in the Soviet Union. For those who watched unseen—and he didn't intend even trying to see them—it would be nothing. For Charlie, it would be a useful reconnoiter for the real thing. If the real thing ever happened.

The streets were drab and uniform and depressing and Charlie thought how crushing it would be to imagine having to spend the rest of his life here. Which was what Sampson would do. Enthusiastically. For how long? Charlie wondered. The stupid bugger was eager enough now, full of cliché and cant, but Charlie couldn't believe that later—a year, maybe two, maybe five, but some time later—he wouldn't realize he'd just changed prisons. Serve the bastard right. Charlie hoped the realization came sooner, rather than later. Christ, how Charlie wished there were some way he could really find out if Sampson were involved in trying to trace the Russian traitor. He thought—he bloody well knew—that he'd rather confront and defeat Sampson in a competition of professional ability than he would compete in the best of three falls in Natalia Fedova. It would be a hell of an experience, falling onto Natalia Fedova. Silly, fantasizing sod, he thought.

The massive expanse of Red Square opened up before him and Charlie experienced a spurt of satisfaction at having found his way unfailingly there. He hoped—after the absence—that all the other abilities were still as good. For the benefit of those dutifully observing, Charlie meandered without any apparent direction through Kitav-Gorod, the oldest part of the Soviet capital. Charlie remembered the Russian for what was now the dominating area, pleased once more that things were coming back so well. It was, he was sure, Krasnaya Ploshchad. And it meant Beautiful Square. And it was beautiful, compared to the drab boxes upon boxes arranged around the regimented rectangles through which he'd walked on his way there. The very center of Soviet history, for four hundred years, reflected Charlie. Here had been enacted slaughters and executions and triumphs and failures. And only a few hundred yards away—

maybe not even that—was the meeting place with an unknown stranger through whom, if he were very clever and very devious and very lucky, he was going to be able to rehabilitate himself completely and go back to a life he should never—in a moment of conceited vindictiveness—have considered abandoning. Another if, held like an admonishing finger. Would Red Square—Beautiful Square—be for him a triumph or a failure? Charlie wondered. And was the Russian really unknown? If it were Berenkov—and circumstantially there were enough pointers—then the man would have been astonished to find Charlie in Moscow. And until his actual appearance at GUM wouldn't anyway know he was the deputed route-master. Charlie hoped very much it was Berenkov.

Charlie had forgotten, from his previous, long-ago visit, how vast the architecture was. Gulliver's houses in the land of Lilliput. No, he thought, unhappy with the impression. All around were the despised edifices of the Czars and Czarinas and the oppressive, heel-crushing rich which the new czars and czarinas and oppressors chose not to hate but to occupy, like grateful hermit crabs warm and safe inside the shells that had once been the homes of bigger, better crabs. Charlie grimaced to himself. He wasn't sure the succeeding impression was any better than the first. Maybe he should stop trying; trying so hard at least.

Lenin's mausoleum didn't accord with the surroundings. The memorial to the goatee-bearded opportunist who chased away the bigger crabs was an ill-fitting apology of a place. If they were going to bother, they should have got it right, thought Charlie. Whether Lenin had been an opportunist or a dedicated revolutionary against an unjust regime—and Charlie thought he was more of an opportunist than dedicated revolutionary—he had caused a pretty dramatic body swerve in world history. So he deserved more than something that looked like a 1940's bomb shelter against a chance air raid. Charlie wondered if the always present, dutifully waiting queue—were they really genuine visiting Soviet-territory tourists or permanently employed actors, on a job for life?—were as disappointed as he was.

Deciding that he had appeared aimless for long enough, Charlie turned away from the unimpressive resting place for the father of the revolution and went at last toward what had now become the object of his visit. Outside of the store, in towering identity, was the full name from the initials of which the acronym is created, Gosudarstvennyy Universal'nyy Magazin. Once, thought Charlie, as he approached, the concentration of more than one thousand different stores, each competing, each surviving. Now, like everything else—almost everything—a collective. But positioned where it was and with the captive market it had, perhaps a more successful collective than most within the system.

The west door, on the third Thursday of any month: those were the instructions. So where the hell was the west door? There appeared to be dozens of doors, all around the place. Utilizing the sense of direction again, Charlie used St. Basil's Cathedral, to the south of Red Square, as a marker. Charlie worked out the geography easily enough but still wasn't sure that it would help. He actually entered the huge store from one of the doors to the west, immediately conscious of the activity inside, a huge, human beehive. And inside this beehive on the third Thursday of succeeding months there was going to be a queen bee who was going to pick him out as a very special worker bee. He hoped. A guidebook wrapped around a rolled-up copy of *Pravda*, Charlie recalled, continuing the instructions. Professionally he decided that the choice of meeting place was good and the book and the newspaper innocuous enough, and the final part of the process—"If I lived in Moscow, I don't think I'd care what the weather was like"—the sort of simple exchange not likely to arouse suspicion. So what would? Charlie had survived for so long—been good for so long—because before embarking upon any operation, any problem, he always approached it from every possible direction because the danger always was that the bad guys would know a route he hadn't thought of and use it to come charging down and scoop him up.

Charlie eased his way through the crowded store, letting the movement of the crowd carry him, taking only seconds to isolate the flaw. Today's visit was okay, and maybe a subsequent one—on the third Thursday of any month, between eleven and noon that time—but anything beyond that would be dangerous. And the guidebook and the newspaper weren't as good as he'd first thought: there would unquestionably have been watchers today. Who would have seen him find his way without maps or directions. So the guidebook would look out of place, if his observers were as good as they should be. Just as it would look out of place if, on succeeding third Thursdays of succeeding months, he kept returning to a regular spot at regular times. Shit, thought Charlie. There was no despair; Charlie was too experienced for that. Having identified the flaws, Charlie immediately began seeking a way around them. It was simply— he hoped to Christ it was simple—a matter of clearing his trail. But doing it better than those watching had ever known before, so that the evasion of pursuit wouldn't be a conscious attempt upon his part but an irritating mistake upon theirs: and be shown to be, at any subsequent inquiry. Having found the resolve, Charlie improved upon it. He wouldn't try to dodge on the first identification visit: nothing was going to happen then—apart, he hoped, from his being identified by whoever it was who would later make contact—so better to let that trip be seen. Better still, he'd make lots of other apparently pointless visits, carrying the guidebook and the newspaper, to lots of other apparently innocent tourist spots. That way there'd be a logical reason for the book—which, the longer and more obviously he carried it, would cease to occupy the attention of those watching, because they would become accustomed to his always having it—and GUM would not register with any more significance than anywhere else he went.

It was going to involve a hell of a lot of walking, thought Charlie, remembering his recurrent personal problem. He actually stopped, looking down at his already throbbing feet too tightly enclosed in the shoes that had been provided for him on the night of the escape. And then he realized he was in the country's biggest store and started to look around with greater attention, seeking the shoe department. There was, in fact, more than one, and Charlie went to them all, looking for anything resembling the familiar Hush Puppies and becoming increasingly disappointed. Bloody amazing, he thought. Maybe it was something to do with all the snow they had in the winter, but Charlie decided in boots like these, snowshoes wouldn't have been necessary to cross the drifts. Some looked big enough actually to walk on water! It was going to be an uncomfortable time.

Charlie made an unhurried exit from the store but didn't immediately leave the area, which again might have marked GUM out as the significant destination. He visited St. Basil's Cathedral and stopped and pretended to admire the monument to Minin and Pozharsky beside it and then went on, ambling down the Razina highway, and decided, when he saw it there, to go into the Rossiya Hotel. Charlie's unthinking intention was to have a drink but then he realized he didn't have any money and recognized again just how much of a prisoner he remained. He sat instead in the downstairs foyer, preparing his feet for the return walk, getting up after half an hour with the awareness that his feet would never be prepared for any sort of walking.

It took him an increasingly uncomfortable hour to get back to the apartment. He boiled some water, diluted it to the right temperature, and gratefully soaked the ache from his feet, savoring the relief and not wanting it to end, so it was almost an hour from his actual return when he went properly into the kitchen and opened the refrigerator and saw that in his absence the flat had been entered and restocked. So the surveillance was as active as it had ever been! He supposed the listening devices would have been replaced, too. He grinned and said loudly "Thanks." In a cupboard in the main room he found a bottle of vodka, which was an addition to the previous supplies, which Charlie supposed to be an indication of acceptance. "Thanks again," he said to the unseen and unknown listeners.

* * *

Charlie crossed and traversed again practically every tourist location in the Russian capital. He read the *Pravda* denunciation of Wainwright and wondered if it were all over anyway, but he still kept the appointment at the GUM department store on the appointed Thursday, hoping that he wasn't presenting himself for arrest and that Berenkov would emerge from the crowd.

He didn't, but he telephoned, actually on the evening that Charlie returned from the store.

"Wondered if you might like to work?" said Berenkov.

Charlie felt the jump of excitement. "You're joking!" he said. "I'm practically going out of my mind with boredom."

"How would you feel about instructing at a spy school?"

Charlie hesitated, although not from the reservation that Berenkov imagined. Bloody marvelous, thought Charlie, realizing the advantages at once. To the Russian he said, "That sounds very interesting."

"You'll do it?"

"Yes," accepted Charlie. "I'll do it."

"It was a great shame about Wainwright," said Wilson.

"More mentally affected than we suspected," agreed Harkness.

"We've made all the arrangements?"

His deputy nodded. "He intended to retire to Bognor, apparently. That's where the funeral has been arranged. The wife died two years ago. But there's a mother, in an old people's home in Brighton: suppose that's one of the reasons he chose to live nearby. I've arranged for his pension to be carried on, so that the fees for the home are paid. Pension people aren't happy about it: they say it's establishing a precedent."

"Damn the pension people," said Wilson. "Let me know if there's a difficulty."

Harkness nodded and said, "I don't think there will be. What about the funeral?"

The Director considered the question. "The Soviets will swamp it, of course," he predicted.

"Inevitably, I would think," said Harkness.

"Better for no one important to go then . . ." Wilson hesitated. "Richardson!" he suddenly decided. "They'll know about Richardson now."

"Might even make them think there was something that Wainwright didn't tell them, after all," said Harkness.

"Good point." Wilson nodded. He paused for several moments and said, "Don't suppose there's any doubt that he didn't tell them everything?"

"None at all, I wouldn't imagine," said Harkness. "They'll expect us to change the code now. Not only because of Wainwright but because they'll know we've detected their alterations, from our listening facilities."

"Let's not designate a sender anymore," ruled Wilson. "I don't want to lose anyone else, in the Russian panic to find out what's happening."

21

General Kalenin was extremely careful preparing his entrapment information because the suspected twelve men who
received it were consummate professional intelligence officers
who would have recognized at once not only if it did not appear
absolutely genuine but if it were something going beyond the
knowledge they were entitled to receive. Which meant, the
KGB chairman accepted with great reluctance, that the material
had to be genuine. He attempted to console himself with the
thought that the accepted cure for oil-well fires was explosions
within the well head itself, extinguishing a destructive blaze
with a bigger—but briefer—conflagration. He tried to limit the
potential damage as much as possible, sifting through what had
already been leaked and where applicable adding tidbits that
would not seriously worsen an already bad situation, but with
twelve possible sources to cover, that was not completely
possible. He had to include intelligence concerning Soviet
preparations in the event of an open, armed conflict with the
Chinese along the border area at Alma Ata and some indication
of troop strength and disposition plans, if a Chinese conflict did
develop, necessary from the need to switch from the Warsaw
Pact front.

The British changed their transmission code within a
fortnight of Wainwright's body being returned to the country.

Kalenin was surprised they didn't do it earlier. He imposed fresh pressure upon the code-breaking cryptologists and underwent two frustrating weeks of uncertainty before the mathematicians found the key. It was another mathematical code, this time based upon a factor of five, and Sampson was again utilized, in an effort to transcribe ripple designation and the prefacing identity line that once more was created from a different code structure. As should have been expected from their exper- tise—and their computers—it was the mathematicians who isolated the ripple figure which made the code work, but it only happened after the suggestion from Sampson that the second formula might be linked to the first. There was no longer the disparaging attitude toward Sampson that there had been before and so the cryptologists listened to the suggestion and acted upon it, taking the activating numeral of the initial code—two— and dividing it into the activating numeral of the second. Which produced a figure of 2.50. Using that as the multiplier, they experimented with their computers for a further week, running random subtractions and multiples, and finally found their entry into the messages by quadrupling the activating 2.50 and then multiplying it by the base figure, with the final multiplication by a further 2.50 for the actual message.

The deciphering experts were hampered by having only three messages upon which to work. The first, when they transcribed it, concerned a difficulty in raising foreign currency from gold sales because of failures in the ore-producing mines of Muruntau. The second recorded the troop dispositions neces- sary to maintain the Soviet control of Afghanistan. Neither had been included in the entrapment messages that Kalenin de- vised. The third, which was electrifying, said the Russian source intended to make contact and use the identifying phrase.

Sampson remained involved through the transcriptions and succeeded in deciphering the identity line ahead of the mathe- maticians' success with the first message. Rose was again the key, which in later discussions with Berenkov when the Russian tried to argue carelessness, the increasingly confident Sampson argued the alternative, the actual cleverness of adapting an existing device because of the logical explanation that they would attempt something completely new. On the second occasion the rose-loving British Director had confined his key to a single species—the centifolia—and when he transcribed it Sampson asked for an immediate meeting with Berenkov, because of the difference he found. Berenkov, conscious of the importance, saw Sampson the same day.

The two men met in Berenkov's office, a conference table cleared and unnecessarily large for the limited file that Sampson brought with him. It was a simple exposition for the Englishman, only a few moments' comparison being necessary.

"No sender?" Berenkov realized at once.

Pedantically Sampson went through the line, wanting to prove his worth. "The first block identifies Wilson, MD again," he said. "The second block is simply a dating and timing configuration. The sender is identified only by the word 'Residency.'"

"So now we don't even have a transmission name at this end."

"We do know that the contact has been maintained. Despite Richardson's withdrawal. And despite Wainwright's death. And something else."

"What?"

"The third message. Reference to an identification phrase," pointed out Sampson. "There's no indication in anything that we've intercepted of what it will be."

Berenkov nodded. "How do you interpret that?"

"Richardson hand-carried it," guessed Sampson. "That's why he was withdrawn." He paused and said, "There's something else about the messages—all of them—don't you think?"

"What?" demanded Berenkov.

Before answering, Sampson laid everything out upon the conference table, the new messages and then all those that had preceded them in the other code. "Ignore the contact message," said Sampson. "Look at all the others very closely and analyze them beyond the decoding. Almost without exception—

just four, to be precise—everything emanates from an operational or planning level. And even the four that don't conform—four devoted entirely to trade decisions—have an operational application so there is probably some cross-referencing somewhere."

Berenkov didn't hurry. He went painstakingly through every message, frequently appearing to refer back to a message he had already examined because the inference was obvious, and at the end he said, "Thank you. That was an extremely astute observation."

It was the judgment that Berenkov repeated, during the later meeting with Kalenin. Like Berenkov before, the KGB chairman examined all the messages and finally looked up stern-faced and said, "Absolutely right. The trade messages threw me off track, but Sampson's absolutely right. It's entirely operational or planning."

"My divisions," acknowledged Berenkov openly.

Kalenin realized it reduced the possible sources from twelve to just seven men. Which was still seven too many but a small improvement. "Yes," he said shortly.

"I would understand if you chose to suspend me until the inquiries are complete," said Berenkov formally.

Kalenin shook his head in immediate refusal. "I need your help, not your absence."

"Why don't we plant something, to get him to reveal himself that way?"

"I've done that already," disclosed Kalenin. "It didn't work."

"Including me?" asked Berenkov.

"Including you," said the chairman.

Berenkov wondered what the material had been. He said, "What then?"

"Greatly increased surveillance," said Kalenin. "Electronic, photographic . . . everything."

"What about suspension from sensitive material until it's resolved. With only seven people, it shouldn't take long."

"It would, if we took away the very reason for contact."

"That's an appalling risk, to allow everything to continue: not to impose some sort of filter."

"I want to find him, whoever he is. Not drive him underground."

"Still an appalling risk."

"But one I've got to take. That I've no alternative but to take."

"Sampson is proving to be brilliant," praised Berenkov.

Kalenin's surveillance included monitoring beyond what was normal and he knew from film and microphones everything that passed between his friend and the Englishman. He nodded and said, "He seems to be the only piece of good fortune that we've had for a long time."

"He realizes the importance of this—the opportunity it's created for him—and he's determined to prove himself. It's become a personal thing," said Berenkov, who had expected and knew Kalenin's study of the meetings.

"It's a personal thing for me, as well," said Kalenin, increasingly morose.

That was proved quicker than the KGB chairman expected. Two days later he was summoned before an unscheduled but plenary session of the Politburo convened specifically to consider the leak. Kalenin went fully aware that although Wainwright's death had occurred outside Soviet jurisdiction he was being blamed for a political mistake, in addition to the increasing—and valid—criticism of appearing powerless to find and stop the activities of a traitor. The Politburo had been provided with a complete report in advance of his personal attendance but they insisted upon Kalenin making a personal presentation—a humiliation further to indicate criticism, he recognized—and then underwent a full hour of questioning, unhappily aware throughout that he had hardly any of the answers.

"This is a situation that has to be resolved," insisted the Politburo chairman, Anatoli Matushin.

"I understand that," said Kalenin, self-angered at his apparent impotence.

"The progress so far is unimpressive."

"For which I personally apologize, Comrade Chairman."

"I am not interested in your apologies," said Matushin. "I am interested in a criminal—a traitor—being brought to justice and the leaking to the West of material essential to our very security being halted. I want results, Comrade General. I want results and I want them quickly. And if you prove unable to achieve them, then the task must be given to someone else."

Charlie decided that things were looking good again. After the hiatus between the first encounter with Berenkov, they moved fast, too. There were two meetings with Berenkov, official this time, out at the familiar American-style building by the ring road, where Berenkov explained the job was to be to brief agents immediately prior to their infiltration into the West and explained the employment would give Charlie some legitimacy, with a three-thousand-ruble-a-month salary and concessionary facilities and possibly an apartment away from the transitional one he currently occupied. Charlie asked the questions he knew he would have been expected to ask and considered the implications as he would have been expected to consider them, all the while thinking instead of the bonus it gave him. To succeed—and if contact were made, Charlie was determined to succeed—in the function which had brought him to Moscow would mean complete rehabilitation, as he had already decided: to be able to return to the West knowing the identities of people in whom the KGB had invested years of training and expertise and infiltrated into Europe and North America would be an even greater coup, making it possible for him to cut off Soviet spying efforts for years. Christ, weren't things looking good!

Apart from the encounters with Berenkov, there were meetings with two separate examination panels, which Charlie instantly recognized as being assessments of his ability. Charlie welcomed the challenge, properly confident, that confidence growing when he realized—from their questions—how ignorant the supposed expert body were about the reality of life outside

Russia. The illegals being sent abroad from the Soviet Union needed further training and advice, if they were setting out with the preconceived biases and downright misunderstandings that some of the questioners showed in their examination of him. Charlie pointed up the ignorance every time, careless of offending anyone because he didn't intend the career to be long enough for the politics of friends and enemies to be important and because every time he did so it proved his ability for the very function for which they were deciding his aptitude.

It was Berenkov who confirmed the appointment, and not at the official building but at Kutuzovsky Prospekt again. This time, with money available, Charlie took flowers and Valentina wasn't as shy as she had been on the first occasion, staying with them longer at the table and afterward and joining more in the conversation. Georgi was absent, cramming the final studies at the academy, before his exchange examinations, and apart from saying he hoped Georgi was successful, Charlie didn't talk much about the boy to either of them, conscious of the feeling between them at the prospect of Georgi going overseas.

Although she spent more time with them, there was still opportunity for Charlie and Berenkov to talk business. Charlie was as critical to Berenkov about the selection committees as he had been to their faces, and the Russian shook his head in weary acceptance and agreed the shortcomings and said that was precisely why he'd thought of Charlie performing the function. Having presented himself at GUM—which meant Berenkov would have recognized his purpose for being there if indeed it was Berenkov—Charlie actually made the pretense of examining the overflowing bookshelves and selecting something of Chekhov's, but Berenkov gave no reaction, not even recalling his use of the books in Britain. Charlie wondered about talking of the accusation in *Pravda* against the British first secretary and decided against it, unwilling to risk too much.

There are espionage schools throughout the Soviet Union but the concentration is around Moscow. The installations that equip Russian agents for overseas work are administered by the

First Chief Directorate, of which a subsection—Directorate S—is responsible for foreign infiltration.

Balashikha is such an installation, actually off the same circumferal highway that Charlie now knew so well, about fifteen miles east of Moscow just off Gofkovskoy Shosse. It is an absolutely restricted, secluded place, behind sensored fences and protected by uniformed guards and dogs. Charlie went the first day under escort, the necessary accreditation and passes actually provided to him during the ride out from the city. The security checks were more stringent than he could remember from England, four separate and intensive checks before he reached the main building, where there was a further examination.

There was a man waiting for him just beyond the reception area and Charlie recognized him as someone who had sat on both the selection panels.

"My name is Krysin," introduced the man. "Andrei Vladimirovich Krysin. I am the director here."

And someone whose ignorance of true conditions in the West he had on at least three occasions shown to be facile, remembered Charlie. Fuck it, he thought. "I'm looking forward to working with you," he said.

"We're looking forward to your being here," said Krysin heavily. "From our apparent ignorance you seemed delighted to expose during what was supposed to be your suitability selection, it would seem we're greatly in need of your expertise."

Why was it, wondered Charlie, that he never got on with anyone in authority? He said, "I hope I don't disappoint you."

"I hope so too," said Krysin, making the threat obvious. "I hope so very much indeed."

Kiss my ass, thought Charlie.

22

Natalia Fedova was the third person to enter the room. Her arrival completely confused Charlie but he was sure there was no outward indication. He remained as he was, lounged over the lectern in the front of the small lecture hall, glad there were more behind, which meant he didn't have to begin immediately, having time to think instead. What the hell was she doing there! Berenkov wouldn't have made contact and he wouldn't have got past the selection interviews or—most indicative of all—been allowed in a place with the security of Balashikha if they didn't trust him. So it couldn't be a test. And if it were a test, then it wouldn't be done like this, with her taking her place sedately in one of the seats confronting him: it would be with microphones and cameras, entrapment devices trying to catch him in an unguarded moment. Maybe it was a move of Krysin's. Charlie recognized he'd made the academy director look a fool in front of the other selectors, so maybe the man was invoking whatever authority he possessed to get Natalia to run another check and maybe make an adverse report, reducing the impression that he appeared to have made with the other examiners.

Charlie was waiting when she finally looked up. He smiled at her. She made no response, instead looking away with the appearance of discomfort. Charlie accepted that his conclusion might be wrong, but it was the best he could manage. Okay, Natalia Nikandrova Fedova, he thought, if you want to see a performance then you'll see a performance. As the one thought came, so did another. Always honest with himself, Charlie realized that he'd enjoy showing off to her.

There were five, in addition to Natalia, one other woman and four men. Although the room was small, it still left a lot of space. They arranged themselves in seats in varying rows: Natalia was third from the front. Charlie waited until they had settled themselves, watching while the other woman and two of the men took out notepads and arranged pencils alongside.

"Dobraya utra," said Charlie.

"Dobraya utra," every one of them replied, and Charlie slapped the desk and said, "You've all just been arrested."

The group assembled in front of him looked among themselves uncertainly and Charlie said, "What you've just done is inconceivable! You are supposed to have qualified from every training course, to be ready to be infiltrated anywhere in the West. You're not Russian anymore. You don't think Russian, speak Russian, you're not Russian."

It had been gimmicky—the oldest gimmick in the book—but it had worked. He had their attention. The fact that they had fallen for the oldest entrapment gimmick didn't say much for their training.

"You," said Charlie, pointing to a fair-haired man nearest to him, in the front row. "What is your name?"

"Belik," replied the young man, "Gennadi Belik."

"What have Zachary Taylor, James Buchanan, and Rutherford Hayes got in common?"

The young man smiled, relieved. "They were all presidents of the United States of America."

Charlie sighed. "Shall I tell you who knows that?" he said. "American historians, academics, know that. A few hundred college students. And foreign agents force-fed facts, in the stupid belief that it gives them cover . . ." If Krysin heard this—and Charlie didn't have any doubt that he would—he'd be even more unhappy. He said to the man, "All right, what should you have said?"

Belik colored, the uncertainty obvious. "I don't know," he admitted, responding to Charlie's question.

"Exactly!" accepted Charlie. "You didn't know. Don't ever go beyond what is absolutely essential to maintain whatever legends you're living. Someone who can recite the names of three obscure presidents of the United States is drawing attention to himself. The essential requirement if you are going to survive—and this is what we're literally talking about, survival—then you must never, under any circumstances, draw attention to yourselves. You become people of whom nobody is aware. You see but are not seen . . ." He pointed to the other woman. "What is your name?"

"Olga Suvorov," replied the woman. She was nondescript and mousy-haired: a good choice, thought Charlie.

He said, "Before entering the room, you assembled, outside?"

She nodded.

"You see but are not seen," repeated Charlie. "Stay looking directly at me, like you are at the moment. Stay looking directly at me and describe how everyone else in the room is dressed."

Olga's eyes flicked sideways and Charlie said, "Look at me!"

Predictably, Olga began with Natalia. "Gray dress," she began awkwardly. "Belted. Shoes . . . I think the shoes were black. The men . . . suits. Two were . . . I think three were gray . . . No, two were . . ."

"Stop," said Charlie. Holding the woman's eyes, he said, "You have an oatmeal dress, brown shoes, and a ladder in the left leg of your stockings. It's not visible now, because of the way you are sitting, but you have a necklace with a black stone pendant, and your earrings don't match. They're dark blue. The other woman in the class is wearing a gray dress. The shoes aren't black, they're dark gray, and if you remembered that the dress was belted you should have remembered also that the front buttons are heavy and black. She has a gold chain at her throat, not earrings, although her ears are pierced. She isn't wearing stockings. The man in the front seat is wearing a green sports jacket and gray trousers, which haven't been pressed. He's a smoker, because the fingers of his left hand are nicotine-stained. That's not the only indication of his being a heavy smoker. Sometimes he does it surreptitiously, holding the cigarette cupped in the palm of his hand. The hand is stained, too . . ." Instinctively Belik moved to cover his hand. Charlie went on: "He has a gray shirt and a gray knitted tie. The left cuff of the shirt is frayed. Sometime in the past his fountain pen leaked: there's a large stain, which was visible when he took out some pencils to take notes, at the beginning of this session. The two men in the back row are wearing suits. One is plain gray, the other with a predominant blue check over gray. Both the shirts are white; one tie is red, the other a pattern, mostly blue. The gray suit is old: there is a repair mark on the left knee. The check isn't new, either. The seat is worn and shiny. Both have black shoes. The man in the gray suit has the nervous habit of biting his nails, left hand more than right . . ." The accused man moved his hands, like Belik had earlier. "The man in the patterned suit also has a nervous mannerism, moving the ring on his left hand. The fourth man in this class is wearing a brown sports jacket with lighter brown trousers, with brogue shoes. The shoes are in need of repair, both badly down at heel. The tie is red, and trying to conform to some earlier instruction, the knot is a wide one, no doubt a style you've been taught is popular in the West, particularly in America. The man in the brown jacket is impatient with this lesson, considering it a waste of time: five times already he's checked the time. He's appeared to make notes but from the movement of the pencil, they haven't been notes. They've been doodles, a way to pass the time . . ."

Charlie broke away from his direct stare at Olga Suvorov, encompassing the class. The face of the man in the brown jacket blazed red and both Belik and the man at the rear sat with their hands beneath the desk now. Gimmicky again, conceded Charlie—later they might even decide it hadn't been such an impressive trick, because he'd had the advantage of looking out at them, even though they'd have to accept that all of them were partially hidden by the desks at which they sat—but it was still effective. They were all looking among themselves, with the exception of Natalia. She met Charlie's gaze this time, the expression on her face one of faint amusement. Was it amusement? wondered Charlie. Or contempt?

To the embarrassed man in the brown jacket Charlie said, "How are you called?"

"Popov," said the man. "Yuri Pavlovich Popov."

"No!" said Charlie. "Listen, for Christ's sake listen! You've been trained to infiltrate countries that speak English. Which means England or the United States or Canada or Australia or New Zealand or—although unlikely—South Africa. No one there, seeking your name, says 'How are you called?' That's English constructed from a foreign language. It's another interrogation trick, like saying good morning in Russian."

"How should we respond, then?"

The question came from Natalia. Charlie looked to her, thinking again how attractive she was: not beautiful, but attractive. A contemptuous question? he wondered, recalling her earlier expression. Or one of genuine interest? He was talking of interrogation—entrapment—and she'd interrogated him. It could be a test. If he proved himself too adept at confronting and resisting interrogation, then she might suspect that he'd tricked her. "Always with innocence," he said. "Because that's what you always are, innocent of whatever stupidity has caused whatever has happened to you. Not anger. Or arrogance. Anger and arrogance fit, of course, but unless they're absolutely genuine they're too easy to detect and undermine. Innocence is the barrier. Because if you're innocent then it's natural to be confused and if you're confused then it's perfectly understandable if you stumble and appear awkward— if you make dangerous mistakes, even." Charlie hesitated, wondering whether to continue. She was concentrating absolutely upon him and Charlie was warmed by the attention. He went on, "But use being a confused innocent . . ." He looked to the brown-jacketed man who had identified himself as Yuri Popov. "'How are you called?' didn't fit, and instead of being anxious to respond, you should have come back at me and asked me what I meant. By doing that, you tilt the balances so that *I* have to provide, to *your* questioning.

"You!" demanded Charlie suddenly, gesturing to the man at the rear in the overchecked suit. "What's the point I'm making?"

The man twitched, unhappy at the sudden unwelcome attention. Blushing at his inability—like Popov had blushed before him—the man said, "I'm not sure," and stopped miserably.

"Good!" praised Charlie, aware of the other man's look of surprise. "You didn't mean it but that was exactly the lesson. Never make the mistake of trying to respond either fully or at once to any question. Always remember you're confused, that you don't understand. Always misunderstand and gain time from it.

"You!" said Charlie, finger-pointing again and continuing the demands, this time to Natalia. "What's been peculiar about everything I've said so far today?"

The relief from everyone else in the room at having avoided such a question was palpable. Natalia showed no discomfort. Nor hurry, either. She actually looked down at her desk, considering the answers, and then she came back to him and said, "Defeat. Everything you've said has been directed toward our detection—the need for us satisfactorily to withstand investigation."

Charlie's reactions were mixed. The first was a satisfaction of his own, that she'd got the answer right. Then there were others. Us, she'd said: the need for us satisfactorily to withstand investigation. Was Natalia really someone under consideration for overseas posting: someone who, when she was posted, he was going to betray? Just once, thought Charlie, he'd like there to be more answers than there were questions in a single day. "Right," he said. "Exactly right."

Natalia flushed, pleased, and Charlie was pleased too.

"You!" he said, schoolmasterly again, to the man in gray whom he'd so far spared. "What are you called?"

The man frowned and said, "I'm sorry. I do not understand."

"Good." Charlie smiled. "Very good. What is your name?"

"Valeri Pavlovich Vlasov," said the man, grateful his test had come last, so that he'd had time to learn.

"So tell me, Valeri Pavlovich Vlasov. Why do you think I've been concentrating upon how to resist interrogation?"

The man's relief seeped away like air from a balloon. "Because it is important," he blurted desperately.

Recalling the earlier instructions, Vlasov said, "To survive."

"Should it have got this far?" said Charlie.

"I don't understand," said the man, trying to flee up the already signposted escape route.

Charlie didn't allow him the escape, but he spread the question to involve everyone in the room. "Why?" he said again. "Why do you imagine that I consider resistance so important, at our very first meeting? You!" He pointed to Natalia. "Tell me what you think."

There wasn't the hesitation this time. "I don't think you've any confidence in our being able to escape detection," she said simply. "I think you imagine that we'd be swept up almost as soon as we arrived."

"You would," said Charlie. "I don't think any of you would stand a chance. You've been taught like animals, to perform tricks. Seals can balance balls on their noses and dogs can balance on their hind legs provided the trick is always demanded in the same way, through the same formula. You've been taught in a formularized way and the easiest way to be detected is to behave to a formula. Agents behave to a formula; not ordinary people. Ordinary people—the sort of people that you're expected to be—make mistakes and get drunk and forget to pay the rent . . ." Charlie raised his hand, seeing the look upon the faces of both Belik and Popov. "Which is not a contradiction of what I said about being unobtrusive. It's in support of it.

Ordinary, unsuspicious wallpaper-on-the-wall people do those things. No one hasn't ever forgotten to pay a bill or parked wrongly on a line or taken too much at a party. Who are the good guys at a party? The drunks or the sober ones, who get remembered afterward?"

"So what are you saying?" asked Natalia, who appeared to be emerging as the spokesman for the group.

"That's better," praised Charlie, almost overeffusively. "Turn as many questions back as you can. What I'm saying is that I think you've all got to relearn—every one of you. I don't mean go back to the basic classes and undergo every course again. I mean that having assimilated the courses, you've got to adapt what you've learned into what it's supposed to make you, a Westerner. And stop being Russians who've been taught to balance balls on their noses when the trick is demanded of them."

Charlie's ability to describe how every one of them was dressed from their initial entry into the room wasn't a trick; not any longer, anyway. It had been, years ago, when the need was first explained to him, a conscious effort at memory, but now it was instinctive. The conscious effort he was making was about their faces, faces he was later going to have to recall, to photofit artists so that complete reconstructions could be made and circulated throughout the security services, for them to be detected. He was fairly confident that he could do it already, from this first meeting. Every succeeding day was going to be an advantage. He said, "I'm going to make you Westerners: instinctive, automatic, easily assimilated Westerners. There are going to be times when you think I am wasting your time . . ." He glanced at Popov, who looked discomfited again. "I won't be wasting your time. I'll be teaching you apparently stupid, inconsequential things and it's what appears stupid and inconsequential that will keep you safe from detection." Charlie smiled around the room, the first time he had appeared to relax. Before they had time to get that impression, he said, "All right. With one exception—because it wasn't demanded—you've all made a mistake. What was it?"

Yet again there were uncertain movements throughout the group, Natalia less than the others.

"You told me your names," said Charlie. "Because I'm standing here, at the head of the class, you assumed I had authority—the right to know—and when I asked, you responded to that authority. Weren't you all provided with pseudonyms when you came here?"

It was a question for later, when he returned to England. While he was at Balashikha he would learn all he could about the training and the instruction. To know precisely how the Russians taught their agents would be invaluable.

From the people in front of him there were nods of agreement.

"Then they were provided for a reason," said Charlie. "For protection, even here. It's the same lesson as before: don't feel the need to respond. Until it becomes an automatic response, consciously look behind every question—every instruction—for a second or third or fourth reason for that question or instructions . . ." Charlie hesitated, remembering the lessons he had learned at the knee of Sir Archibald Willoughby, the Director under whom he had worked for so long. Recalling one verbatim, Charlie said, "There is never a straight line in espionage. Always too many conflicting lines."

Charlie generalized for a further hour and it was a more subdued group that prepared to leave than the one that had entered. As they gathered their things, Charlie said to Natalia, "Can I speak to you?"

The woman appeared embarrassed at being finally singled out from the rest, smiling at them apologetically and then turning back to Charlie. When they were alone Charlie said, "I was surprised."

"So was I."

"You didn't know?"

"Not that it would be you . . . just that it was an extra course. Something special . . ." She hesitated, smiling at him this time, and said, "Should I be looking for a second or third or fourth reason in the questions?"

He grinned back at her. "Maybe we both should."

"I don't know if it's possible, but I think it would be best if I applied to be taken off the course, don't you?"

Did that mean she really was undergoing overseas instruction? He said, "Would it really be difficult for you?"

"Obviously," she said, appearing surprised at his question. "Wouldn't it for you?"

"I don't know," said Charlie. "I don't think so." Having reestablished contact, he didn't want to lose it. He said, "Why don't we talk about it further . . . somewhere other than here?"

"I'm not sure that's a good idea, either."

"We don't seem sure about anything, do we?"

"I think you upset everybody," said Natalia.

"Seems to be a habit I have," said Charlie.

"Having you here is an innovation, instructions from outside."

Berenkov, Charlie presumed. He said, "Resented?"

"The other instructors didn't appear very keen. Today's group were supposed to be graduate level."

Charlie wished he could categorize Natalia's place in all this. He said, "And supposed to test me?"

She nodded. "You were very impressive."

Charlie felt a physical reaction to her praise, a stomach tightening. He said, "They weren't."

"Maybe they thought it was going to be too easy. Relaxed too much."

"That isn't any sort of excuse. Explanation even," said Charlie professionally.

Her face closed against him and Charlie wished he hadn't spoken so curtly. "That wasn't meant to be a rebuke," he said.

"I should be joining the others."

"I can do it now," said Charlie, purposely obtuse.

She frowned back at him. "I don't understand."

"During one of the debriefings I said I couldn't invite you

out to dinner because I didn't have any money. This job pays. What are you doing tonight?"

She smiled at him again, shaking her head. "No," she said.

"Why not?"

"You know why not."

"No, I don't," said Charlie, still intentionally awkward. If she refused him now, then any subsequent refusal would be easier for her.

"It wouldn't look right."

"Who'd be looking?" If they knew, they'd both probably be surprised, he thought.

"Going out to dinner in Moscow isn't easy, like it is in the West."

She was weakening, Charlie realized. "I'd still like to try," he said. "Please."

Natalia hesitated. Then she said, "All right."

Charlie felt the stomach tightening come again.

Kalenin set out his miniature tanks to recreate Montgomery's confrontation in North Africa against Rommel, fully familiar with the ploys and the strategies of the battle. Having assembled them, he remained staring down. There had been a sandstorm, he remembered; a blinding, concealing sandstorm, and Montgomery had utilized the advantage.

Was he being deflected by a sandstorm? wondered the KGB chairman. Kalenin knew he had done all the right things and made all the right moves to try to locate his traitor. But he still couldn't see anything. So what was he doing wrong? What was blinding him from looking in the right direction?

Kalenin turned away from his game, uninterested. The order had come from the Politburo for regular reports. Kalenin was aware that rarely—at any time during his career—had he been so exposed.

23

Charlie was happy to let Natalia lead in everything because attracted to her though he was and genuine though he believed her to be, he didn't believe in coincidence, any more than he believed Father Christmas came down chimneys every December, and he couldn't reconcile himself to her appearance at Balashikha. He was curious at her choice of the Rossiya because it was the hotel to which he'd gone after the rebellious outing which had included the GUM store, but pleased with the top-story restaurant because of its magnificent view of central Moscow. The wine list was restricted to products within the Soviet Union and he wondered what Berenkov would have ordered: at least, he thought, it prevented him making any mistakes. He selected a red, from Georgia, and it tasted good and he was relieved; he didn't want to show himself up in front of her. His attitude—which, objective as always, he recognized as one of nervousness—intrigued Charlie because the nervousness wasn't because of his uncertainty about her true function but just about being in her company. Having been lucky with the wine, he deferred to her over the food. They started with assorted cold fish and then goulash, which was excellent. The service was typically Russian, slow, but Charlie wasn't in any hurry and he welcomed the delay: before the goulash arrived, he'd ordered the second bottle of wine. The lecture-hall reservation remained initially between them, so that although Charlie had decided to let her lead in the choice of where and what to eat, he had to prompt the conversation, coaxing her out, bit by bit. Almost at once, tauntingly, she asked from how many sides she should look at his questions, and he extended one finger toward her, and guessing the response, she met hers with his and Charlie said it signified a pact, for neither to be suspicious of the other, comfortable with his own hypocrisy. Gradually she began to talk. She told him of her hometown of Penza but of moving to Moscow very young, within the first year of her university entrance, because the KGB personnel selectors had already received reports of her ability, particularly with languages. Charlie got the impression she clearly enjoyed being in the service, for the advantages it meant. She explained how the training had been extensive and her grades impressive, so impressive that the offer was made— and accepted—that she should extend her studies to include psychology, for the function for which she was ultimately groomed. Presented with the opening, Charlie asked outright whether that grooming was now being further extended to mean her posting abroad, the only explanation for her presence on the course. This time she offered her finger and Charlie, enjoying the game, touched back—enjoying, too, the actual touch of her—and she admitted it wasn't. Making no effort to conceal the pride, Natalia said she was the senior psychologist in the debriefing section and that her appointment to the sessions was to provide the final assessment, on the suitability of the other five selected for overseas emplacement. Charlie's initial, abrupt reaction was one of relief because it meant that at some time in the future he wouldn't be entrapping her, for arrest and imprisonment—the awfulness of imprisonment that he had known—in England or America. But at the same time, that other part of his brain—the never-resting, never-sleeping, never-relaxing professional part—saw the flaw.

"Then it didn't mean anything, did it?" he demanded.

She looked up at him, face creased with uncertainty. "What didn't?"

"What you said in the lecture room, about applying to be taken off the course. Because you also said it was special, an innovation. There weren't any other courses to which you could be transferred."

She smiled at him admiringly. "I also said you were impressive," she said. "I hoped you wouldn't remember."

"Why not?"

"Because it was a lie. I meant what I said, about being surprised at seeing you when I walked into the hall today. I didn't know how to respond: I hadn't been given any warning. I don't know why they didn't warn me. It was stupid, not to have done so. And because I was uncertain, I just carried on with the charade, until I could get out to get some guidance."

"From Krysin?"

"Yes," she said.

"Did you tell him we were meeting tonight?"

She frowned again. "Is there any reason why I shouldn't have done?"

Instead of answering her question, Charlie asked another. "What would you have done if Krysin had said no, you couldn't come?"

"I told him as a matter of courtesy," she qualified. "I'm equal to Krysin in rank. And influence. He hasn't the authority to forbid me."

"What would you have done if he talked against it?" persisted Charlie.

Natalia looked down into her wineglass. "I don't know," she admitted. "I think I would have come, but I'm not sure."

"So he could influence you?"

"Not about my private life, no," she said in further qualification. "I would have listened to Krysin if I'd thought my becoming involved with you could in any way have caused difficulty with the other five in the class: they're the important consideration, not your or my social life."

"Are we becoming involved?" seized Charlie.

"No," she said at once.

Almost too sharply, Charlie thought. Seeing the opening for an unasked question, Charlie said, "Are you married?"

"Would it have any importance, if I were?"

"Wouldn't that be a decision for you?"

"Why?" she demanded. "What a bourgeois question! What can conceivably be wrong in a married man or a married woman dining together?"

"The roles have reversed again," said Charlie.

His evasion confused her, as it was supposed to do. "What do you mean?"

"You're in charge again," he said.

She smiled, reluctantly. "Answer the question," she insisted.

"No," he said. "There can be absolutely nothing wrong. Now answer mine—is it happening?"

Natalia sighed but Charlie didn't think it was an expression of irritation. She said, "I was married during my first year here in Moscow. He was a major in our Border Guard division. An incredible man, in every way. The most active way was sexual and he expected me to understand the other women, but I couldn't. So I divorced him."

"It sounds as if you still love him," said Charlie.

"Oh, I do," she admitted at once. "Very much."

Disappointment engulfed Charlie, like a blanket suddenly thrown over his head, blocking out the light. "Why not try to get back together?" said Charlie.

"I tried," said Natalia, honest still. "He isn't interested."

"I'm sorry," said Charlie, carelessly.

"Why should you be?"

He smiled at her, recovering. "One of those stupid, inconsequential Western reactions," he said.

"At least there's Eduard," she said. "He's ten now. A very clever boy. I'm lucky, with the benefits of what I do. He's at a boarding academy, getting a wonderful education."

It would be a KGB-run school, Charlie guessed. There seemed something obscene, battery-feeding a child that early into intelligence. It was the same, he supposed, with seminaries, although he didn't imagine priests would have liked the comparison. "How often do you see him?" asked Charlie.

"Not enough," said Natalia. "I'd prefer to have him home, but it's better for him, the way it is."

Neither wanted anything after the goulash. Charlie ordered coffee and brandy, Russian again. "Well?" he said.

"Well what?"

"Has it been so bad?"

"No," she said. "It's been very nice. Thank you."

Her apartment was far more central than his, just off Mytninskaya. There was the customary concierge on the ground floor and Natalia gave no reaction when Charlie walked confidently by, accompanying her to the elevator and then up to the apartment door. No smells, noted Charlie. At the door she turned and said "No."

"No what?" he said innocently.

"Just no." She extended her hand formally and said, "Thank you again. I've enjoyed it very much."

Charlie took her hand, thinking how much better it was than finger touching but regretting this was all it was going to be. "Me too," he said. "Don't be late for school in the morning."

"Were they bad?" she said seriously. "As bad as you made out?"

"Bloody awful," said Charlie.

With his customary ebullience Berenkov insisted upon a celebration dinner and with her customary obedience Valentina complied. Berenkov, naturally, made himself responsible for the wines. There was imported French champagne for the repeated toasts, and the dinner wine and brandy were French, too. Georgi, who still had to learn to know his father, was overawed by the flamboyance and further embarrassed by the congratulations that Berenkov kept proposing, praises for passing the examinations with almost-maximum marks and forecasts of the successes that Georgi was going to know in whatever Western university accepted him. The boy drank slightly too much and went unsteadily to bed and after he left the table Valentina said,

"I can't reconcile myself to it. I've tried—believing it will be as good for him as you tell me it will—but I can't reconcile myself to it."

"It'll be different from before," assured Berenkov. "Before, we didn't know when we were going to be together again, you and I. It won't be like that this time."

"How long will it be?" the woman demanded, wanting specifics.

"Two years," said Berenkov. "I'm sure it won't be any longer than two years."

"Two years without seeing him!"

"Maybe we'll be able to see him earlier than that; maybe it won't be a two-year gap."

"You mean he'll be able to come home on vacations?"

"I mean we'll see him," said Berenkov. "Of course we'll see him."

24

Charlie was a relentless, unremitting instructor because he had to be. To win. And to survive. Concentrating upon survival first—which he always did—Charlie knew from Natalia's warning that those he was teaching, who were after all supposed to be qualified, would report back to Krysin or someone else at Balashikha if he didn't appear to be giving everything and more. And by giving everything and more he won, because it enabled him to learn just how good they were—and therefore the standard of their training—and a lot about the installation off Gofkovskoy Shosse, all of which he intended carrying back to England. Under the pretext of improving their technique, he had them take him through all their tradecraft, how they established cells and communicated within those cells, how they created message drops and contact procedures and—most important—how they'd been taught to maintain relations with Moscow. All the time he corrected and modified—confident they would never have the opportunity to utilize the expertise he was giving them—all the time aware that in addition to winning and surviving, he was the focus of Natalia's attention and increasing admiration.

Charlie tempered—although only to himself—his initial impression of their ability. They'd been taught well, in some respects impressively. But by rote, with rarely any advice on how to improvise or adapt if the circumstances for which they had been prepared didn't accord with the expected pattern. Charlie thought those to whom he would subsequently report in London were going to be intrigued by how little individual initiative Moscow allowed its operatives.

And intrigued, too, by his account of Balashikha. Charlie wasn't aware of anything like it in England. He supposed the CIA's training facility at Camp Peary, in Virginia, was similar but guessed even that fell short of what was available here. It was an enclave-within-enclave design and Charlie estimated that in total it occupied several thousand acres. The lecture halls and administration offices were the hub. Operatives lived within the installation, in dormitory accommodation which adjoined the central block. In the grounds there had been constructed complete replicas of typical streets and houses in Western towns. Insisting he should monitor his class's trade craft in as proper a setting as possible, Charlie managed to gain access to reproductions of English, American, Canadian, and French townships. There were parts to which he was not permitted admission, but from one section the explosions and noise were obvious and Charlie realized that at Balashikha the *spetnaz* units were trained, too. He wondered, in passing, if Letsov and the other commando who had got him out of England had received their training here.

Krysin remained hostile but Charlie ignored the man's attitude, determined to take back with him as much as he could about the staff as well as the installation. He forced himself upon them in the recreation and dining areas and invented acceptable queries about the earlier training of those he was now instructing to intrude into their lecture halls and offices until finally Krysin summoned him and told Charlie that he was ignoring regulations and that all inquiries should be channeled through him, as director. Charlie was able to say—quite honestly—that he was unaware of any such regulations and Krysin had to admit to not having told him, which was further cause for ill feeling between them. Charlie didn't care. By then he had the named identities of five other instructors in addition to Krysin and, by barging unannounced and uninvited into a classroom, a mental picture of four more agents undergoing infiltration training.

Every time he invited Natalia out in the evenings, she agreed. They ate Azerbaijan food at the Baku and went to a recital at the Central Concert Hall, and at her insistence, because she said he would never have seen anything like it, went to the Moscow State Circus and Charlie admitted she was right. At the end of each evening, at the door to her apartment, she politely extended her hand and Charlie politely shook it: after the circus he tried to kiss her but she turned her face, so that gesture ended in a peck on the cheek, further politeness.

Charlie planned for the contact Thursday. He knew Krysin had tried hard to find fault—and been unable to apart from his intruding where he shouldn't—so the director's resistance to the suggestion was predictable. Charlie prepared for it, arguing the need for them to put their training to practical street use, and by setting it out as a challenge—putting their earlier instruction against his subsequent training—finally obtained the director's agreement. He set it out as a challenge to the class, too, warning them on the Wednesday that the following day he was going to be the hare to their hounds and within an hour clear his trail completely of their pursuit. It hadn't really been necessary to challenge them, Charlie knew; he just wanted to impress Natalia.

Charlie made extensive use of the metro, crisscrossing the city and consciously losing Popov and Olga Suvorov by appearing to leave the train at the Kazan interchange and then reboarding at the last minute. He did change, twice, and emerged at street level at the Kiev station. He was lucky because a riverboat was about to depart up the Moskva River and he hurried toward it, sideslipping into the last of the crowd, and Belik tried to anticipate him and was at the rail, looking desperately around him, when the boat left with Charlie still ashore. He went underground again, traveling this time as far as the Kursk station. The Museum of Oriental Art was ideal, a large, rambling building with many confusing rooms, and he used the emergency exit to get out, not onto the main Obukha Street, but into a side alley. He used the park alongside the Yauza River, actually entering the sanatorium that had been created from the mansion in the grounds there and finding another side entrance so that he could avoid reemerging from the same door. He chanced a street bus from the park, consciously going away from the direction he intended, leaving after two halts and backtracking, still by bus, until he saw a convenient metro station and went underground again. He switched trains twice, remaining the second time on the same line, and emerged from the Arbatskaya station near the Kremlin. He didn't approach the GUM store direct but consciously went around Dzerzhinsky Square, gazing up at the goatee-bearded statue of the man after whom it was named and who established the Soviet secret service, and then beyond, to the uneven facade of the headquarters of the KGB itself. He hadn't got inside, as Wilson had hoped. Too much to have hoped for anyway. He'd got to Berenkov, which was as good. And penetrated Balashikha, which was also good. Bloody good. If only he could make the contact and pull the whole damned thing off. Charlie moved on, still with the building in view. It was conveniently situated to GUM if the informant were actually inside, he reflected.

Charlie entered the enormous store through the prescribed door and loitered with the identifying guidebook and copy of *Pravda* in his left hand, feeling uncomfortably conspicuous. He waited a full fifteen minutes and then went further inside. Charlie's feet throbbed from the exercise of losing his pursuers. At first without conscious intention but then with increasing determination he went to the shoe department, the one on the second floor, and looked this time with greater concentration than before. They all still seemed to be big, but he finally found a pair that appeared to be made of something resembling the suede of the Hush Puppies that were so kind to him. He tried them on, wiggling his toes to test the restriction and then embarking on a brief trial walk. Not bad, he thought; they'd spread and be better than the ones he had. He paid and kept them on, having the ones he had been wearing put into the bag.

He went back to the deputed area and spent a further fifteen minutes there, alert for contact. Come on! he thought in sudden exasperation. Whoever it was had to be a professional. And Charlie decided that if the man were a professional then he'd had ample opportunity to establish there was no surveillance to concern him. He looked about the store, seeking the familiar face of Berenkov. Around him, the shoppers swirled: at an adjoining counter an American couple debated the merits of engraved glass as souvenirs and decided against buying. Charlie moved his feet, hunching them inside his new shoes, trying immediately to mold them. He couldn't see Berenkov anywhere.

"Is there a prize?"

Although he was prepared—actually waiting for the approach—Charlie still jumped at the familiar voice.

Natalia smiled back at him.

"What is it?" The smile faded into a frown of concern.

"Startled me," said Charlie, honestly. Could it be? She was in the service: but with the sort of access that Wilson indicated? Why not? As a debriefer and assessor she'd range over more than one department. Ideally placed, in fact. It didn't have to be Berenkov. The questions crowded in, one jostling the other.

"That's conceited," she said.

"What?" said Charlie, regaining control.

"Imagining you'd be able to lose everyone."

It was, if she'd genuinely followed him: dangerous, too, because he'd checked constantly and been unaware of her. "From the beginning?" he said.

Natalia nodded, pleased with herself. "I almost lost you on the metro at Ploshchad Nogina. Only saw you switch at the last moment."

Still needing time, Charlie took her arm and began to walk her from the store. Where was the Chekhov quote that was going to confirm everything for him? Outside, he actually shivered, to make it obvious—and easy—for her, and said, "It's cold, suddenly."

"I kept warm enough, chasing you," she said.

For him to make the approach would be against every rule and precaution. He said, "There is a prize." Nodding toward the Rossiya Hotel where they'd had their first meal, he said, "A congratulatory drink."

The uncertainties remained, irritating him. If her being in the store were as she claimed to be—simply the result of her expertise—then there was a good chance that the would-be defector, if he were watching, would have been frightened away by witnessing his being approached. Which would mean that he had been conceited. Worse, that he'd probably cocked everything up. He took her to the roof bar, adjoining the restaurant, and said, "I'm impressed."

"I wanted you to be," she said, in an abrupt moment of seriousness.

Charlie waited hopefully, but she didn't go on. He said, "I thought you were trained as a psychologist and as an assessor."

"A complete assessor," she expanded. "Practical as well as everything else."

She didn't have the identification phrase, Charlie realized. So it had been her expertise. And his ineptitude. He was unhappy at the awareness that she was his street equal: he didn't think anyone was. Conceited, like she'd accused him of being. He waited for their wine to be served, raised his glass, and said, "Congratulations."

She giggled, recognizing his attitude. "You're offended!" she said, pleased.

"No I'm not," said Charlie defensively.

"You are! I know you are. You thought you were better than anybody else."

Bloody psychologist, he thought. He said, "The others failed. All of them. So we'll have to do it again. And you. Bet I'll beat you next time."

"A bet," she accepted, extending her hand to confirm it.

Charlie joined in the playacting and said, "I'm getting fed up, shaking hands all the time."

There was another moment of abrupt seriousness and Natalia said, "So am I."

They stayed looking directly at each other for several moments and Charlie felt the nervousness he'd known with her before. He said, "It was scheduled to be an all-day exercise: we don't have to go back to Balashikha."

"No," she agreed.

"My apartment is a long way out," said Charlie. "The neighbors cook cabbage all the time."

She rose, without saying anything, and they didn't talk on the way to her apartment. They walked by the familiar concierge and Natalia had the key ready when they reached the door. It was neat and fastidious, like Natalia, a small place with a couch that came out to form a bed, turning the living area into a bedroom. She made the conversion, appearing embarrassed now that he was actually in the apartment with her, unwilling to look at him. When she turned from the bed, still not looking, he held out his hand so that she had to stop, and then he brought her to him. He could feel her trembling. He kissed her, not very well at first, and then her nervousness started to go and she responded and it was better. Charlie was nervous too, particularly about trying to make love to her because it had been such a long time and he didn't do it well the first time and that made him more nervous. Her breasts were very full, like he'd known they would be, and he kept caressing her and she reacted and Charlie knew he could make love again, which pleased him. It was much better the second time: they were getting used to each other, each matching the other's pace. She climaxed ahead of him and that pleased him too, and when it was over she clung to him tightly, not letting him withdraw.

"Wonderful," she said. "That was really wonderful."

"For me too," said Charlie.

"I'd almost forgotten."

"So had I."

"Charlie."

"What?"

"I want to tell you something. About my being in the class."

She released him as she spoke, so that he was able to move beside her: he lay propped up on his arm, so that he could look down at her. "What about it?"

"It wasn't just to assess the others," she said. "I had to assess you, as well. Compare what happened against how you behaved during the debriefing."

"So you did know I would be there, that first day?"

She nodded. "It was done to off-balance you."

And sodding well succeeded, thought Charlie. He said, "Why the hell let me into the place, if they don't trust me?"

"They trust you, as far as they're able. They just wanted to be absolutely sure."

"Have you made the report?"

She nodded again, turning to look directly up at him. "I told them I didn't consider there was any cause whatsoever to doubt you. That I thought you were fantastic. Which I do."

That would turn out to be a damning opinion in a few months' time, Charlie thought in sudden realization. He said, "Thanks."

"Are you angry? You've the right to be."

"No," he said. "It's just business."

"It's not now though, is it?"

"No," he agreed. "Not any longer."

"I'm glad it's happened," said Natalia. "I was frightened of it happening, but now it has, I'm glad."

"So am I," said Charlie sincerely. "Very glad."

"I won't lie to you again, Charlie. I promise."

Charlie swallowed, covering the awkwardness he felt by leaning forward to kiss her. Why the hell couldn't it have been Natalia who wanted to cross to the West? he thought bitterly.

With no fresh interceptions, there was no alternative but to reexamine those that had already been made and try to discover an indicator that had been overlooked. Edwin Sampson was retained at Dzerzhinsky Square, in the office close to that of

Berenkov, and went unsuccessfully through everything they had. There were empty, daily conferences with Berenkov, and having gone through every message without discovering anything new, Sampson said, "It's hopeless: there's nothing to indicate who it is. Just that it's someone here, in this building."

"I suppose there's some satisfaction to be gained from the fact that the transmissions have stopped," said Berenkov.

"Perhaps whoever it is is frightened. Thinking we're getting close."

Berenkov snorted. "I wish that we were!"

"It'll happen," predicted Sampson. "So far he's been lucky. But he'll make a mistake. It's inevitable that he'll make a mistake."

"Maybe he'll be clever enough not to," said Berenkov.

25

Life for Charlie became an existence in separate, settled compartments, and the most settled of all developed with Natalia. He was allocated another apartment, smaller but better than the first, and nearer the center of the city, and they alternated between the two, sometimes at her place, sometimes his. At the weekends they stayed together all the time, sometimes going on river trips or journeys into the hills outside Moscow in her Lada car and sometimes not bothering to do anything at all, remaining in whichever apartment they had chosen, to read or listen to music, just enjoying each other. On a weekend when Eduard was released from school they went to the circus again—and slept apart, which seemed unnatural, so accustomed to each other had they become—and Charlie tried to make friends with the boy but Eduard remained distant and reserved, instinctively sensing competition for his mother's affections.

Charlie didn't mean it to develop like it did. It wasn't how he conducted affairs, not even when Edith had been alive and he'd been cheating. He'd always been a slam-bam-thank-you-ma'am operator, fun on both sides—and fully recognized to be just that—and no tears or regrets when the time came to say good-bye. He'd actually tried to keep it light, at the very beginning, but the awkward artificiality had been obvious and so he'd let everything grow, knowing it was pointless and knowing it was stupid but not wanting it to stop. Which was selfish—as well as pointless and stupid—and worst of all, dangerous.

It was because of his growing awareness of the danger to her that he changed his mind about asking her to accompany him when the next invitation came from Berenkov, quite apart from the difficulty she might have felt in the presence of someone so high in the service. Charlie dutifully congratulated Georgi on his examination results and was amused at Berenkov's boastful pride, joining in the toasts upon which Berenkov insisted, careless of the boy's blushing discomfort. It was the first opportunity to thank the Russian since his appointment to the spy school, and Charlie said how much he was enjoying it and Berenkov said he was impressed by what Charlie was doing, and Charlie wondered if it were Natalia's report to which he was referring. He didn't think any praise would have come from Krysin.

His existence at the spy school was another compartment. The barrier still existed between Charlie and the other instructors but gradually, with their increasing and difficult-to-avoid acknowledgment of his expertise, some of them strayed beyond it and Charlie cultivated the approaches, draining everything he could from them.

He staged another pursuit exercise on the next contact Thursday and evaded them all again and won his bet with Natalia, because she lost him this time. By then he didn't feel any competition between them, so it didn't seem much of a victory. More important was the time he spent lingering in the department store, waiting for an approach which never came. Charlie's feeling about that was ambivalent. Professionally he wanted the meeting. He wanted to identify the informant and make the crossing arrangements and to go back to England in complete and well-deserved triumph. But if that happened it would mean leaving Natalia and increasingly the thought of leaving Natalia was becoming a burden. So as well as disappointment there was also relief when nothing happened in the GUM store that day, and the relief was greater when he went there again, on the next appointed time, and nothing happened then either. By the time of that visit, he'd been given fresh operatives to work through their final training. It meant that the initial batch disappeared and he assumed might have been immediately infiltrated into Britain or America, which slightly unsettled Charlie, because he'd never actually intended them the opportunity to practice what he had taught them. He'd wanted to be back, in advance, able to issue the warnings and complete the photofits and get them swept up or turned. It also meant that Natalia left the class, which Charlie welcomed because by the end, when they were together every night and every weekend, having to adopt the role of lecturer to pupil during the day became practically a farce. Charlie's dismay at suspecting some of those he had trained were already working, undetected, was tempered by the awareness that the second batch, six again, meant there were more agents whom he would subsequently be able to identify: and those that had gone ahead wouldn't be able to do much damage, anyway. An essential part of his training had been that the primary requirement for their being successful was first of all completely to install themselves in their country of placing, to obtain bona fide jobs and bona fide accommodation and—as far as possible—apparently bona fide respectability. He tried to reassure himself by the thought that even if they had been put into place, it would be six months, maybe as long as a year, before they began properly to operate.

And he'd be out in a year, thought Charlie. Which naturally brought him back to thinking about Natalia, and having avoided and sidestepped and looked the other way for so long, Charlie forced himself properly to think about it. Was he using her: enjoying the comfort and the security and the normality of an affair in an uncomfortable, insecure, abnormal situation? Or was it more than opportunism: love? Charlie confronted the word, one he'd avoided most of all. Charlie was frightened of love. Of admitting it. He'd always thought of being in love as exposing part of himself he didn't want anyone else to see, like sitting on a crowded bus with a trouser zip undone. Apart from the brief and soon-past excitement of variation, a lot of the affairs when Edith had been alive had been Charlie wanting to feel that he wasn't dependent upon one woman. Which he had been and which— too late—he'd accepted. Charlie, who always derided rules and formulae, wished to Christ there was a listed chart he could consult, a mathematically unarguable square root of love.

He kept the fifth date at the GUM store, as unsuccessful as all the others, and as he made his way back across Dzerzhinsky Square and past the headquarters of the KGB Charlie realized that according to the arrangements he'd made with Wilson, seemingly years before in the prison governor's office, he only had a month left. At once Charlie found an alternative argument. Six months had been an arbitrary period, plucked from nowhere and agreed anyway because by then he'd expected things to be difficult. Charlie carried the reflection on. He'd been concentrating upon the risk of his own detection. What if the informant had been found, weeks or months before? There'd been the highly publicized affair with the British first secretary: that was unusual. The detection of the would-be defector would be an explanation—the obvious one—for there not having been any contact. Logical, as well as obvious. Except that one logic extended to another. If the Russians had got their man, they'd have broken him, and if they'd broken him then Charlie would not have been allowed to hang around Moscow stores unarrested.

So where was he?

Charlie recognized he was incredibly well-placed, gaining intelligence of an incalculable value, increasingly trusted and in no danger. He'd actually considered, within the first few days of being in Moscow, that he might have to remain longer than the period he'd agreed with the British Director. So he'd stay on, Charlie determined. Just for a while longer, if no approach were made. He was, after all, a complete professional; and to stay would be the professional thing to do. And meant he didn't have to consider the thought of losing Natalia. Shit, he thought; why was nothing ever easy?

* * *

The absence of any further messages did nothing to relieve the pressure from the Politburo upon Kalenin and therefore his demands upon those answerable to him. Rather, they increased. The Politburo insisted on explanations the KGB chairman didn't have, and his insistences permeated through his immediate deputies to division directors and their subordinates and spread the uncertainty not just throughout Dzerzhinsky Square but to the other divisional buildings in the capital. Even Charlie was aware of a change of attitude from Krysin but was unable to discover the reason, so he wrongly assumed it was just a further indication of alienation between them.

Because of the indications that the leaks were coming from the operational or planning divisions, the concentration evolved particularly onto Berenkov. Edwin Sampson made a further examination, as unsuccessful as those before, and separate competing committees were set up independent of each other—and the Briton's efforts—to carry out their own inquiries. And were unsuccessful, too. The surveillance upon the British embassy became positive harassment. A car carrying an archivist and a secretary on a perfectly innocent outing to the Tchaikovsky Concert Hall on Sadovaya Street was actually involved in a crash with a KGB observation group and the Britons were held for three hours in police custody before diplomatic pressure released them.

It is one of the anomalies of diplomacy that while no Soviet embassy in any Western capital will accept foreign nationals in any support capacity, in Moscow Western embassies employ Russian general help. The attempt was clumsily blatant and was realized almost at once by the internal-security staff, who discovered two maids and a male cleaner within a week trying to install listening devices. The Foreign Office in London extended the protests beyond the natural complaint in Moscow itself by summoning the Russian ambassador personally to Whitehall. In addition they released the details to the media and there was extensive newspaper coverage, to which the Kremlin responded with their clichéd rejection that it was anti-Soviet propaganda.

Berenkov recognized the intrusion but knew he had no alternative, because his official position required him to inform Kalenin. He chose the end of their now customary daily inconclusive conference after Kalenin had cast aside the equally inconclusive reports and suggested the vodka, the chairman's intake of which was noticeably increasing while the crisis continued unresolved.

Kalenin frowned when Berenkov began to talk of his son's qualification successes, not immediately understanding, so that Berenkov had to repeat himself and Kalenin said, "Overseas?"

"There's a place for him in Boston," said Berenkov. Remembering there were towns in both countries and conscious of the chairman's apparent distraction, Berenkov hurriedly added, "Boston, America, not Boston, England."

There was no immediate reaction from Kalenin. He finished pouring and handed Berenkov his glass and said, "Going to the West?"

"I think he would benefit," said Berenkov.

"Are you sure that's wise?"

"Which is why I felt I should officially raise it with you," said Berenkov.

"What do you imagine would happen if the Western intelligence agencies were to discover who his father was?" said Kalenin.

"I did not think that was a serious risk," said Berenkov.

"Then I don't think you've considered it sufficiently," said Kalenin. "The American Central Intelligence Agency actively recruits from universities: apparatus exists, for talent spotting. And if they're that well-organized they'd naturally focus upon visiting Russian students. I'd consider there would be a serious risk of Georgi becoming compromised."

"Are you telling me officially that he can't take up the place?" asked Berenkov miserably.

"I'm saying that I want to think further about it," said Kalenin. "That maybe we both should."

"He's worked extremely hard," said Berenkov emptily.

"We're currently experiencing enough difficulty," said Kalenin. "You're a deputy within the Committee for State Security, at the very highest echelon. And someone known in the West. I think we should seriously consider the risk of any embarrassment beyond that which we are already suffering."

That suffering—and that embarrassment—worsened.

The messages to London resumed in a sudden flurry, three intercepted by the KGB monitoring services on succeeding nights. Each formed part of a sensational whole, the complete identities—and their cover designation—of virtually the entire Soviet espionage system within Britain, from the embassy-based resident under diplomatic title down through every other diplomatic listing and extending to the Soviet trade mission at Highgate.

The last of the three messages promised further identities of agents in the United States and France. And concluded, "Shortly intend making promised personal contact."

In London Wilson said, "Well. Here we go."

"We hope," said the cautious Harkness.

Moscow intercepted London's radioed reply. It was "People don't notice whether it's winter or summer when they're happy."

26

All his life Charlie felt he had been running; often literally. He had run in the department, always to stay ahead of the supercilious sods with their nose-lifted accents. He had run, to survive, when those same sods set him up. And run again, to survive again, after he set them up, instead. He'd run in prison, like a trapped animal runs, blindly, from one corner to another corner. And was aware he should have the impression of running here, involved in the most difficult and dangerous operation he'd encountered. But he didn't. He felt unhurried. Relaxed even. As if there were time—all the time in the world—to rest, with no danger of anyone catching up. It was Natalia, he knew. Just as he knew—without having the rules to guide him, because there were no rules—that he loved her. He loved her completely and absolutely and he wanted never to spend a moment of his no-longer-running life apart from her. Which meant staying. Which he couldn't. Any more than he could consider leaving.

The conflicts—of feelings and loyalty and attitudes and professionalism—crowded in upon him and every time he got halfway toward solving one he tripped over another. Keeping Natalia from the consideration—which would have been a clash of love against professionalism—Charlie became increasingly convinced, after two more failed rendezvous, that there never would be any contact. What had appeared in the Soviet newspapers about the British first secretary was inadequate and inconclusive, like accounts always were in Soviet newspapers, but Charlie guessed whatever had happened involved the person he was supposed to meet at the GUM store. The unanswerable was why, if they'd swept the defector up, he'd remained unaffected. But Charlie recognized there could be explanations, like the man dying rather than face arrest. Or dying under questioning. Or going mad under that same questioning, before he'd been able to disclose and therefore endanger the meeting spot. If that conjecture was correct, then there was no further purpose in remaining in Moscow—another conflict—teaching intended Soviet spies to be better than they were, which was a further conflict. Professionally, he should get out. Professionally, he should stop buggering about and start running again. Would she run with him? The idea had been a long time coming—too long—but why not? She hadn't said so— which he hadn't either, nervous of actually saying it—but Charlie was absolutely sure that Natalia loved him. Why the hell couldn't it have been her, that day in GUM, who wanted to defect? Or Berenkov, to whom all the signs pointed but who hadn't committed himself? If it had been Berenkov, then Charlie would have been gone months ago, before getting so hopelessly entangled. He shook his head, a physical movement of irrita- tion. What sort of thinking was that, wishing things had or hadn't happened, like some child! It hadn't been Natalia and it hadn't been Berenkov and he had fallen in love and he had to sort it out by logical, sensible thinking, not flights of fancy. It wasn't just Natalia, of course. There was Eduard. She wouldn't consider leaving the boy—why the hell should she?—so he'd have to get both of them out at the same time. Difficult but not insurmount- able. Charlie consciously braked the flow of thought. How difficult? Officially he was still British. But Natalia and Eduard weren't. They were Russian and Charlie doubted the British embassy would consider flying them out if they simply walked into the embassy with him. There would have to be diplomatic this and diplomatic that and a damned good chance that they'd hand them back if the Russian pressure became too heavy. Which it unquestionably would. Practically insurmountable then. What if he lied? What if he took Natalia and Eduard into the embassy and conned London that she was the source for which they were so anxious? They'd bend the rules then and smuggle her out eagerly enough. But what would happen when they got back to London? The Russians would chase, because Natalia was high-ranking and because they always chased anyway. And when he realized he had been cheated, Wilson and the department wouldn't provide any sort of protection. So it would be like it had been before, with Edith, harassed and terrified, from place to place and country to country. Charlie knew he couldn't stand that. He couldn't stand it and he couldn't ask Natalia to endure it: certainly not with a young kid.

A further class came and went at the spy school, and Charlie knew he couldn't delay much longer. His confusion and distraction increasingly came between the two of them, like a barrier, marring the earlier tranquillity, and there were arguments—not serious rows, but quarrels of irritability just the same—and it put Charlie under fresh pressure because he didn't want her to misunderstand and imagine the reverse of his feelings and that he was tired of the relationship.

He tried to plan the occasion. He took her to the Rossiya, where they had had their first meal and from which, on the subsequent occasion, they'd left to go back to her apartment and make love. Everything about Natalia had affected Charlie, but a tangible part of their being together had been the reduction in the extent of Charlie's drinking. That night, however, he drank more than usual with her, needing the support, but stayed far short of getting drunk. Completely confident with Russian now, Charlie ordered for them and it was a good choice, and seeking omens, he decided it was a good augury for later.

She was conscious of his effort and Natalia tried, too, so that the tenseness that had developed between them in the recent days and weeks eased away. Charlie was relieved that Natalia was relaxed again and relieved too that after all the unconcluded agonizing the moment had come to be open with her.

"I've something to tell you," he said when the meal was over and they had started their coffee.

"What?"

"I love you."

Natalia winced, which wasn't the response Charlie expected.

"I said I love you," he repeated.

"Yes."

"Is that all, just yes?"

Natalia looked away, refusing his look. Surely he hadn't got it wrong! Not this. He was convinced how she felt. The silence lasted for a long time and eventually Charlie said, "I see."

"No," she blurted, hurriedly now. "No, you mustn't misunderstand."

"You haven't said or done anything that allows me to understand or misunderstand," said Charlie.

"I love you," said Natalia, looking fully at him at last. "I love you completely: more than I ever thought it was possible to love anyone. I thought I loved my first husband, but now I realize it was nothing like love . . ."

The relief came back to Charlie, so strong that he was glad they were sitting because it was an impression of physical weakness. "Then . . ." he started, but she shook her head, refusing him the interruption.

"I didn't, at first," she said. "I thought you were cocky and conceited . . ." She hesitated, seeking the word. "Awful," she said at last, inadequately. "But not for very long. You made me laugh, although you didn't know it. I always intended to go out with you that night, when you first asked me. I just didn't want you to know how much I wanted to say yes. And I always knew that eventually we'd become lovers. I wanted that, too, but I equally didn't want you to think it was casual. Something that didn't matter. Because it mattered very much to me . . ." There was another pause. "You matter very much to me."

"Everything is going to be all right," promised Charlie. "It's going to be wonderful. I know it is." He reached across for her hand and although she let him take it there was no answering pressure. He frowned down at her lifeless hand and said, "What is it?"

"I'm Russian, Charlie," she said. "Do you know what that means?"

"Of course you're Russian," said Charlie, laughing uncertainly.

"What it means," she insisted. "The actual feeling it engenders, in its people."

"Maybe not," conceded Charlie.

"It's stronger than in any other nationality. The loyalty: that's what I'm talking about."

"I see," said Charlie, who thought he did but didn't want to.

"I'd never betray that loyalty," said Natalia. "Not even for anyone I loved to the exclusion of everything else. Not even for Eduard—whom I love differently but just as much—could I make that choice."

Charlie sat gazing down into his emptying wineglass. Appearing aware of it, he poured more from the bottle, not knowing what to say.

"You lost the bet, Charlie," said Natalia quietly.

He frowned up. "What bet?"

"The second pursuit," said the woman. "You did lose me, once. But I picked you up again, quite by chance, at the Marksa metro. You didn't seem to be making many checks, by then . . ."

Because by then I'd lost everyone, thought Charlie. And was actually going toward the store. He felt a numbness of uncertainty.

"I didn't try to follow you, in case you spotted me," continued Natalia. "I took a chance on GUM. Saw you waiting there, in the same place as you waited before. It wasn't right, according to any tradecraft principles, for you to return to the same place as before. That's why I didn't challenge you. And then we went out and I enjoyed you, although I didn't realize then just what that enjoyment was going to develop into. I was in the GUM store again, Charlie; saw you when you visited the next time, and then I recognized there was a pattern so I followed it too. And you conformed, every time. Every third Thursday of every month, between eleven and noon. Always with a copy of *Pravda* and a guidebook. Always in your left hand."

"What are you going to do?" said Charlie, dry-voiced.

"If I were going to do something, don't you imagine I would have done it by now?" said Natalia. "I made the decision a long time ago. I decided to clutch on to what I had—what we had—for as long as I possibly could. Knowing that it couldn't last forever but not wanting it to stop. Just have every day and every night and try not to think of the one that followed, in case it didn't follow . . ." She stopped momentarily and then said, "I've dreaded this moment, Charlie. I've dreaded all the indications of a special occasion: the time when it would be obvious that you'd made a particular effort. And most of all I've dreaded you saying something like 'I've got something to tell you.' I've longed to hear you say you love me but I've always known there would be something else and I don't want to know what that something else could be."

"It could be all right," repeated Charlie in hollow desperation. "Everything could be all right. I promise."

Natalia shook her head, quite positively. "It wouldn't, Charlie. For all the reasons I've tried to explain and all the reasons you know. We had it—we have it—but we can't keep it." She was crying now, unashamedly, without any sound but with the tears pathing down her face.

"I *love* you!" insisted Charlie.

"I love you too," said Natalia. "But that isn't enough."

Britain made the maximum capital out of the spy expulsion. The Prime Minister personally named forty in the House of Commons and when Moscow made the necessary protestations the Foreign Office the following day itemized another thirty who would be expelled as well. The Soviet ambassador was summoned to the Foreign Office and warned personally by the British Foreign Secretary that if Russia attempted the predictable response—mass expulsion of Britons from the Soviet capital—then there were twenty-five further Soviet spies who could be declared *persona non grata* and that if that occurred, London would declare unacceptable fifty replacements, diminishing the stature of the embassy.

In Moscow Berenkov conducted the meeting with Edwin Sampson with the impression of Kalenin standing at his shoulder, guessing that the KGB chairman would be watching the television-monitored meeting live from the control room at the end of the corridor behind the security-guarded doors.

Sampson gestured to the last of the intercepted messages, the British identification response to the promised contact with the Soviet spy. "It's Chekhov," identified Sampson. "It comes from *The Three Sisters*."

"I'm aware of that," said Berenkov. "I was once very familiar with the works of Chekhov." The huge Russian paused and said, "Are you familiar with another quotation, 'When a lot of remedies are suggested for a disease, that means it can't be cured'?"

"No," said Sampson.

"It's from *The Cherry Orchard*," said Berenkov. "I always preferred *The Cherry Orchard*."

The interview with Kalenin took place the same evening, a difficult encounter between friends.

"There will have to be a suspension, initially."

"Of course."

"I'd recognized it a long time ago, of course. Hoped that it wouldn't happen."

"It's wrong, you know?" said Berenkov.

Kalenin raised his hand, halting the other man, not wanting to prolong the meeting any longer than was absolutely necessary. "Please," he said. "Let's leave it until the formal inquiry."

27

They both tried hard—futilely—to maintain some sort of form to their relationship, but it was hollowed out inside and with every day, like something hollowed out inside, it collapsed further in upon itself. Charlie refused, at first, to believe he couldn't make her change her mind, but as she had that night in the rooftop restaurant with its view of Moscow, Natalia refused even to let him explain, demanding—with increasing anger—that he shouldn't make things any more difficult for her than they already were. Evenings and days which had been relaxed and easy became tense and then hostile. They made love like strangers, mechanically, and then they stopped doing that, more and more becoming strangers.

Charlie considered missing the Thursday meeting but it was only two days from the initial confrontation with Natalia and Charlie's professionalism didn't allow him. It was as pointless as every other one had been but this time he concentrated, looking to see if Natalia would check. He didn't detect her, but then, he hadn't on the other occasions. He didn't ask her and she didn't volunteer the information.

It finally convinced Charlie that there was no further purpose in him going again. And as the difficulties grew with Natalia, he realized, too, that it meant he had to leave. With belated honesty Charlie conceded to himself that for a long time she had been the only reason for his staying anyway. As with everything else, for so long the apparent answer to one problem created another. He couldn't just go, like he'd arranged with Wilson. He'd become involved with Natalia and guessed the authorities would be aware of it. And if they weren't already, they soon would be, when they investigated his flight; and they would investigate it, aware of the damage he could cause because of his admission to the spy school. To flee, as he now had to flee, would mean Natalia being arrested and interrogated and probably jailed. The awareness spurred Charlie into trying to make fresh approaches to her, to warn her, but always she refused the conversation. It led to one of their biggest arguments so far. He accused her of sticking her head into the sand, like an ostrich refusing to face reality, and she yelled back that Russia was her reality and that with its head in the sand an ostrich at least remained where it was. The outburst meant she knew—or at least guessed—what he wanted to say, and assuming that, Charlie argued that she didn't know the risks she was taking. Distraught—actually crying—Natalia said she did and that she didn't care, and when he accused her of being stupid and childlike and not even making sense, she fled, locking herself in the bathroom. Which added another level to the barrier growing between them because it meant eventually she had the embarrassment of unlocking the door and emerging again. She only did so after shouting through the door that she didn't want to talk about it anymore. Charlie's instinct was to say they hadn't talked about anything, but instead he agreed and they sat in silence, not even looking at each other, and Charlie fully accepted just how completely things had ended between them.

He still refused to abandon her, however. He spent nights away from her, alone in his own apartment, needing the relief as much as Natalia did but needing more the solitude to find a seemingly impossible way to save her from any retribution. She wasn't the only one facing retribution, he realized. From the early meetings with Alexei Berenkov Charlie knew that the permission to appoint him to the spy school in the first place had been approved by someone else, but Berenkov had clearly been the instigator. So he'd suffer. Charlie sighed, trying to rationalize. But then, Berenkov had always been going to suffer. Whether the attitude was cynical or professional or both, Charlie had known from the very first moment of contact—contact he couldn't have refused—that the moment he entered the embassy gates, Berenkov would be the loser. That was business, decided Charlie, confronting the familiar thought. About Berenkov he could have done nothing—do nothing—but he'd knowingly pursued an involvement with Natalia—although not guessing what it would come to mean to him—and she didn't deserve to suffer because of it. And she'd protected him. She'd said nothing about the GUM visits, when she could have done. And still wasn't saying anything when, even if things weren't actually out in the open, they were at least understood.

When the idea occurred to him, Charlie snatched at it like a drowning man at a lifebelt. But having got its support, he looked around, like the same drowning man might look for the lurking shark that would pull him down again to destruction. It wasn't perfect, Charlie recognized, with his ingrained objectivity. In fact, for a lifebelt it was pretty waterlogged, but it had a chance. Timing would be important. Absolute and utter timing, so there would be incontrovertible proof of her loyalty. Which meant—finally—that she had to hear him out. If it meant physically holding her down and keeping her hands away from her ears, she had to hear him out.

"No," she said at once, when she answered his telephone call. "I don't want us to meet again. I've thought about it and I think it should end, now."

"We must meet," said Charlie with quiet insistence, determined against any dispute that would harden her refusal. He added, "We must meet, for the last time."

"Oh," she said.

"Do you understand what I'm saying?" he said anxiously.

"I think so."

"It's important," insisted Charlie. Determined to get her to agree, he said, "It's not just you, Natalia. There's Eduard."

"Yes," she said. "There's Eduard. There's always been Eduard."

To have gone to a restaurant would have made it into something it wasn't, and neither wanted to meet at their respective apartments, determined at the moment of parting upon pleasant memories instead of final unhappiness. They just walked—although nowhere near Red Square and GUM, because of other unpleasant recollections—choosing the embankment, watching the scurrying river craft and the misted insects. Natalia held his hand, schoolgirlish, her arm consciously touching his, the reserve of the immediate past weeks gone, and Charlie felt the despair lumped in him, having physically to swallow against the emotion, at the complete awareness of what he was giving up and could never hope to get again. He'd lost Edith and now he was going to lose Natalia, and in a rare but lasting moment of self-pity Charlie wondered why he always had to lose and why, just once, he couldn't win, just a little bit.

"I don't think you properly heard the words on the telephone," she said.

"I did," said Charlie. "And it wasn't words. It was just one word."

"I think myself I'd take the chance," said Natalia. "I have taken the chance. I can't risk Eduard."

Resigned now, Charlie still tried. "What if it wasn't a risk to Eduard?"

"Can you guarantee that?" she asked, almost desperately. "Can you guarantee that you could protect us both, forever?"

They were at the Kalininskiy bridge. There were bordering seats and resting places and without any discussion they went toward a seat and sat upon it, all the while without Charlie talking.

"You haven't answered," she said.

"No."

"So?"

"I was thinking," said Charlie. "I was thinking that if I didn't love you so much how easy it would be to lie. To say yes, that I could guarantee it."

"I'm glad you didn't," said Natalia. "Because I'd know it was a lie and I don't want you to lie to me, not anymore."

"I didn't lie," said Charlie.

She felt out for his hand, all the comfort and contentment back between them now. "Stop it," she said, softly chiding, not angry like she had so often been recently. "I know there was no other way. We just shouldn't have got involved, not like we did. Lost people shouldn't find lost people, that's all."

"I want you to listen now," said Charlie. "I'm concerned for you because I love you, but I want you to listen because of Eduard, too. Because if anything happens to you, then it happens to him, as well."

Natalia sat with her head forward, not even looking at the river, but she didn't protest about not wanting to know as she always had in the past. Charlie was glad of her attitude, which he hadn't expected but which made it easier, because it made him sure of her and by the same token know that she was sure of him. So she wouldn't doubt him. And she couldn't doubt him, not for a moment, if she were properly to withstand the interrogation and the pressures that were going to come.

Charlie lied easily, because they were easy lies, just slight but vitally important deviations from the truth that fitted all the facts and all the circumstances. He knew how good she was—what her training was—and although he appeared to be as deeply enclosed as she was, Charlie was alert for any reaction from her: for the sort of challenge that her questioners would make, very soon now. There was no dispute from Natalia and Charlie hoped more desperately than he had ever hoped for anything that it meant it would work and there wouldn't be any way she could be exposed.

"It means I made a mistake," she said. At once, defensively, she said, "I wasn't given enough time. Everything was rushed."

"Then it's not your fault."

"No," she said doubtfully. "It wasn't my decision."

"There's us," he pointed out.

"Yes," she said.

And then Charlie told her how to account for that, as well, on easier ground now because outright lying wasn't involved. He was still tensed for her to expose a fault but she didn't and when he finished Charlie hoped it was because that part of the story was as good as the earlier account and not because her emotions and feelings were clouding her usual alertness.

"Now?" she said emptily.

"Now," said Charlie. He felt the surge of despair and fought against it because it was too late for despair now. They'd recovered what they'd known before because of their acceptance of the end; there was no turning back because there was nowhere to which they could turn. Conflict upon conflict, ifs upon ifs. "You understand the importance of the timing, don't you?" pressed Charlie. "The timing's got to be precisely right."

"Yes," said Natalia. "I understand about the timing."

They remained unspeaking on the embankment seat. The light was going now and the shadow from the vast Comecon building stretched like a barrier across the Moskva River, a hurdle for the still-busy boats to cross. Her hand was still in his and Charlie didn't want to let it go.

"I love you, Natalia," said Charlie.

"I love you, too, my darling," said Natalia. She stopped and then she said, "And I know I'm going to regret what I've done—or what I haven't done—for the rest of my life."

Charlie turned to her hurriedly, about to speak, but she squeezed her fingers with his and said, "No! Don't say it. Please don't say it."

"Why can't you come?" he said, ignoring her plea.

"Why can't you stay?" she said, defeating him. "My loyalty isn't the only barrier. There's yours. I've already given more than you have. Why can't you give?"

"You know I can't."

"Then you know I can't."

The shadows on the river got deeper, obscuring the smaller boats altogether. They remained side by side, their hands linked, neither wanting to be the first actually to break the final, inevitable contact.

"Timing is important," repeated Charlie.

"Then you should go."

"Yes."

"I wish we could make love," Natalia blurted suddenly. "Not like last time. Not like a lot of times recently. Like it was before, when we were like this."

"It doesn't have to be tonight," said Charlie.

"Yes it does," she said immediately. "Trying to hold on to what we've got now, this moment, won't work . . ." She gestured out toward the river, where the evening mist was already forming, in competition to the insect swarms. "It's like that," she said. "Like the evening fog."

Charlie made the moment of parting, knowing he had to. He withdrew his hand positively, not looking at her, and said, "It's lucky that we chose to walk along the river."

"Yes," said Natalia, consciously trying to put the briskness in her voice. "Morisa Toreza is quite near."

Charlie stood, forcing himself like she was doing. "Remember the time," he said. "They'll know almost immediately. Don't wait."

For a moment they remained looking at each other, Natalia still on the bench, Charlie standing but apart from her, not trusting himself to be too close.

"I don't want you to kiss me," she said.

"No."

"Just don't say anything. Do anything."

Charlie stayed where he was for a few more moments, knowing that he would never see her again and wanting to etch everything into his mind, and then he turned and found the main highway and walked toward the British embassy on the Morisa Toreza. He walked shoulder-slumped, for once in his life careless of anything around him, reluctant actually to get to the security of the British legation but committed now because Natalia's safety depended upon him reaching it at a certain time. He knew for a long way she would be able to see him—and he her—but he never turned back. By the time he reached the embassy the professionalism had taken over but much of it automatic, right up until the actual moment of entry, which had to be right.

There were still cars and people about, which he wanted, and in passing Charlie wondered how much of the passing traffic was genuine and how much official. He crossed carefully, long before the embassy entrance, approaching on the same side but appearing to take no interest in the approaching building. There were uniformed Soviet personnel near the entrance, which Charlie hadn't expected and couldn't remember from his previous time in Moscow. He strode on, confidently, with no break in his stride, the turn into the compound abrupt yet still confident, a man accustomed to the route and unprepared for any challenge.

None came.

Charlie hurried into the vestibule, anxious to gain official British territory. There was the reception desk and security personnel, but British this time. The receptionist was a man. He looked up, blank-faced, toward Charlie and said, "Can I help you?"

"Yes," said Charlie. "I want to go home."

Pending the investigation, Alexei Berenkov was held in Lefortovo prison, the same jail in which, months earlier, Cecil Wainwright had been broken into admitting his cowardice. It was not a usual concession and Berenkov guessed at Kalenin's intervention and was grateful: on the third week he was permitted a visit from Valentina. The small woman appeared even smaller in the echoing surroundings of the prison, cowed by everything around her. She perched, fittingly birdlike, on her chair and blinked through the grille at her burly husband behind it, and Berenkov ached for her fear.

"They say I can only stay for a few moments; that I'm lucky to be here at all."

"Yes," said Berenkov. He wanted so much to be able to reach out to touch her, to caress away her terror. "You mustn't worry," he said. "I haven't done anything wrong."

"You're in jail!" she said.

"I've been in jail before," he said. "It's easier, this time."

"I don't understand what's going on, Alexei," pleaded the woman. "I don't understand why you've been arrested and put in jail and I don't understand why Georgi's examination has been rescinded and his exchange facilities withdrawn."

"When did that happen?" asked Berenkov sadly.

"Last week," said Valentina. "There was no explanation. Just a letter from the principal. He's asked for an interview but it's being refused."

"It will be," said Berenkov sadly.

"Tell me something, Alexei," insisted his wife. "Tell me something honestly. Have you done anything wrong?"

"No," said Berenkov at once.

"Then what's happened?" shouted the woman, in unusual anger.

"I don't know," said Berenkov.

28

The reaction was very quick and although Charlie was distracted—Natalia and his worry about her constantly intruding
into his mind—he was impressed. There was only one telephone call from the vestibule and within minutes he was taken
to a man who identified himself as Hollis and another named
Greening. Both young, urgent, and anxious, Charlie recognized; he wondered, in passing, if he'd been like that at the
beginning. They took him to a part of the embassy Charlie
recognized from his earlier, official visit as the intelligence
residency, but he was kept in an outer office while Hollis kept
appearing and disappearing, for what Charlie presumed was
contact with London. The reaction there was quick, too, little
more than an hour before Hollis reemerged finally and said,
"We're getting out right now: before there's time for any official
protest or action. We're lucky with British Airways."

They arrived at Sheremetyevo with an hour before the
scheduled departure, Charlie tight between the two escorts,
the hurriedly issued diplomatic passport clutched in his hand. It
got them past the initial customary checks, and the local British
Airways manager seemed to expect them. An advance call from
the embassy, Charlie supposed. The airport official took them
out ahead of normal embarkation to a specially curtained part of
the first-class section.

The Russians made their snatch-back attempt thirty minutes before takeoff, when the other passengers were boarding, a sudden, pushing arrival of men whom Hollis and Greening confronted at the door. Charlie, already strapped into his seat, heard most of the argument, the demands for his handing over, and the shouted refusal from Hollis to surrender a British national. The Russians, whom Charlie couldn't properly see because of the way they were blocked at the entrance, insisted Charlie was wanted for a crime and Hollis demanded a formal copy of the charge and when that couldn't be produced said that a warrant was in existence in England against Charlie on a charge of murder and produced what appeared to be a paper setting out the formal indictment. The dispute raged while the embarking passengers milled on behind and the pilot and the first officer apprehensively joined in, uncertain completely what was happening.

Hollis was very good, thought Charlie. The man insisted he had jurisdiction—which technically he did—and that the aircraft was British territory, which Charlie thought was a more debatable claim. It appeared to impress the captain, who announced after consultation with the escorting airport manager that unless an official documented reason was produced which superseded the British official documentation, he intended to depart. The Russians made the mistake of trying to rush the aircraft. They were easily blocked in the narrow entrance and the desperation convinced the captain that the Soviets were bluffing. He ordered the rear doors to be closed against any secondary assault and then joined in the physical rebuff of the still-jostling Russians, to enable the door into the first-class section to be secured.

There was further argument that Charlie was aware of through the open door, refusal of the control tower to grant leaving permission, and finally the captain moved the aircraft away from the terminal, apparently without ground assistance.

"Don't worry," assured the still-breathless Hollis from the adjoining seat. "It's going to be okay."

Charlie realized, for the first time, that he hadn't been

worried. It had been—still was—the time when he was most likely to be seized and he didn't feel any fear. The emptiness was still too strong for that, too strong to allow relief when the aircraft actually lifted and he knew he was safe. Safe from Russia, at least. He hadn't expected there to be an outstanding warrant alleging murder against him, although—considering it—he supposed it was logical. Surely to Christ it hadn't all been for nothing; that he hadn't trapped himself into going back to jail! Even the thought of that, at the moment, didn't seem to matter. It would later, if it happened, Charlie knew; but not now.

"Know what this means?" asked the conversational Hollis, beside him.

"What?" asked Charlie dully.

"I can't go back . . ." Hollis turned to Greening, sitting behind. "We'll neither be acceptable any longer, after this."

"Thank Christ for that," said the man behind.

Charlie refused any food or drink or even conversation, gazing out of the windows at the night's blackness, staring at his own reflection. It would have happened by now, he decided. Would Natalia be under formal arrest? Or just interrogation? God, he hoped she would be all right. The agony—now and forever—was that he was never going to know.

There was a squad waiting at London airport, four men who hurried officiously onto the aircraft and more in waiting cars, and from the immediate subservience and dismissal into other vehicles of Hollis and Greening, Charlie knew they were higher-ranking. There were no introductions from the squad or any official immigration formalities, just bustled, arm-holding progress along side corridors and through side doors. Charlie obeyed every nudge and instruction, still uninterested. It was only when the cavalcade gained the M4 and was heading toward London that Charlie consciously attempted to push aside the ennui and concentrate on what might be about to happen.

He'd failed.

But not in a way that meant he should feel guilt. He'd told Wilson that day in the governor's office that it was practically impossible, and the Russians had got the first secretary before he'd properly had time to get organized: Charlie was sure the diplomat's arrest was the key to no contact ever having been made. They'd have reason to be disappointed, but not critical. Certainly not critical when he told them everything about the spy school and what he'd done, to get out. He wouldn't tell them about Natalia, Charlie determined. Not for any particular reason—there were no problems it could cause her—but he just decided not to.

"Never thought we'd get you back," said an anonymous man to his right.

Charlie recognized at once the official, accusing voice. "Life's full of surprises," he said, knowing the apparent absence of fear would irritate the man. Running time again, he thought. What about the murder warrant that had been announced at Moscow airport? Charlie looked out at the yellow-lighted streets of London and wondered how soon it would be before he saw them again, without an escort.

The men who had met him at the airport remained grouped about him as he got from the car, at the building that had once been so familiar to Charlie. Instinctively Charlie hesitated, looking up at the features he had so often thought about nostalgically, and the man behind wasn't expecting the pause, colliding with him.

"Come on," said the man brusquely, and Charlie moved on, going inside. Nothing seemed to have changed. There were the same brown-painted, sighing radiators and the chipped, yellow-washed walls and the ancient mesh-faced lifts that snatched uncertainly upward, as if they were unsure they'd complete the journey.

Wilson's office was different. Willoughby had occupied rooms at the rear of the building, on the fourth floor, and Cuthbertson inherited them. Sir Alistair Wilson's suite was on the top floor at the front and as Charlie entered he saw the necklace of lights through the uncurtained window and realized it overlooked the river. The Director was standing beside his desk, with Harkness behind him, nearer the window. There was a vase of roses on the desk and a flower that matched the display in the Director's buttonhole. The perfume permeated the room.

"Charlie!" greeted Wilson, someone greeting an old and much-missed friend. "Charlie!"

The man stumped forward, stiff-legged, hand outstretched, and Charlie stayed just inside the door, utterly confused. Hesitantly he took the greeting, aware of Wilson's head jerk of dismissal to those who had accompanied him from the airport. The less-effusive Harkness advanced too and offered his hand, and Charlie shook that, as well.

"You made it, Charlie! And got back. Congratulations! Damned well done," said Wilson.

The older man seized Charlie's shoulders, moving him further into the room. What was happening: what the bloody hell was happening! thought Charlie. Surely they realized it had all gone wrong, with the first secretary's arrest.

Charlie stood by the chair that Wilson offered, not immediately sitting. "It didn't work," he said. "There was never any contact."

"No," accepted Wilson at once. "Of course not."

"So it was the first secretary?" said Charlie. "I guessed that was how it was blown. There were reports in the papers of his arrest; of the destruction of a major spy cell."

Wilson turned, to look briefly at Harkness. "One of the tragedies of the whole affair," he said, momentarily distant. Having read the Soviet reports, as Charlie had, Wilson said, suddenly reminded, "You wouldn't know, of course: it wasn't reported there. Wainwright committed suicide, in our own embassy, after the Russians released him."

"Did they break him?" demanded Charlie at once.

"Of what he knew," said Wilson. "He was the initial control. We'd switched."

So that's how he'd been able to go to GUM undetected, apart from Natalia! At once came another thought. All the contacts had been blind, Wilson had said that day in jail. Which meant Wainwright hadn't known an identity to disclose to his questioners. So the defector was undetected, just obviously holding back until the pressure lessened. Oh God, thought Charlie: he'd got out too soon!

"I said there was never any contact," he reminded the older man.

Wilson smiled apologetically. "There couldn't have been."

Charlie slowly sat, knowing it was time to stop guessing. "Couldn't have been?" he said.

"There never was a spy, Charlie. Never anyone for you to meet," said the Director. He leaned forward demandingly. "Tell me something," he said. "Something important. Did you manage to meet Berenkov?"

Charlie frowned doubtfully. "Yes," he said. "Several times. And that's why the operation wasn't a complete failure. Berenkov arranged for me to teach at a spy school. I've got the complete layout of Balashikha: identities of staff and at least twenty agents. Training methods, too. But I don't understand, about there never being a spy."

"You couldn't, Charlie," said Wilson, apologetic again. "You had to be blind, like Wainwright. I knew Wainwright would break, under interrogation. Planned for it to happen, although not for him to take his own life. And you might have got caught, although that wasn't planned for. And if you were caught, I couldn't take the chance of your breaking too . . ." Wilson raised his hand. "I know you wouldn't have given in easily, but everyone's got their breaking point."

"I still don't understand," protested Charlie.

Wilson arranged himself against the radiator, injured leg straight out before him. "You were part—a vital, additional part—of one of the most complicated operations that we've ever devised," said the man. "Five years ago, when I became director, I decided to hit the Russian service. Hit it and cause as much damage as I could. It was, as I say, a complicated scheme but actually one of a certain simplicity. I was lucky, because some of the groundwork had already been done. Just before he was replaced as director, Willoughby, whom I know you greatly admired, set up a classic disinformation operation with a brilliant and very brave operative. In Beirut he had Edwin Sampson let himself be approached and apparently suborned by the Russians . . ."

"What!" erupted Charlie.

Wilson made his hand-stopping gesture. "I expected you to be surprised, Charlie. Hear me out. Hear just how brilliant and brave Sampson is. I decided to build upon what Willoughby had started. It meant giving a lot away, of course, but I decided the prize was worth the investment. When the Russians were completely convinced of Sampson's loyalty to them, they asked him to get himself transferred back here. I agreed, of course. Got him on the Soviet desk and again let him give them a lot of good, genuine stuff, to keep on convincing them. They actually made him a major, did you know that?"

Charlie nodded, not trusting himself to speak.

"Then we got you," said Wilson. "We got you and I decided how the operation could be made doubly effective. We knew by then, of course, that Berenkov had been taken into Dzerzhinsky Square, promoted officially to deputy. I saw the way to hit the Russian service harder than I ever thought possible . . ." Wilson paused, smiling his apologetic smile. "I had you under a microscope in jail, Charlie. I knew, from all the assessment reports and from what you did to Cuthbertson, what sort of a person you were, but I had to know for myself, to be sure. I knew from week to week how you refused to give in and fought back against everyone and everything, and I decided it would work. From here I had the trusted Sampson tell Moscow he believed they had a spy, someone so high that I was dealing directly with him, running control. And then we had a cultural attaché named Richardson put a contact note into the pocket of his colleague, Cecil Wainwright . . ." Wilson hesitated again. "Richardson was told as much as was necessary, but Wainwright had to remain blind, like I said, for it to work. Weeks before what Wainwright believed to be a genuine approach at the Bolshoi, I'd pouched to Moscow a top-security code, to be used in the event of something really important. I wanted the Russians to intercept, to know that something was happening. Having got Sampson to light the fuse, we pretended to catch him. It was all timed, practically to the minute, for the moment when we knew you were getting close to breaking point. We went through the pretense of a trial, which wasn't difficult because it was in camera, of course. Got Sampson sent to Wormwood Scrubs and put in the same cell as you and made him cultivate you, like he did . . ." Wilson shook his head in admiration. "Like I said, a brilliant and very brave man. Did he make you hate him?"

"Yes," said Charlie. He was dry-throated and the confirmation croaked from him.

"He had to, of course," said Wilson. "For it to work, later: for now, when you've come back. The Russians had to know of the loathing that existed between you, so that he wouldn't be endangered . . ."

"He shot a policeman," said Charlie, groping to understand. "He beat up one of the good prison officers and shot a copper. I saw him."

"Wait," said Wilson. "Hear it fully out. Despite your official assessments which were on record here and the monitor from the prison governor, I still had to satisfy myself completely about you. We could still have aborted your part in the operation, even then. The Soviets are always bloody good about getting their people out. We knew when they made contact, initially through the newspaper and then through the radio he'd been told to get brought in. His telling you was the test, Charlie. If you hadn't done exactly as you did, got to the governor and tried to stop it . . . agreed to go along, instead, then I'd have arranged a simple cell change and let Sampson go on alone."

"What would have happened to me?" demanded Charlie, suddenly attentive.

This time there was no smile from Wilson. "If you hadn't reported the escape plan and decided to get out, to Moscow, then you'd have been a traitor, wouldn't you, Charlie? You'd have served the rest of your sentence, with no parole, no reduction of sentence . . ."

"Jesus!" said Charlie emptily.

"But you're not a traitor, Charlie. I always knew it . . ." The smile came back. "That's when I knew it was all going to work . . . stood a chance of working, at least. It was important to guarantee your return, of course. That's why the business with the policeman was important . . ."

"You allowed a policeman to be killed!"

Wilson shook his head. "The warder had to be beaten. It was unfortunate but necessary. You had to believe it. We planted the policeman: he was one of our people."

"Blanks?" said Charlie.

Wilson nodded.

"The Russians demanded the gun," remembered Charlie. "If they'd checked the magazine, it would have been over before it started."

"No," said Wilson, unoffended. "I've told you, Charlie. We planned everything to the last detail. Two of the shots were blanks. The first one, which appeared to bring the man down. And the second, to finish him off. The other bullets were genuine, just in case they did check. By that time the Russians had to believe the killing, as well."

"But why?" demanded Charlie.

"To allow the murder warrants," explained Wilson gently. "If getting you out hadn't gone as smoothly as it did—and I think we were lucky there—we had a warrant alleging murder against you. Moscow couldn't have demanded to keep a murderer, could they?"

"Sampson pretended to kill a copper to protect me!"

"Yes," said Wilson.

"Oh God," Charlie said.

"All you really had to do, to make your part of the operation work, was actually get to Moscow and then get back again," said Wilson. "The business with GUM was just to make you believe there was a point in your going . . ." Wilson broke away. "Getting into that spy school was a hell of a bonus, by the way. Well done."

"Berenkov fixed it," repeated Charlie.

Wilson nodded. "He was the target," said the Director. "All

the messages were carefully planted, pointed to Berenkov's division. I wonder if we haven't taken too much of an obvious chance, making the supposed identification Chekhov quotations. We've no news of any move against him: won't have for months yet."

"The messages," said Charlie. "How could you make the supposed information you were getting out of Moscow genuine enough to hope to convince them?"

Wilson shifted against the radiator, pulling his stiff leg into a more comfortable position. "Had to be very careful there," he conceded. "Drew on America a lot, although they don't know it. Asked for special help, from their satellite surveillance system. If the Soviets knew—instead of believing it came from one of their own people—they'd realize just how effective and complete that satellite spying is. All the stuff from Baikonur and about crop yields came from satellites. The American NSA and our own radio-and-telephone-intercept people at Cheltenham helped a lot, too—again not knowing just how much—and we managed to get quite a bit more from that. The information I told you about in jail, about Politburo decisions, actually came from microwave intercept. We made a big fuss, finally. We blanketed the Soviet embassy here and over the course of several months—while you were still in jail and actually before Sampson got sentenced—began to identify their agents here. We pouched the information to Moscow and had them transmit it back and then expelled most of them, a couple of months back."

"My coming out turned the key completely on Berenkov?" said Charlie, the picture practically formed in his mind now. "We'd known each other here. The messages—the indication that the informant wanted to defect—pointed to him. My going to Moscow—then getting out—would confirm the final suspicion?"

"That's right," said Wilson.

"Did you know about Georgi?"

"Georgi?"

"His son passed an examination qualifying him for an

exchange-course education somewhere in the West," explained Charlie.

"Marvelous!" said Wilson enthusiastically. "I didn't have any idea but that's a hell of a bonus, too. Like your actually getting to him. I thought it might happen but I recognized it as a long shot."

"Poor Alexei," said Charlie wistfully.

Wilson frowned at the sympathy. "Can't you understand how this will turn the Russian service on its head!" he demanded. "Everything with which Berenkov has been involved since his return and rehabilitation in Russia will be suspect. And not just that. Everything he ever sent from here, as well. It'll take them years to sort out, and send them in more wrong directions than we can count."

"Yes," agreed Charlie. "It's very clever." He stopped and then began again. "What about Sampson?"

"He does what it was always intended he should do when I took over the Willoughby operation. I always intended to stage his arrest, to get him repatriated to Russia . . ." Wilson paused, in further admiration. "I don't think I know of a man with more courage or conviction. I didn't force the decision upon him, you understand. I gave him weeks to make his mind up. Set it out as clearly as I could that he was committing himself to a situation that I didn't think many men could endure. He insisted on going through with it. There's a chance he would have been involved in their attempts to find out who the supposed defector was: he sent the first warning message, after all. If he is, then he can further tilt everything in Berenkov's direction. But that again would be a bonus and I think we've had enough of those. What we're hoping for is that he'll get brought into their service . . ." There was another smile. "And then we'll have what the Russians think we've already got. We'll have a spy in place."

"Christ!" said Charlie.

"He won't be able to go on forever, of course," said Wilson. "The same murder warrant exists against him. The understanding is that he can run whenever he wants. Knowing Sampson, I expect him to stay for the agreed period. Five years. For five years he's going to feed us everything he can. And when he gets back here I'm personally going to see that he gets every reward and honor it's possible for him to have."

"You should have told me," insisted Charlie, flat-voiced. "You really should have told me."

The relevant times were logged and the evidence was in her favor and Kalenin decided the woman had made a desperate attempt to stop the escape. It had been his mistake wrongly to send the seizure squads to the spy school and to Charlie Muffin's apartment. Only later—too late—did he identify from photographs the stranger whose abrupt entry into the British embassy was probably timed thirty minutes after Natalia Fedova's attempted approach to him, an approach Kalenin now realized he should have responded to earlier. By the time the photograph had been identified as that of Charlie Muffin, the damned man was already aboard the aircraft at Sheremetyevo. Kalenin had been halfway to the airport when the report came in on the car radio that the aircraft had taken off. They were fools not to have stormed it or to have shot the tires out instead of standing helplessly around waiting for orders from higher authority. In his fury, Kalenin determined they would regret that indecision for the rest of their imprisoned days. The KGB chairman stopped the reflection, coming back to the woman sitting nervously in front of him.

"Again," insisted Kalenin. "Tell me the salient points again."

"I encouraged the affair between us," repeated Natalia. "Without having any evidence I could bring before you or anyone else, I was unhappy with the initial interviews and again with his performance at Balashikha." Natalia paused, unsure if she were fully expressing herself as she intended. "Never any evidence; no proof. Just a feeling. When we were together there was always an attitude, an uncertainty. Again, only a feeling. I started to follow him. Twice it was the same rendezvous, the GUM department store. It was obviously a point of contact. I followed him there again today, because I wanted positive proof that something was not as we suspected it. I knew he saw me. There was no obvious indication, but I knew I had been identified."

"So he fled," said Kalenin reflectively. "He penetrated us, because of the stupidity of someone who should have known better. Damn Alexei Berenkov!" He looked up at Natalia. "You've no doubt at all about the person you saw him meet on every occasion?"

"None," said Natalia. "I knew, of course, why my debriefing was cut short. Knew what Edwin Sampson was being called upon to do. It was definitely Sampson, at every meeting. Despite all the indications to the contrary, that they disliked each other, they retained contact."

"Charlie Muffin is a survivor," mused Kalenin. "A professional survivor. Knowing you'd identified him, he'd have cut his losses and abandoned everything: better to save part of an operation than nothing at all."

"There's still Sampson."

"Yes," said Kalenin, his fury returning. "There's still Sampson, and by the time his interrogation is over there is absolutely nothing that Sampson will not have told us."